LOST MARS

The Golden Age of the Red Planet

LOST MARS

The Golden Age of the Red Planet

edited by

MIKE ASHLEY

BRITISH LIBRARY

First published 2018 by
The British Library
96 Euston Road
London NW1 2DB

Introduction and notes copyright © 2018 Mike Ashley

Cataloguing in Publication Data
A catalogue record for this book is available from the British Library

ISBN 978 0 7123 5240 6

Frontispiece from *Astronomie populaire*
by Camille Flammarion, Paris, 1880.

Typeset by Tetragon, London
Printed and bound in England by TJ International

CONTENTS

When, in July 1965, the American probe *Mariner 4* flew past Mars at a distance of less than 10,000 kilometres (about 6,200 miles) the pictures it took showed an arid, desert-like and apparently dead world. It seemed to put an end to the centuries of speculation that there might have been life on Mars, perhaps even intelligent life. Eleven years later the two *Viking* probes landed on the Martian surface and undertook a series of soil tests and biological experiments, and from the results scientists deduced that there were no microorganisms in the soil and that in all likelihood there was no life on Mars, and might not have been for millions of years. That conclusion has since been challenged, and the search for some form of microbial life continues, but there now seems no chance that any aliens, whether "little green men" or octopoid creatures housed in fighting machines, exist or ever existed.

It is a bitter pill to swallow for all those visionaries who hoped we might have some form of life in our solar neighbourhood, and while the search continues, both on Mars and on other planets and moons, we can nevertheless look back and reflect on the way writers considered the possibilities of life on Mars or our colonisation of the planet.

The Golden Age of Martian fiction really began in 1882 when the work of Italian astronomer Giovanni Schiaparelli leaked into the public domain. Following an extensive study of the planet he announced that there were many straight lines on the Martian surface, which he called *canali*, or channels. However, this was interpreted as "canals", thereby creating a vision of a planet with vast waterways constructed to bring water from the polar ice caps across an otherwise arid landscape. The American astronomer Percival Lowell explored these ideas in his 1895 book *Mars*, with the concept of the planet bearing intelligent life, which he further developed in *Mars and its Canals* (1906) and *Mars as the Abode of Life* (1908). Though Lowell's theories were frowned on by most fellow scientists they fuelled the public interest in Mars, an interest that had also been stimulated by H. G. Wells's novel of a terrifying Martian invasion, *The War of the Worlds* (1897).

This anthology brings together a selection of the more diverse science fiction that has been set on Mars in those years from the 1880s to the 1960s. Among the many settings based on Mars, two favoured ones emerged. There was the Mars of the planetary romance, popularised by Edgar Rice Burroughs and continued by many authors. At the other extreme was the harsh reality of a dead or dying Martian landscape, where attempts to adapt the planet were both dangerous and near impossible, as depicted in the stories by E. C. Tubb and Walter M. Miller. The classic image of Mars is also represented by one of Ray Bradbury's *Martian Chronicles* stories, while attempts to rediscover the past of Mars are explored in the stories by Marion Zimmer Bradley and J. G. Ballard. The ecological aspect of whether we should plunder Mars or protect it was one that was considered early, most notably in the story by P. Schuyler Miller from 1932, while a look at the unique environment of Mars—admittedly a rather more romantic one—will be found in the classic story by Stanley G. Weinbaum, voted the most popular story of the 1930s in the Science Fiction Hall of Fame.

The stories collected here are but a small sample and in order to understand the rich heritage of Martian fiction I'd like to explore its origins and development in the following section, which shows not only the first stories to explore Mars, but also how this fiction exploded in the late nineteenth century encouraged by the ideas of Schiaparelli and Lowell.

THE MARTIAN PIONEERS

The first fiction about Mars arose from speculation about its moons. Although Mars was one of five planets known to the ancients (along with Mercury, Venus, Jupiter and Saturn) nothing was known about it except for its fast and often erratic movement about the heavens— the very word "planet" comes from the ancient Greek for wanderer. But no details could be discerned of any of these planets until the invention of the telescope. When Galileo focused his telescope on the planet Jupiter in 1610 he saw four attendant satellites. The first of Saturn's moons, Titan, was discovered in 1655, with four more over the next thirty years. Astronomers suspected there were further moons to find, many of which, as the natural philosopher William Derham surmised in *Astro-Theology* (1714), would be too small to see with the strength of the telescopes at the time. Nevertheless, at the time he was writing, it was known that since the Earth had one moon, Jupiter four and Saturn five,* it seemed logical that Mars must have at least one and more likely two. So while it seemed remarkable when Jonathan Swift revealed in *Gulliver's Travels* in 1726 that the astronomers of Laputa had discovered the two moons of Mars, Swift was only repeating what many already suspected.

Just eighteen years after *Gulliver's Travels*, in July 1744, the German astronomer Eberhard Christian Kindermann believed he

---

* Jupiter is, at the time of writing, believed to have 67 moons and Saturn 62.

had discovered at least one Martian moon, though quite what he saw remains uncertain, as his description of it was far too large. Kindermann's study of the skies, *Vollständige Astronomie* ('Complete Astronomy', 1744), had just been published so, in order to proclaim his discovery, he speculated upon it in a story, 'Der Geschwinde Reise' ('The Speedy Journey'), which he issued before the end of the year. Although Kindermann presented the story as fiction, almost like a fairy tale, he nevertheless endeavoured to root it in as scientific a basis as contemporary knowledge allowed, making it a genuine science-fiction story. Five individuals (with the names of the five senses) create an airship based on the design proposed in 1670 by the Italian Jesuit mathematician Francesco Lana de Terzi. He believed that a ship with a sail could fly through the air supported by four globes from which the air had been evacuated. Kindermann's ship has six globes, just to be sure, and is equipped with oars so it can be rowed through the air.

Kindermann was aware that Mars was at least thirty million miles distant and, as the airship was travelling at around 460 miles per hour, the journey would have taken over seven years, yet it seems to happen in an instant. Moreover, while the travellers believe they have been away from Earth for only a short period they learn their adventure had lasted well over twenty years, rather like "time-in-faery".

With the help of an angelic spirit guide, the five travellers make their way to the Martian moon. The inhabitants are humanoid and the travellers present themselves as gods. Much of the discussion with the natives is about religion. It transpires that this moon was the first object created by God. Indeed, the natives seem to have a special relationship with God. At the time Kindermann was writing there was much speculation about the plurality of worlds, a subject given considerable attention by the French philosopher Bernard Le Bovier de Fontenelle in *Entretiens sur la pluralité des mondes* ('Conversations on the Plurality of Worlds') in 1686, and widely translated, including a German edition in 1725. In this highly influential work, Fontenelle discusses in a friendly, open style the nature of the heavens and the possibility of life elsewhere. He was, alas, rather dismissive of Mars, saying "it contains nothing calculated to arrest our attention", though he did wonder if the planet had phosphorescent rocks that lit up at night. He also speculated that Mars had vast seas that periodically washed over all of the land.

Others followed in Fontenelle's wake. In *De Telluribus in Mundo Nostro Solari* ('Concerning the Earths in Our Solar System', 1758) the Swedish philosopher Emanuel Swedenborg believed that all the planets in our solar system were variants of Earth and that the Martian inhabitants were among the best and most honest, with no central government. There had been a similar idyllic planet in the anonymous *A Voyage to the World in the Centre of the Earth* (1755), where Mars is portrayed like ancient Greece, with the spirits of heroes, lawgivers, musicians and poets. A more war-ravaged Mars, in keeping with being named after the Roman god of war, is envisaged in both Marie-Anne de Roumier-Robert's *Voyages de Milord Céton dans les sept planètes* ('The Voyages of Lord Seaton to the Seven Planets', 1765), where the planet is the home of reincarnated soldiers, and the anonymous *A Fantastical Excursion into the Planets* (1839), in which Mars is depicted as the location of an industrial holocaust, with weapon-making and slaughter. In Benjamin Lumley's *Another World* (1873), Mars is shown as having once been war-torn, but with its population later controlled through a close monitoring of children.

None of these works seeks to explore Mars in any scientific sense, making Kindermann's early work all the more remarkable, but an explosion of interest came after the conjunction of Mars in 1877, when the planet was some 35 million miles from Earth. It was at that time that Asaph Hall discovered the two tiny moons, soon named Phobos and Deimos, and it was also when Giovanni Schiaparelli believed he had observed straight lines on the surface, his so-called *canali* or channels. His findings, amplified by further observations, were discussed in the scientific community, but Schiaparelli did not claim that these channels had been constructed artificially, and even when the news leaked to the press in 1882 it did not cause an immediate stir. The London-born astronomer Richard A. Proctor, who had just relocated to the United States, had been studying Mars for nearly twenty years and had published his own map of the surface in 1867. He had noticed no such straight lines, and wrote to *The Times* in London in April 1882 exercising caution and noting that they could be an optical illusion.

Others were more enthusiastic about their significance and there were several noted scientists who took the prospect of intelligent life on Mars seriously. Chief among these was the American astronomer Percival Lowell, who stated that he had seen these "canals" and studied them extensively. Over the next two decades he compiled three books on the subject: *Mars* (1895), *Mars and Its Canals* (1906) and *Mars as the Abode of Life* (1908). Lowell was inspired not only by Schiaparelli but by the French astronomer Camille Flammarion, whose detailed study, *La planète Mars*, was published in 1892. Flammarion had earlier written a collection of narratives, *Uranie* (1889), which includes a section where the astronomer visits Mars in a dream-state and is lectured by two humanoid inhabitants over Earth's failure as a civilisation because it is too warlike.

It was this growing scientific speculation on the potential for life on Mars that inspired writers and visionaries. The general view that prevailed was that the Martians were technologically advanced over humans, and might have other powers. In Percy Greg's novel *Across the Zodiac* (1880), they are telepathic. In Edward Bellamy's short story 'The Blindman's World' (1886) they have knowledge of the future. In W. S. Lach-Szyrma's *Aleriel* (1883) and its sequels—a sample of which is included in this anthology—they have developed a virtuous, harmonious society. They are likewise gentle and technologically advanced in Robert Cromie's *A Plunge into Space* (1890) and James Cowan's *Daybreak* (1896).

Mars became an ideal location for speculating on whether an advanced civilisation might have overcome its base instincts and developed a near-perfect society. In *The Man from Mars* (1891) by Thomas Blot they are far advanced over inhabitants of Earth, and have built domed cities to protect themselves. In *Unveiling a Parallel* (1893) published as by 'Two Women of the West', the alias of Alice Ilgenfritz Jones and Ella Merchant, we find Marsians [*sic*] who are handsome and intelligent, and a place in which woman are totally liberated—in short, a feminist utopia. Another feminist utopia appears in *A Woman of Mars* (1901) by the Australian writer Mary Moore-Bentley. In *The Inhabitants of Mars* (1895), inventor and electrical engineer Willis Mitchell was convinced electricity was the answer to everything and makes Mars an electrical utopia.

Mitchell's Martians are extremely religious, and the idea that religion helped develop the perfection of Mars recurs in other books. In *A Dream of a Modest Prophet* (1890), American lawyer Mortimer Leggett broached the idea that the Martians had had their own Christ-like Messiah in the past, and had unified to disavow war. The little-known Charles Cole was even more daring in *Visitors from Mars* (1901), in which he drops the bombshell that Jesus had been raised and educated on Mars and was sent to Earth to help. The Martians rescued him at his crucifixion and brought him back to Mars. Jesus had also been present on Mars four centuries before, in Henry Wallace Dowding's *The Man from Mars* (1910).

By the end of the nineteenth century the image of Martians as scientifically advanced had become standard. In most cases they were also benign, almost saintly, but one novel would change all that: H. G. Wells's *The War of the Worlds*, serialised during 1897. The Martians, desperate to colonise elsewhere because their own world is dying, invade Earth, and their advanced technology is too much for Earth's weak military powers. On one level Wells's novel was part of the sub-genre of future war/invasion stories prevalent at that time, demonstrating how ill-prepared Britain was against any nation with military prowess. But it did much more. Hitherto all Martians had been portrayed as humanoid, often taller than ourselves, sometimes weaker because of the lesser gravity, and sometimes with additional powers, but generally benign. However Wells depicted them as utterly alien, octopoid creatures that need the strength of their walking fighting machines to allow them to operate in Earth's stronger gravity. They are totally merciless and devoid of feelings towards human or animal life, and are bent on conquest. There had been Martians on Earth in earlier stories, such as Thomas Blot's *The Man from Mars* (1891) and Robert Braine's *Messages from Mars* (1892), in which they are on a remote island in the Indian Ocean, but they were always friendly. By the late 1890s, though, this began to change.

The impact of Wells's novel was such that it immediately generated a sequel, much to the author's annoyance. When the novel was serialised in the United States Wells had insisted it be reprinted with no change of location. However, the two newspapers that ran the story, the *New York Evening Journal* and the *Boston Post*, both changed the setting to their own locale and made other changes as suited them. To add insult to injury, the *New York Evening Journal* then commissioned its science reporter, Garrett P. Serviss, to write a sequel, which became 'Edison's Conquest of Mars'.* Although the original Martian invaders (now giant humanoids rather than octopoid creatures) have all died there is fear the Martians will try again, and so the world's scientists, headed by Thomas Edison, pool their brainpower to create super-weapons capable of defeating the Martians. A huge armada is built (funds are no object) and Edison leads it in the war against Mars. Eventually almost the entire Martian civilisation is wiped out. It is also learned that the Martians had come to Earth centuries before and built the pyramids and the Sphinx.

At the time that Wells's novel appeared, two other works also showed interest in Mars and Martian powers. The noted artist and novelist George du Maurier (grandfather of Daphne du Maurier), author of *Trilby* (1894), penned a society novel, *The Martian*,† in which a Martian spirit, between reincarnations, becomes something of a guardian angel to an ailing British wastrel. Little is revealed about the Martians until late in the novel when we learn that they evolved from seal-like creatures, are vastly superior to humans and communicate telepathically. Du Maurier's novel may have inspired a very successful stage play, *A Message from Mars* by Richard Ganthony, which ran for sixteen months from 22 November 1899.

---

* Although this was serialised daily in the *Evening Journal* from 12 January to 10 February 1898, it did not appear in book form until 1947, just after Wells's death and eighteen years after Serviss's.

† Serialised in *Harper's Monthly Magazine* during 1896, it had a special limited edition in the USA in 1897, but was not published in Great Britain until 1898. Du Maurier did not live to see any of these printings.

Bearing similarities to Charles Dickens's *A Christmas Carol*, the play shows how the spirit of a scientifically advanced Martian helps reform a selfish egotist.

Meanwhile in Germany the physicist and educator Kurd Lasswitz published his profound novel *Auf Zwei Planeten* ('Of Two Planets', 1897). Here humanoid Martians (identifiable only by their huge eyes) have recently created bases at Earth's North and South Poles, unbeknown to humans until explorers stumble across them. The Martians have space stations hovering above both Poles, powered by an antigravity device. The Martians are benign and are scientifically far superior to Earth's inhabitants, and want to help educate humanity in exchange for air and energy to supplement their own planet's diminishing supplies. Alas, the crass stubbornness of the English results in hostilities erupting. The Martians did not want a war, and their superior power soon overwhelms Earth and they establish a protectorate over the planet. Despite their efforts to improve Earth, problems arise and further hostilities erupt. Lasswitz's message demonstrated the corrupting consequences of colonialism, despite the improving potential of science and technology.

Although Lasswitz's novel proved highly popular in Germany and was translated into many European languages, it has never been published in Great Britain, and its first English translation was of an abridged edition published in the United States in 1971. Thus, although science-fiction devotees knew of the book through occasional references and by word of mouth, it had little influence on the development of science fiction in Britain or America. Yet it had a significant impact in Germany, not least on the German rocket scientist Wernher von Braun, the inventor of the V2 rocket during the Second World War and the developer of the *Saturn V* rocket in the American space programme. Von Braun later wrote, "I shall never forget how I devoured this novel with curiosity and excitement as a young man." In 1949 von Braun wrote his own novel of an expedition to Mars, though it remained unpublished until 2006 when it appeared as *Project Mars: A Technical Tale*. It is, indeed, full of technical data as von Braun, true to his reputation, strove to demonstrate accurately how to reach Mars.

Lasswitz was not the first to envisage Martians colonising Earth's polar regions. In *Journey to Mars* (1894) the American physician Gustavus W. Pope had a sailor discover a Martian colony at the South Pole. He is taken back to Mars where he falls in love with a young princess and finds himself embroiled in a power struggle over the throne. Mars, it transpires, has three different races—red-, blue-and yellow-skinned—and Pope suggests that on Mars, which is very Earth-like, life developed much as it had on Earth by parallel evolution.

The idea that life on Mars would evolve along similar lines to Earth was one way in which Victorian writers could reconcile their religious views with Darwinism. It also proved a useful convenience to have humanoid Martians speaking English. That's how they appear in some of the more absurd novels of the late Victorian period, such as *Bellona's Bridegroom* (1887) by the American William James Roe (writing as Hudor Genone) and *Mr. Stranger's Sealed Packet* (1889) by the Scottish mathematician Hugh MacColl. Interestingly this last work also has blue-and red-skinned Martians, which might have influenced Pope, and more significantly, it might have influenced H. G. Wells. A Martian female who returns to Earth succumbs to Earth's diseases, just as the Martians did in *The War of the Worlds*. The antigravity device featured in MacColl's novel is also similar to that used by Professor Cavor in Wells's *The First Men in the Moon*, as is the way in which the spaceship is lost at the end.

The American insurance broker Elmer Dwiggins (writing as Ellsworth Douglass) used his business knowledge for the plot of *Pharaoh's Broker* (1899), where parallel evolution has brought Martian history to the equivalent period of the ancient Egyptian civilisation on Earth. As its history exactly parallels that of Earth, the wily explorers who have financed a journey to Mars (using antigravity) have a foreknowledge of the Martian future, with the pharaoh's dream of the twelve fat years and twelve lean years (as recorded in Genesis 41:1–13), and use this to their initial advantage. Dwiggins see Mars as another example of God's wisdom in how life has developed according to its environment.

The blending of Martian civilisation with religion continued into the twentieth century, with probably two of the best-known books about Mars: *Out of the Silent Planet* (1938), the first book in what became known as the Cosmic Trilogy by C. S. Lewis, and *Stranger in a Strange Land* (1961) by Robert A. Heinlein. Lewis's novel could be seen as an allegory, with the lead character, Ransom, representing the "ransom sacrifice" that God made of Jesus on behalf of mankind. Ransom is kidnapped and taken to Mars as a sacrifice so that mankind, which has proved so evil and warlike, can live again on Mars and other planets. Mars has remained in a state of godliness, and Lewis contrasts the spiritual outlook of the Martians with that of the humans. In Heinlein's novel a young boy, the only survivor of an early expedition, is raised by Martians, and when he returns to Earth he acts with the religious and psychic beliefs of the Martians. He is regarded as a messiah by certain religious zealots on Earth and, like Lewis, Heinlein is able to show how human traits will inevitably contaminate Martian ideals. These and other novels continue a concept that dates back almost to the dawn of space fiction: that Mars remains in a state of grace, from which Earth has fallen.

It is evident by now that the wealth of Martian material in novels was creating a stream of influence, and many of the ideas reappeared in later works. Of particular interest is *Lieut. Gullivar Jones: His Vacation* (1905) by the British writer Edwin Lester Arnold. This is more fantasy than science fiction, since our hero, a lieutenant in the United States Navy, is whisked off to Mars on a magic carpet. He discovers an Earth-like environment and humanoid Martians, and falls in love with a beautiful princess whom he rescues. The Martian names are Egyptian, though the civilisation is not. The rest of the novel is primarily a romance that takes place against various cultural, physical and dynastic odds, and on its own is of little significance. Yet various authorities have speculated that this novel could have inspired Edgar Rice Burroughs with his own Martian novels.

Another possible influence is *A King of Mars* (1908) by the American artist Avis Hekking, who wrote it while an art student in Paris. Two artists discover a globe sent from Mars, which contains a story written by a slave about her role in the power struggle on the planet between the king and the "arch-traitor" Anayru.

There is, alas, no evidence that Burroughs read any of these earlier works, despite the mostly superficial similarities that arise— rather the opposite. Alongside Jules Verne and H. G. Wells, Edgar Rice Burroughs must be ranked as one of the most influential of all pioneers of science fiction.

His first Martian novel was serialised as 'Under the Moons of Mars' in 1912, and published in book form as *A Princess of Mars* in 1917. Captain John Carter, a Confederate Civil War veteran fleeing from American Indians, hides in a cave and is overcome by strange fumes. He has an out-of-body experience and his astral self travels to Mars. Mostly a desert land, irrigated by canals, and with a thin atmosphere, Carter finds he has great strength and agility because of the lesser gravity. He learns that there are essentially two types of Martian: a green-skinned race with two sets of arms, who are warriors, apparently the product of a failed genetic experiment; and the more scientifically inclined red-skinned race, a co-mingling of other races. They are scientifically advanced and telepathic, but still prefer swords over their other weapons in battle. Carter rescues a beautiful princess, Dejah Thoris, but they are separated, and most of the first novel concerns Carter's efforts to rescue her from various warring factions and technological disasters. It's an exciting adventure story, which set the trend for the planetary romance. There have been many imitators since, most notably Otis Adelbert Kline, Robert E. Howard, Lin Carter, Philip José Farmer, Michael Moorcock (as Edward P. Bradbury), C. L. Moore and Marion Zimmer Bradley, though the real Queen of the Planetary Romance was Leigh Brackett—who, while relishing the freedom of the planetary romance, nevertheless introduced a more rigid scientific rationale.

There's little chance that Burroughs read *Le Prisonnier de la Planète Mars* (1908) or its sequel *La Guerre des Vampires* (1909) by Gustave Le Rouge, as neither was translated into English until 2008 (as *Vampires of Mars*), but these were also in the developing planetary romance sub-genre. An engineer, Robert Darvel, is sent to Mars by the psychic powers of Hindu Brahmins and undergoes many adventures featuring a wide range of native creatures. Hitherto most novels had focused on the humanoid or intelligent inhabitants of Mars. Le Rouge took note of other likely dangers, including reptilian mermen with long tentacular arms, bat-winged vampirical humanoids and macrocephalic gnomes. Over the next few years only the occasional novel considered the other wildlife of Mars, including the German boys' book *Wunderwelte* (1911) by Friedrich W. Mader, translated in 1932 as *Distant Worlds*. This surprisingly advanced book, which takes its adventurers as far as Alpha Centauri in a "World-Ship" which, powered by magnetic repulsion, can travel faster than light, first takes in several of the planets. They find that Mars has no canals (they were an optical illusion), but is covered with red vegetation in which lurk many horrors including giant insects and worms. There are bat-winged birds and boars covered in hedgehog quills. The native Martians have been all but wiped out by earthquakes. In *Last and First Men* (1930) Olaf Stapledon described Martians as amoeboid cloudlets with a group mind. However, the real turning point in describing Martian flora and fauna came with 'A Martian Odyssey' (1934) by Stanley G. Weinbaum. One of the most popular sf stories from the pulps of the 1930s, it is included in this anthology. The idea of respecting the local creatures and protecting them was rarely considered in early science fiction, which is what makes P. Schuyler Miller's story 'The Forgotten Man of Space' (1933), also included here, so remarkable.

While the planetary romance theme was developing there were other explorations of Martian culture. The Red Planet became an obvious setting for a communist state in *Krasnaia Zvezda* ('Red Star', 1908) and its sequel *Inzhener Menni* ('Engineer Menni', 1912) by Alexander Bogdanov. Although reasonably well known in Russia, especially at the time of the revolution in 1917, and notoriously because of its reference to free love on Mars, it was not translated into English until 1984. Kim Stanley Robinson claimed it served as an influence for his own novel, *Red Mars* (1992), the first of his trilogy about terraforming the planet. Although the emphasis in Bogdanov's stories is on the benefits of socialism, he took trouble to make the science as realistic as possible. The egg-shaped rocket to Mars is powered by atomic energy. His Mars is Schiaparellian, with canals that have forests planted along their full length, explaining why they are visible from Earth. He also went to great lengths to explain how the topography of Mars, and the fact that it was twice as old as Earth, allowed social evolution to develop gradually and more effectively, with planet-wide communication and thus a single language.

The American clergyman William Shuler Harris emphasised the class divide in *Life in a Thousand Worlds* (1905). Once all Martians lived together, he tells us, but then "a few schemers" used their "inventive genius" to build curtains from mountain ridge to ridge, allowing the privileged to live on the mountain tops, in the sun, while the toilers lived in the valleys, did all the work, and had to pay a fee to the rich. The toilers rebelled, which led to them becoming isolated, and eventually the slaves had no idea there were others living on the mountains above.

The great pulpster Homer Eon Flint, whose imagination was way beyond most writers of his brief heyday, also used Mars to explore his ideas of social inequality in 'The Planeteer' (1918). In the future Earth is overpopulated and facing famine, and one entrepreneurial scientist believes the only way ahead is to colonise the other planets. The Martians have a similar idea, as their world is dying. Martian society is portrayed as having a small elitist upper class, with all others being oppressed workers who are executed once they can no longer perform. Elsewhere in the solar system, cosmic events have already turned Saturn into a small sun, and although the Martians believe they will benefit by moving Mars closer to Saturn, their plan fails and Mars is destroyed.

Flint's story was an early example of the super-science that would dominate the pulps in the 1920s and 1930s. In 'The Man Who Saved the Earth' (1919) Flint's erstwhile collaborator, Austin Hall, has Martians trying to draw up the Earth's water into giant globes and transport it back to a dying Mars, but a super-scientist uses the power of the

Sun to disrupt the Martian's plans. In 'Across Space' (1926), Edmond Hamilton reveals that Martians have long been based on Earth (on Easter Island) and have produced a ray that will draw Mars towards Earth and allow the surviving Martians to fly across. Their plans are thwarted, however, and Mars is left to drift through the solar system.

It was necessary for writers to refocus and consider the realistic nature of Mars and any possible native life. In 1926 Hugo Gernsback launched the first science-fiction magazine, *Amazing Stories*. In the previous two decades he had published some science fiction in his technical magazine *The Electrical Experimenter*, including his series 'The Scientific Adventures of Baron Münchausen' (1915–17). The second half of the series is set on Mars and Gernsback, always keen to promote the potential of science, considered in detail what the Martian world, as then understood, might really be like. The Martians communicate with Münchausen telepathically and explain the scientific status of the planet. They have atomic energy and have harnessed the power of the Sun, from which they generate rays that perform most major tasks, like excavating the canals. They have also mastered antigravity and use it for their entertainment. Gernsback was the first author to seriously consider the problem of Martian sandstorms, and he describes how the Martians' elevated cities and roads cope with them. The Martians are tall and barrel-chested, as a result of the weak atmosphere. Gernsback did not complete the series, but in the final episode he commented on how the Martians use giant power plants to purify the air, and questioned how long Earth would cope with polluting the atmosphere from burning fossil fuels.

Gernsback wanted to keep scientific rigour to the forefront when he launched *Amazing Stories*, but he found that difficult as readers wanted more action-oriented fiction. This was evident when Gernsback published a new novel by Edgar Rice Burroughs, 'The

Master Mind of Mars', complete in the *Amazing Stories Annual* for 1927. It has a degree of hard science at its core—the matter of brain transplants and body regeneration—but it is still essentially a sword-and-ray-gun adventure. Cosmic super-science took over in the pulps, and it was some years, and a change of magazines, before Gernsback was able to rein in his writers and encourage them to write more realistic fiction, taking account of the hazards of space travel and the consequences of colonisation. In addition to 'The Forgotten Man of Space', reprinted here, Gernsback ran such stories as 'A Conquest of Two Worlds' (1932) by Edmond Hamilton, which showed how Mars needed to be protected against the excesses of colonialism, and Laurence Manning's serial 'The Wreck of the Asteroid' (1933), in which pioneer explorers who crash on Mars struggle to survive its harsh environment.

The romantic image of Mars, though, was tenacious, and few writers could resist its charms. Leigh Brackett took on the mantle of Edgar Rice Burroughs as the Queen of the Planetary Romance, but whereas Burroughs went for unbridled adventure and heroics, Brackett brought to the field both a mystical depth and a sense of dislocation that made her stories, which began with 'Martian Quest' (1940), alien yet sentimental. Brackett's close friend and one-time collaborator, Ray Bradbury, also brought a sentimental view to the planet in a series of stories, most of which were collected as *The Martian Chronicles* (1950). Bradbury charted the human colonisation of Mars, which results in the passing of the true Martians in much the same way as the American continent was overrun by European colonists. Bradbury succeeds admirably in considering the tragedy of this alongside the hope. By the end of the book it is the humans who have become Martians. One of his *Martian Chronicles* stories is included in this anthology.

The years after the Second World War, which ushered in the Atomic Age, brought a more realistic treatment of Martian colonisation—as demonstrated in this anthology by the stories by Walter M. Miller and E. C. Tubb—but it also brought a new hope, that maybe there was still a romantic aspect to Mars. Arthur C. Clarke managed to blend the two objectives in *The Sands of Mars* (1951), which looks at a balanced and appropriate way to develop a Martian colony, while in *Outpost Mars* (1952), Judith Merril and Cyril Kornbluth (writing as Cyril Judd) contrast the dilemma between trying to establish a suitable colony and the determination to make it pay through plundering the planet's resources. My own childhood memories of the BBC radio series *Journey Into Space* by Charles Chilton (particularly the 1954 serial *The Red Planet*) impressed on me how the Martians might be struggling to survive and would turn to Earth for salvation.

Despite recognising the hostile environment of Mars, most writers still clung to the idea that there was some form of native life, such as the Bleekmen in Philip K. Dick's *Martian Time-Slip* (1964) or the Amsirs in Algis Budrys's *The Iron Thorn* (1967), the origins of which introduce another fascination among writers, of an ancient colonisation of Mars.

So even as the *Mariner* and *Viking* probes began to dismantle our romantic vision of Mars, authors continued to provide hope. In *Welcome to Mars* (1967) James Blish even turned back the clock to the good old days to have a young boy discover antigravity and fly to Mars followed by his girlfriend, and between them work out how to survive on the planet and make some remarkable discoveries. Authors also explored how humans would adapt to Mars, such as in Frederik Pohl's *Man Plus* (1976), or how the planet would adapt to humanity, as in Ian McDonald's *Desolation Road* (1988) or Kim Stanley Robinson's trilogy starting with *Red Mars* (1992). Maybe the Chinese will colonise Mars first, as Paul J. McAuley explored in *Red Dust* (1993). Authors have looked back into the Martian past to see if it ever was inhabited, as in Ben Bova's *Mars* (1992) or whether it houses secrets that will reveal more about our place in the universe, as in Allen M. Steele's *Labyrinth of Night* (1992). As many books—if not more—are being set on Mars as ever, showing how the ingenuity of humans can combat whatever Mars throws at them, as in Geoffrey A. Landis's *Mars Crossing* (2000) or Andy Weir's *The Martian* (2011).

The realisation that Mars might not host life has not diminished our desire to reach the planet, despite the overwhelming challenges of the journey and the environment. Mars will continue to exert its fascination as much as it has for the last century, and the stories selected here are a reflection of that desire to explore those hopes and dreams.

MIKE ASHLEY

THE CRYSTAL EGG

H. G. Wells

As discussed in the Introduction, the author who really brought science fiction alive and, in particular, the potential horrors of an invasion by aliens with superior technology, was H. G. Wells (1866–1946). Regarded by many as the Father of Science Fiction, Wells was able to express thoughts on how technology might affect individuals and society rather than focus solely on the technology itself. His fascination with evolution and Social Darwinism was evident from some of his earliest writings, such as 'The Man of the Year Million' (1893) which, along with his first short novel, The Time Machine (1895) presented a vision of what humankind might be like in the far future. In the years from 1893 to 1904 he produced a considerable number of short stories and novels, which are now classified as science fiction but which Wells called his "scientific fantasia". The War of the Worlds, first serialised in Pearson's Magazine from April to December 1897, might well be the most popular of these novels and certainly the best known, what with several film adaptations, the musical adaptation by Jeff Wayne, and the notorious 1938 radio adaptation by Orson Welles which allegedly sent listeners into panic. Wells brought home to readers as never before how helpless we are in the face of alien technology and power.

What is sometimes forgotten is that Wells wrote another story, which serves as a kind of precursor to The War of the Worlds, allowing someone on Earth to see what Mars itself was like. 'The Crystal Egg', first published in The New Review for May 1897 is also one of those stories that fits into the sub-genre of "magic shop" fiction. And in case anyone wonders, the £5 mentioned in the story would be the equivalent of over £500 today.

THERE WAS, UNTIL A YEAR AGO, A LITTLE AND VERY GRIMY-looking shop near Seven Dials, over which, in weather-worn yellow lettering, the name of "C. Cave, Naturalist and Dealer in Antiquities," was inscribed. The contents of its window were curiously variegated. They comprised some elephant tusks and an imperfect set of chessmen, beads and weapons, a box of eyes, two skulls of tigers and one human, several moth-eaten stuffed monkeys (one holding a lamp), an old-fashioned cabinet, a fly-blown ostrich egg or so, some fishing-tackle, and an extraordinarily dirty, empty glass fish-tank. There was also, at the moment the story begins, a mass of crystal, worked into the shape of an egg and brilliantly polished. And at that two people who stood outside the window were looking, one of them a tall, thin clergyman, the other a black-bearded young man of dusky complexion and unobtrusive costume. The dusky young man spoke with eager gesticulation, and seemed anxious for his companion to purchase the article.

While they were there, Mr. Cave came into his shop, his beard still wagging with the bread and butter of his tea. When he saw these men and the object of their regard, his countenance fell. He glanced guiltily over his shoulder, and softly shut the door. He was a little old man, with pale face and peculiar watery blue eyes; his hair was a dirty grey, and he wore a shabby blue frock-coat, an ancient silk hat, and carpet slippers very much down at heel. He remained watching the two men as they talked. The clergyman went deep into his trouser pocket, examined a handful of money, and showed his teeth in an agreeable smile. Mr. Cave seemed still more depressed when they came into the shop.

The clergyman, without any ceremony, asked the price of the crystal egg. Mr. Cave glanced nervously towards the door leading into the parlour, and said five pounds. The clergyman protested that the price was high, to his companion as well as to Mr. Cave—it was, indeed, very much more than Mr. Cave had intended to ask when he had stocked the article—and an attempt at bargaining ensued. Mr. Cave stepped to the shop door, and held it open. "Five pounds is my price," he said, as though he wished to save himself the trouble of unprofitable discussion. As he did so, the upper portion of a woman's face appeared above the blind in the glass upper panel of the door leading into the parlour, and stared curiously at the two customers. "Five pounds is my price," said Mr. Cave, with a quiver in his voice.

The swarthy young man had so far remained a spectator, watching Cave keenly. Now he spoke. "Give him five pounds," he said. The clergyman glanced at him to see if he were in earnest, and when he looked at Mr. Cave again, he saw that the latter's face was white. "It's a lot of money," said the clergyman, and, diving into his pocket, began counting his resources. He had little more than thirty shillings, and he appealed to his companion, with whom he seemed to be on terms of considerable intimacy. This gave Mr. Cave an opportunity of collecting his thoughts, and he began to explain in an agitated manner that the crystal was not, as a matter of fact, entirely free for sale. His two customers were naturally surprised at this, and inquired why he had not thought of that before he began to bargain. Mr. Cave became confused, but he stuck to his story, that the crystal was not in the market that afternoon, that a probable purchaser of it had already appeared. The two, treating this as an attempt to raise the price still further, made as if they would leave the shop. But at this point the parlour door opened, and the owner of the dark fringe and the little eyes appeared.

She was a coarse-featured, corpulent woman, younger and very much larger than Mr. Cave; she walked heavily, and her face was flushed. "That crystal *is* for sale," she said. "And five pounds is a good enough price for it. I can't think what you're about, Cave, not to take the gentleman's offer!"

Mr. Cave, greatly perturbed by the irruption, looked angrily at her over the rims of his spectacles, and, without excessive assurance, asserted his right to manage his business in his own way. An altercation began. The two customers watched the scene with interest and some amusement, occasionally assisting Mrs. Cave with suggestions. Mr. Cave, hard driven, persisted in a confused and impossible story of an inquiry for the crystal that morning, and his agitation became painful. But he stuck to his point with extraordinary persistence. It was the young Oriental who ended this curious controversy. He proposed that they should call again in the course of two days—so as to give the alleged inquirer a fair chance. "And then we must insist," said the clergyman. "Five pounds." Mrs. Cave took it on herself to apologise for her husband, explaining that he was sometimes "a little odd," and as the two customers left, the couple prepared for a free discussion of the incident in all its bearings.

Mrs. Cave talked to her husband with singular directness. The poor little man, quivering with emotion, muddled himself between his stories, maintaining on the one hand that he had another customer in view, and on the other asserting that the crystal was honestly worth ten guineas. "Why did you ask five pounds?" said his wife. "*Do* let me manage my business my own way!" said Mr. Cave.

Mr. Cave had living with him a step-daughter and a step-son, and at supper that night the transaction was re-discussed. None of them had a high opinion of Mr. Cave's business methods, and this action seemed a culminating folly.

"It's my opinion he's refused that crystal before," said the step-son, a loose-limbed lout of eighteen.

"But *Five Pounds!*" said the step-daughter, an argumentative young woman of six-and-twenty.

Mr. Cave's answers were wretched; he could only mumble weak assertions that he knew his own business best. They drove him from his half-eaten supper into the shop, to close it for the night, his ears aflame and tears of vexation behind his spectacles. Why had he left the crystal in the window so long? The folly of it! That was the trouble closest in his mind. For a time he could see no way of evading sale.

After supper his step-daughter and step-son smartened them-selves up and went out and his wife retired upstairs to reflect upon the business aspects of the crystal, over a little sugar and lemon and so forth in hot water. Mr. Cave went into the shop, and stayed there until late, ostensibly to make ornamental rockeries for gold-fish cases, but really for a private purpose that will be better explained later. The next day Mrs. Cave found that the crystal had been removed from the window, and was lying behind some second-hand books on angling. She replaced it in a conspicuous position. But she did not argue further about it, as a nervous headache disinclined her from debate. Mr. Cave was always disinclined. The day passed disagree-ably. Mr. Cave was, if anything, more absent-minded than usual, and uncommonly irritable withal. In the afternoon, when his wife was taking her customary sleep, he removed the crystal from the window again.

The next day Mr. Cave had to deliver a consignment of dog-fish at one of the hospital schools, where they were needed for dissection. In his absence Mrs. Cave's mind reverted to the topic of the crystal, and the methods of expenditure suitable to a windfall of five pounds. She had already devised some very agreeable expedients, among others a dress of green silk for herself and a trip to Richmond, when a jangling of the front door bell summoned her into the shop. The customer was an examination coach who came to complain of the non-delivery of certain frogs asked for the previous day. Mrs. Cave did not approve of this particular branch of Mr. Cave's business, and the gentleman, who had called in a somewhat aggressive mood, retired after a brief exchange of words—entirely civil, so far as he was concerned. Mrs. Cave's eye then naturally turned to the window; for the sight of the crystal was an assurance of the five pounds and of her dreams. What was her surprise to find it gone!

She went to the place behind the locker on the counter, where she had discovered it the day before. It was not there; and she immediately began an eager search about the shop.

When Mr. Cave returned from his business with the dogfish, about a quarter to two in the afternoon, he found the shop in some confusion, and his wife, extremely exasperated and on her knees behind the counter, routing among his taxidermic material. Her face came up hot and angry over the counter, as the jangling bell announced his return, and she forthwith accused him of "hiding it."

"Hid *what*?" asked Mr. Cave.

"The crystal!"

At that Mr. Cave, apparently much surprised, rushed to the window. "Isn't it here?" he said. "Great Heavens! what has become of it?"

Just then Mr. Cave's step-son re-entered the shop from, the inner room—he had come home a minute or so before Mr. Cave—and he was blaspheming freely. He was apprenticed to a second-hand furniture dealer down the road, but he had his meals at home, and he was naturally annoyed to find no dinner ready.

But when he heard of the loss of the crystal, he forgot his meal, and his anger was diverted from his mother to his step-father. Their first idea, of course, was that he had hidden it. But Mr. Cave stoutly denied all knowledge of its fate, freely offering his bedabbled affidavit in the matter—and at last was worked up to the point of accusing, first, his wife and then his stepson of having taken it with a view to a private sale. So began an exceedingly acrimonious and emotional discussion, which ended for Mrs. Cave in a peculiar nervous condition midway between hysterics and amuck, and caused the step-son to be half-an-hour late at the furniture establishment in the afternoon. Mr. Cave took refuge from his wife's emotions in the shop.

In the evening the matter was resumed, with less passion and in a judicial spirit, under the presidency of the step-daughter. The supper passed unhappily and culminated in a painful scene. Mr. Cave gave way at last to extreme exasperation, and went out banging the front door violently. The rest of the family, having discussed him with the freedom his absence warranted, hunted the house from garret to cellar, hoping to light upon the crystal.

The next day the two customers called again. They were received by Mrs. Cave almost in tears. It transpired that no one *could* imagine all that she had stood from Cave at various times in her married pilgrimage… She also gave a garbled account of the disappearance. The clergyman and the Oriental laughed silently at one another, and said it was very extraordinary. As Mrs. Cave seemed disposed to give them the complete history of her life they made to leave the shop. Thereupon Mrs. Cave, still clinging to hope, asked for the clergyman's address, so that, if she could get anything out of Cave, she might communicate it. The address was duly given, but apparently was afterwards mislaid. Mrs. Cave can remember nothing about it.

In the evening of that day the Caves seem to have exhausted their emotions, and Mr. Cave, who had been out in the afternoon, supped in a gloomy isolation that contrasted pleasantly with the impassioned controversy of the previous days. For some time matters were very badly strained in the Cave household, but neither crystal nor customer reappeared.

Now, without mincing the matter, we must admit that Mr. Cave was a liar. He knew perfectly well where the crystal was. It was in the rooms of Mr. Jacoby Wace, Assistant Demonstrator at St. Catherine's Hospital, Westbourne Street. It stood on the sideboard partially covered by a black velvet cloth, and beside a decanter of American whisky. It is from Mr. Wace, indeed, that the particulars upon which this narrative is based were derived. Cave had taken off the thing to the hospital hidden in the dog-fish sack, and there had pressed the young investigator to keep it for him. Mr. Wace was a little dubious at first. His relationship to Cave was peculiar. He had a taste for singular characters, and he had more than once invited the old man to smoke and drink in his rooms, and to unfold his rather amusing views of life in general and of his wife in particular. Mr. Wace had encountered Mrs. Cave, too, on occasions when Mr. Cave was not at home to attend to him. He knew the constant interference to which Cave was subjected, and having weighed the story judicially, he decided to give the crystal a refuge. Mr. Cave promised to explain the reasons for his remarkable affection for the crystal more fully on a later occasion, but he spoke distinctly of seeing visions therein. He called on Mr. Wace the same evening.

He told a complicated story. The crystal he said had come into his possession with other oddments at the forced sale of another curiosity dealer's effects, and not knowing what its value might be, he had ticketed it at ten shillings. It had hung upon his hands at that price for some months, and he was thinking of "reducing the figure," when he made a singular discovery.

At that time his health was very bad—and it must be borne in mind that, throughout all this experience, his physical condition was one of ebb—and he was in considerable distress by reason of the negligence, the positive ill-treatment even, he received from his wife and step-children. His wife was vain, extravagant, unfeeling, and had a growing taste for private drinking; his step-daughter was mean and over-reaching; and his step-son had conceived a violent dislike for him, and lost no chance of showing it. The requirements of his business pressed heavily upon him, and Mr. Wace does not think that he was altogether free from occasional intemperance. He had begun life in a comfortable position, he was a man of fair education, and he suffered, for weeks at a stretch, from melancholia and insomnia. Afraid to disturb his family, he would slip quietly from his wife's side, when his thoughts became intolerable, and wander about the house. And about three o'clock one morning, late in August, chance directed him into the shop.

The dirty little place was impenetrably black except in one spot, where he perceived an unusual glow of light. Approaching this, he discovered it to be the crystal egg, which was standing on the corner of the counter towards the window. A thin ray smote through a crack in the shutters, impinged upon the object, and seemed as it were to fill its entire interior.

It occurred to Mr. Cave that this was not in accordance with the laws of optics as he had known them in his younger days. He could understand the rays being refracted by the crystal and coming to a focus in its interior, but this diffusion jarred with his physical conceptions. He approached the crystal nearly, peering into it and round it, with a transient revival of the scientific curiosity that in his youth had determined his choice of a calling. He was surprised to find the light not steady, but writhing within the substance of the egg, as though that object was a hollow sphere of some luminous vapour. In moving about to get different points of view, he suddenly found that he had come between it and the ray, and that the crystal none the less remained luminous. Greatly astonished, he lifted it out of the light ray and carried it to the darkest part of the shop. It remained bright for some four or five minutes, when it slowly faded and went out. He placed it in the thin streak of daylight, and its luminousness was almost immediately restored.

So far, at least, Mr. Wace was able to verify the remarkable story of Mr. Cave. He has himself repeatedly held this crystal in a ray of light (which had to be of a less diameter than one millimetre). And in a perfect darkness, such as could be produced by velvet wrapping, the crystal did undoubtedly appear very faintly phosphorescent. It would seem, however, that the luminousness was of some exceptional sort, and not equally visible to all eyes; for Mr. Harbinger—whose name will be familiar to the scientific reader in connection with the Pasteur Institute—was quite unable to see any light whatever. And Mr. Wace's own capacity for its appreciation was out of comparison inferior to that of Mr. Cave's. Even with Mr. Cave the power varied very considerably: his vision was most vivid during states of extreme weakness and fatigue.

Now, from the outset, this light in the crystal exercised a curious fascination upon Mr. Cave. And it says more for his loneliness of soul than a volume of pathetic writing could do, that he told no human being of his curious observations. He seems to have been living in such an atmosphere of petty spite that to admit the existence of a pleasure would have been to risk the loss of it. He found that as the dawn advanced, and the amount of diffused light increased, the crystal became to all appearance non-luminous. And for some time he was unable to see anything in it, except at night-time, in dark corners of the shop.

But the use of an old velvet cloth, which he used as a background for a collection of minerals, occurred to him, and by doubling this, and putting it over his head and hands, he was able to get a sight of the luminous movement within the crystal even in the day-time. He was very cautious lest he should be thus discovered by his wife, and he practised this occupation only in the afternoons, while she was asleep upstairs, and then circumspectly in a hollow under the counter. And one day, turning the crystal about in his hands, he saw something. It came and went like a flash, but it gave him the impression that the object had for a moment opened to him the view of a wide and spacious and strange country; and turning it about, he did, just as the light faded, see the same vision again.

Now it would be tedious and unnecessary to state all the phases of Mr. Cave's discovery from this point. Suffice that the effect was this: the crystal, being peered into at an angle of about 137 degrees from the direction of the illuminating ray, gave a clear and consistent picture of a wide and peculiar country-side. It was not dream-like at all: it produced a definite impression of reality, and the better the light the more real and solid it seemed. It was a moving picture: that is to say, certain objects moved in it, but slowly in an orderly manner like real things, and, according as the direction of the lighting and vision changed, the picture changed also. It must, indeed, have been like looking through an oval glass at a view, and turning the glass about to get at different aspects.

Mr. Cave's statements, Mr. Wace assures me, were extremely circumstantial, and entirely free from any of that emotional quality that taints hallucinatory impressions. But it must be remembered that all the efforts of Mr. Wace to see any similar clarity in the faint opalescence of the crystal were wholly unsuccessful, try as he would. The difference in intensity of the impressions received by the two men was very great, and it is quite conceivable that what was a view to Mr. Cave was a mere blurred nebulosity to Mr. Wace.

The view, as Mr. Cave described it, was invariably of an extensive plain, and he seemed always to be looking at it from a considerable height, as if from a tower or a mast. To the east and to the west the plain was bounded at a remote distance by vast reddish cliffs, which reminded him of those he had seen in some picture; but what the picture was Mr. Wace was unable to ascertain. These cliffs passed north and south—he could tell the points of the compass by the stars that were visible of a night—receding in an almost illimitable perspective and fading into the mists of the distance before they met. He was nearer the eastern set of cliffs; on the occasion of his first vision the sun was rising over them, and black against the sunlight and pale against their shadow appeared a multitude of soaring forms that Mr. Cave regarded as birds. A vast range of buildings spread below him; he seemed to be looking down upon them; and as they approached the blurred and refracted edge of the picture they became indistinct. There were also trees curious in shape, and in colouring a deep mossy green and an exquisite grey, beside a wide and shining canal. And something great and brilliantly coloured flew across the picture. But the first time Mr. Cave saw these pictures he saw only in flashes, his hands shook, his head moved, the vision came and went, and grew foggy and indistinct. And at first he had the greatest difficulty in finding the picture again once the direction of it was lost.

His next clear vision, which came about a week after the first, the interval having yielded nothing but tantalising glimpses and some useful experience, showed him the view down the length of the valley. The view was different, but he had a curious persuasion, which his subsequent observations abundantly confirmed, that he was regarding the strange world from exactly the same spot, although he was looking in a different direction. The long façade of the great building, whose roof he had looked down upon before, was now receding in perspective. He recognised the roof. In the front of the façade was a terrace of massive proportions and extraordinary length, and down the middle of the terrace, at certain intervals, stood huge but very graceful masts, bearing small shiny objects which reflected the setting sun. The import of these small objects did not occur to Mr. Cave until some time after, as he was describing the scene to Mr. Wace. The terrace overhung a thicket of the most luxuriant and graceful vegetation, and beyond this was a wide grassy lawn on which certain broad creatures, in form like beetles but enormously larger, reposed. Beyond this again was a richly decorated causeway of pinkish stone; and beyond that, and lined with dense red weeds, and passing up the valley exactly parallel with the distant cliffs, was a broad and mirror-like expanse of water. The air seemed full of squadrons of great birds, manoeuvring in stately curves; and across the river was a multitude of splendid buildings, richly coloured and glittering with metallic tracery and facets, among a forest of moss-like and lichenous trees. And suddenly something flapped repeatedly across the vision, like the fluttering of a jewelled fan or the beating of a wing, and a face, or rather the upper part of a face with very large eyes, came as it were close to his own and as if on the other side of the crystal. Mr. Cave was so startled and so impressed by the absolute reality of these eyes that he drew his head back from the crystal to look behind it. He had become so absorbed in watching that he was quite surprised to find himself in the cool darkness of his little shop, with its familiar odour of methyl, mustiness, and decay. And as he blinked about him, the glowing crystal faded and went out.

Such were the first general impressions of Mr. Cave. The story is curiously direct and circumstantial. From the outset, when the valley first flashed momentarily on his senses, his imagination was strangely affected, and as he began to appreciate the details of the scene he saw, his wonder rose to the point of a passion. He went about his business listless and distraught, thinking only of the time when he should be able to return to his watching. And then a few weeks after his first sight of the valley came the two customers, the stress and excitement of their offer, and the narrow escape of the crystal from sale, as I have already told.

Now, while the thing was Mr. Cave's secret, it remained a mere wonder, a thing to creep to covertly and peep at, as a child might peep upon a forbidden garden. But Mr. Wace has, for a young scientific investigator, a particularly lucid and consecutive habit of mind. Directly the crystal and its story came to him, and he had satisfied himself, by seeing the phosphorescence with his own eyes, that there really was a certain evidence for Mr. Cave's statements, he proceeded to develop the matter systematically. Mr. Cave was only too eager to come and feast his eyes on this wonderland he saw, and he came every night from half-past eight until half-past ten, and sometimes, in Mr. Wace's absence, during the day. On Sunday afternoons, also, he came. From the outset Mr. Wace made copious notes, and it was

due to his scientific method that the relation between the direction
from which the initiating ray entered the crystal and the orientation
of the picture were proved. And, by covering the crystal in a box
perforated only with a small aperture to admit the exciting ray, and
by substituting black holland for his buff blinds, he greatly improved
the conditions of the observations; so that in a little while they were
able to survey the valley in any direction they desired.

So having cleared the way, we may give a brief account of this
visionary world within the crystal. The things were in all cases seen
by Mr. Cave, and the method of working was invariably for him to
watch the crystal and report what he saw, while Mr. Wace (who as
a science student had learnt the trick of writing in the dark) wrote
a brief note of his report. When the crystal faded, it was put into
its box in the proper position and the electric light turned on. Mr.
Wace asked questions, and suggested observations to clear up difficult points. Nothing, indeed, could have been less visionary and
more matter-of-fact.

The attention of Mr. Cave had been speedily directed to the
bird-like creatures he had seen so abundantly present in each of his
earlier visions. His first impression was soon corrected, and he considered for a time that they might represent a diurnal species of bat.
Then he thought, grotesquely enough, that they might be cherubs.
Their heads were round and curiously human, and it was the eyes
of one of them that had so startled him on his second observation.
They had broad, silvery wings, not feathered, but glistening almost
as brilliantly as new-killed fish and with the same subtle play of
colour, and these wings were not built on the plan of bird-wing or
bat, Mr. Wace learned, but supported by curved ribs radiating from
the body. (A sort of butterfly wing with curved ribs seems best to
express their appearance.) The body was small, but fitted with two

bunches of prehensile organs, like long tentacles, immediately under the mouth. Incredible as it appeared to Mr. Wace, the persuasion at last became irresistible that it was these creatures which owned the great quasihuman buildings and the magnificent garden that made the broad valley so splendid. And Mr. Cave perceived that the buildings, with other peculiarities, had no doors, but that the great circular windows, which opened freely, gave the creatures egress and entrance. They would alight upon their tentacles, fold their wings to a smallness almost rod-like, and hop into the interior. But among them was a multitude of smaller-winged creatures, like great dragon-flies and moths and flying beetles, and across the greensward brilliantly-coloured gigantic ground-beetles crawled lazily to and fro. Moreover, on the causeways and terraces, large-headed creatures similar to the greater winged flies, but wingless, were visible, hopping busily upon their hand-like tangle of tentacles.

Allusion has already been made to the glittering objects upon masts that stood upon the terrace of the nearer building. It dawned upon Mr. Cave, after regarding one of these masts very fixedly on one particularly vivid day that the glittering object there was a crystal exactly like that into which he peered. And a still more careful scrutiny convinced him that each one in a vista of nearly twenty carried a similar object.

Occasionally one of the large flying creatures would flutter up to one, and folding its wings and coiling a number of its tentacles about the mast, would regard the crystal fixedly for a space—sometimes for as long as fifteen minutes. And a series of observations, made at the suggestion of Mr. Wace, convinced both watchers that, so far as this visionary world was concerned, the crystal into which they peered actually stood at the summit of the end-most mast on the terrace, and that on one occasion at least one of these inhabitants of this other world had looked into Mr. Cave's face while he was making these observations.

So much for the essential facts of this very singular story. Unless we dismiss it all as the ingenious fabrication of Mr. Wace, we have to believe one of two things: either that Mr. Cave's crystal was in two worlds at once, and that while it was carried about in one, it remained stationary in the other, which seems altogether absurd; or else that it had some peculiar relation of sympathy with another and exactly similar crystal in this other world, so that what was seen in the interior of the one in this world was, under suitable conditions, visible to an observer in the corresponding crystal in the other world; and *vice versa*. At present, indeed, we do not know of any way in which two crystals could so come *en rapport,* but nowadays we know enough to understand that the thing is not altogether impossible. This view of the crystals as *en rapport* was the supposition that occurred to Mr. Wace, and to me at least it seems extremely plausible...

And where was this other world? On this, also, the alert intelligence of Mr. Wace speedily threw light. After sunset, the sky darkened rapidly—there was a very brief twilight interval indeed—and the stars shone out. They were recognisably the same as those we see, arranged in the same constellations. Mr. Cave recognised the Bear, the Pleiades, Aldebaran, and Sirius; so that the other world must be somewhere in the solar system, and, at the utmost, only a few hundreds of millions of miles from our own. Following up this clue, Mr. Wace learned that the midnight sky was a darker blue even than our midwinter sky, and that the sun seemed a little smaller. *And there were two small moons!* "like our moon but smaller, and quite differently marked," one of which moved so rapidly that its motion was clearly visible as one regarded it. These moons were never high in the sky, but vanished as they rose: that is, every time they revolved they were eclipsed because they were so near their primary planet. And all this answers quite completely, although Mr. Cave did not know it, to what must be the condition of things on Mars.

Indeed, it seems an exceedingly plausible conclusion that peering into this crystal Mr. Cave did actually see the planet Mars and its inhabitants. And if that be the case, then the evening star that shone so brilliantly in the sky of that distant vision was neither more nor less than our own familiar earth.

For a time the Martians—if they were Martians—do not seem to have known of Mr. Cave's inspection. Once or twice one would come to peer, and go away very shortly to some other mast, as though the vision was unsatisfactory. During this time Mr. Cave was able to watch the proceedings of these winged people without being disturbed by their attentions, and although his report is necessarily vague and fragmentary, it is nevertheless very suggestive. Imagine the impression of humanity a Martian observer would get who, after a difficult process of preparation and with considerable fatigue to the eyes, was able to peer at London from the steeple of St. Martin's Church for stretches, at longest, of four minutes at a time. Mr. Cave was unable to ascertain if the winged Martians were the same as the Martians who hopped about the causeways and terraces, and if the latter could put on wings at will. He several times saw certain clumsy bipeds, dimly suggestive of apes, white and partially translucent, feeding among certain of the lichenous trees, and once some of these fled before one of the hopping, round-headed Martians. The latter caught one in its tentacles, and then the picture faded suddenly and left Mr. Cave most tantalisingly in the dark. On another occasion a vast thing, that Mr. Cave thought at first was some gigantic insect, appeared advancing along the causeway beside the canal with extraordinary rapidity. As this drew nearer Mr. Cave perceived that it was a mechanism of shining metals and of extraordinary complexity. And then, when he looked again, it had passed out of sight.

After a time Mr. Wace aspired to attract the attention of the Martians, and the next time that the strange eyes of one of them appeared close to the crystal Mr. Cave cried out and sprang away, and they immediately turned on the light and began to gesticulate in a manner suggestive of signalling. But when at last Mr. Cave examined the crystal again the Martian had departed.

Thus far these observations had progressed in early November, and then Mr. Cave, feeling that the suspicions of his family about the crystal were allayed, began to take it to and fro with him in order that, as occasion arose in the daytime or night, he might comfort himself with what was fast becoming the most real thing in his existence.

In December Mr. Wace's work in connection with a forthcoming examination became heavy, the sittings were reluctantly suspended for a week, and for ten or eleven days—he is not quite sure which—he saw nothing of Cave. He then grew anxious to resume these investigations, and, the stress of his seasonal labours being abated, he went down to Seven Dials. At the corner he noticed a shutter before a bird fancier's window, and then another at a cobbler's. Mr. Cave's shop was closed.

He rapped and the door was opened by the step-son in black. He at once called Mrs. Cave, who was, Mr. Wace could not but observe, in cheap but ample widow's weeds of the most imposing pattern. Without any very great surprise Mr. Wace learnt that Cave was dead and already buried. She was in tears, and her voice was a little thick. She had just returned from Highgate. Her mind seemed occupied with her own prospects and the honourable details of the obsequies, but Mr. Wace was at last able to learn the particulars of Cave's death. He had been found dead in his shop in the early morning, the day after his last visit to Mr. Wace, and the crystal had been clasped in his stone-cold hands. His face was smiling, said Mrs. Cave, and the velvet cloth from the minerals lay on the floor at his feet. He must have been dead five or six hours when he was found.

This came as a great shock to Wace, and he began to reproach himself bitterly for having neglected the plain symptoms of the old man's ill-health. But his chief thought was of the crystal. He approached that topic in a gingerly manner, because he knew Mrs. Cave's peculiarities. He was dumbfounded to learn that it was sold.

Mrs. Cave's first impulse, directly Cave's body had been taken upstairs, had been to write to the mad clergyman who had offered five pounds for the crystal, informing him of its recovery; but after a violent hunt, in which her daughter joined her, they were convinced of the loss of his address. As they were without the means required to mourn and bury Cave in the elaborate style the dignity of an old Seven Dials inhabitant demands, they had appealed to a friendly fellow-tradesman in Great Portland Street. He had very kindly taken over a portion of the stock at a valuation. The valuation was his own, and the crystal egg was included in one of the lots. Mr. Wace, after a few suitable condolences, a little off-handedly proffered perhaps, hurried at once to Great Portland Street. But there he learned that the crystal egg had already been sold to a tall, dark man in grey. And there the material facts in this curious, and to me at least very suggestive, story come abruptly to an end. The Great Portland Street dealer did not know who the tall dark man in grey was, nor had he observed him with sufficient attention to describe him minutely. He did not even know which way this person had gone after leaving the shop. For a time Mr. Wace remained in the shop, trying the dealer's patience with hopeless questions, venting his own exasperation. And at last, realising abruptly that the whole thing had passed out of his hands, had vanished like a vision of the night, he returned to his own rooms, a little astonished to find the notes he had made still tangible and visible upon, his untidy table.

His annoyance and disappointment were naturally very great. He made a second call (equally ineffectual) upon the Great Portland Street dealer, and he resorted to advertisements in such periodicals as were lively to come into the hands of a *bric-a-brac* collector. He also wrote letters to *The Daily Chronicle* and *Nature*, but both those periodicals, suspecting a hoax, asked him to reconsider his action before they printed, and he was advised that such a strange story, unfortunately so bare of supporting evidence, might imperil his reputation as an investigator. Moreover, the calls of his proper work were urgent. So that after a month or so, save for an occasional reminder to certain dealers, he had reluctantly to abandon the quest for the crystal egg, and from that day to this it remains undiscovered. Occasionally, however, he tells me, and I can quite believe him, he has bursts of zeal, in which he abandons his more urgent occupation and resumes the search.

Whether or not it will remain lost for ever, with the material and origin of it, are things equally speculative at the present time. If the present purchaser is a collector, one would have expected the enquiries of Mr. Wace to have reached him through the dealers. He has been able to discover Mr. Cave's clergyman and "Oriental"—no other than the Rev. James Parker and the young Prince of Bosso-Kuni in Java. I am obliged to them for certain particulars. The object of the Prince was simply curiosity—and extravagance. He was so eager to buy because Cave was so oddly reluctant to sell. It is just as possible that the buyer in the second instance was simply a casual purchaser and not a collector at all, and the crystal egg, for all I know, may at the present moment be within a mile of me, decorating a drawing-room or serving as a paper-weight—its remarkable functions all unknown. Indeed, it is partly with the idea of such a possibility that I have thrown this narrative into a form that will give it a chance of being read by the ordinary consumer of fiction.

My own ideas in the matter are practically identical with those of Mr. Wace. I believe the crystal on the mast in Mars and the crystal egg of Mr. Cave's to be in some physical, but at present quite inexplicable, way *en rapport,* and we both believe further that the terrestrial crystal must have been—possibly at some remote date—sent hither from that planet, in order to give the Martians a near view of our affairs. Possibly the fellows to the crystals on the other masts are also on our globe. No theory of hallucination suffices for the facts.

LETTERS FROM MARS

W. S. Lach-Szyrma

The suggestion by Giovanni Schiaparelli that he had seen straight lines, or canali, on Mars prompted the speculation that Mars might have canals, carrying water from the polar regions to irrigate more arid areas, and that in turn implied there was intelligent life there. It was from this thought, fuelled by the American astronomer Percival Lowell, that the late Victorian belief grew that Mars was the home of intelligent beings; a belief that lasted for over eighty years. One of the first authors to consider the canals was Wladislaw Somerville Lach-Szyrma (1841–1915).

The author was born and raised in Devon, the son of a Polish soldier and philosopher who had immigrated to England in 1832. His son entered the Church, and at the time he was writing these stories he was vicar of St. Peter's at Newlyn in Cornwall. He was clearly well read and believed that life, in one form or another, was almost certainly universal throughout the cosmos. He wrote a small book, A Voice from Another World, *in 1874 to put forward these views, which he did from the vantage point of Aleriel, a winged native of Venus, who has travelled through the cosmos in his ether-ship. The book was well received and in 1883 he reissued it with additional material as* Aleriel, or a Voyage to Other Worlds. *This takes place several years later, when the narrator receives a report from Aleriel about his adventures since they last met, which included a visit to Mars. On that first visit Aleriel barely mentions the canals. Instead the 1883 account talks about the planet's red vegetation and green seas, and the devout nature of the tall Martians, who had also had a saviour from*

God. Lach-Szyrma clearly enjoyed writing these didactic pieces, as he returned to Aleriel in 1887 and wrote an occasional series of 'Letters from the Planets' for Cassell's Family Magazine, which ran until 1892. The series gave updates on Aleriel's travels, including his home life, and the following educational return to Mars.

D EAR FRIEND,—I HAVE THOUGHT OF MENTIONING TO YOU
one of the sights I saw on Mars, which may interest you,
and be of use as suggesting what man might effect if only he learnt
wisdom. Your Arctic regions are useless; left to the Polar bear, or the
whale and walrus. Man's dominion does not extend to them, even
to those realms nearest to the most cultured lands of Europe. As for
your Antarctic regions, you actually know less of them than of the
Antarctic realms of Mars, for these you can see in your most powerful telescopes—you can at least discern the outlines of land and sea.
But of the Antarctic realms of the earth no man can tell whether
they are land or sea, whether the Antarctic continent is a fable or a
fact, though probably it is the former.

When I arrived at the Mitchell Mountains, in the Antarctic zone of
Mars, I was struck with the vast scene of icy desolation there—very
like the mountain regions of Greenland, only that the sea around
was green, and not blue. After traversing some hundreds of miles of
their snowy peaks and cliffs, and magnificent wild Arctic scenery (not
unlike the Arctic scenery of earth), I was suddenly struck with the
sight of a trail of rich red vegetation of several miles in the midst of
the eternal snows. I approached with curiosity this oasis in the frozen
desert. As I approached I felt the air suddenly grow less icy, or rather
the icy blasts were relieved by warmer air currents, and these currents
seemed to rise from what appeared to be a huge crater of a volcano
(very like the volcanoes of earth or the extinct ring mountains of the
moon, and, on a smaller scale, like our ring mountains). "Surely," I

thought, "here is volcanic action." Still I noticed no eruption, nor geysers, nor lava current.

The night came on. The Martian moon Phoibos was dimly visible near the horizon. All else was dark and calm, save the stars above. From an opening in the mountain, in the very centre of the warmer oasis, a light issued; but not the ruddy light of molten lava, nor sulphurous flickering flame, but the calm white electric light. It appeared issuing from the ground. I approached, and then I saw it came from a vast chasm, which, however, was not opened perpendicularly down into the depths, but seemingly sloped downwards into an angle. As I drew near, I noticed some hundreds of Martians busy about the opening.

It was difficult to enter the chasm without being perceived, but as I noticed the electric light only illumined well the lower part of the slope—*i.e.*, that near the ground—and that the overhanging rocks were at a great height in comparative darkness, I resolved to make the attempt.

I flew in the shadow right into the tunnel. Then I felt the air was warmer, and as I went on, going onward and onward, it grew warmer and warmer still. I flew forward thus several miles, the tunnel manifestly sinking deeper and deeper by its decline in the slope. The light was less, and the electric lamps grew further and further apart. By them, however, I noticed cars of the Martians hurried forward into the tunnel, and descended by it deeper and deeper into the planet's interior. It was, in fact, like a huge adit of a colossal mine.

So I thought for a time that it might be, until having gone some ten miles into the huge tunnel, and I should think some three or four miles down into the depth of the planet, below the level of the Arctic Sea, I came to a gigantic cavern about a mile high, and the limits of which I could not see on any side. Before me was a huge lake of evidently half-boiling water, through which there flowed a stream of burning lava, or rather that liquid rock which in Mars represents the lava of the earth. Through this lake there was a huge causeway, on which the Martian cars were carried onwards with their living freight. I flew onwards over the lake, and here and there on its dark steaming waters were the electric ships of the Martians, while in certain places lighthouses were placed, which gave with the blaze of their electric lights a calm to a scene which otherwise might have been terrible. I followed the line of the causeway, and came at last to a shore, where was a well-illuminated city.

Here were hosts of factories, of vast machines, of smelting opera-tions, of huge furnaces, deriving heat from the great lava streams issuing out of the depths of the planet. The air, instead of being cold, as on the surface above, was heated. Busy works were going on, and myriads of the Martians could be seen following in the city divers industries. It was a wonderful scene of activity.

When I looked at it, I thought, "Is not this more advanced planet representing to me what in future ages may be seen in the Arctic regions of the earth? Those realms are now cold, bound down, and frozen with intense eternal cold. They are useless to mankind. Yet if the surface be so frozen, it does not follow that the depths are so likewise. Nay, Hecla itself teaches how beneath frozen Iceland is a region of eternal fires of burning heat, such as might smelt all the metals of Birmingham.

"On earth man leaves these Arctic regions waste and barren, because he confines himself to the cold frozen surface; but the Martians are wiser—their Arctic regions, indeed, are even colder than those on earth, but they can obtain heat beneath the surface.

A few miles below Siberia or Labrador are regions hotter than man can bear. I have met miners on earth who, in latitudes north of 50° on earth, have told me that in the coldest winters, when the surface of the earth is frozen and covered with the white snows, they have been so hot that they have had to labour with their clothes off, almost naked, on account of the heat. Why not utilise these subterranean fires? Underneath Manchester or Glasgow, or far colder regions, are subterranean fires, more potent than all the coal of the Lancashire or Staffordshire coal measures could produce. Intense heat is to be found a mile or two beneath earth's surface. Why should that heat be all useless? How absurd of man to lament the chimerical trouble that the coal measures can be exhausted by human industry, when the earth's heat alone offers a greater heat than the burning up of all the coal measures of their world can produce; just as the force of the tides of earth's oceans, now utterly wasted, even in England itself, could produce a thousand times greater power (capable of being converted into the master-force of electricity) than all the steam-engines of earth could produce—a mighty, almost immeasurable force!"

In those regions not far from the Mitchell Mountains in the hilly country of Cassini Land, I saw another quaint scene no less wonderful, which may be regarded as the natural outcome of the immense power over nature (to mould it to their will) which the Martians possess, and which man may in time attain when mechanical arts are further advanced than they are now, should the instinct of mound-building ever revive on earth. I noticed in those more favoured regions of the Martian south temperate zone, as I approached Cassini Land over the green waves of the Zollner Sea, what looked like colossal statues of gigantic Martians, several hundred feet high. These enormous statues struck me as very singular. I approached them and saw that they were natural hills cut into shapes of gigantic size many times larger than the huge Colossus of Rhodes, or the figure of Liberty at New York. In one case, indeed, a gigantic crouching figure was so vast that its head was surmounted with a crown, within the border of which a little city had been erected. Another hill was cut into the form of one of the Martian trees, and on each leaf there stood a house, looking like a flower or bud. In another hill two projecting peaks had been fashioned into two hands, and in each hand a house was built. "Here," I thought, "is something of the state of things that might have even now occurred on earth, had the present civilised inhabitants shared the desire of moulding hills into the form of natural objects which once existed among the Mound-builders of Wisconsin and Ohio. Had those Mound-builders, instead of being exterminated by superior races, left descendants capable of carrying out their ideas and of utilising the steam-engine, and dynamite, and the various forces of civilisation, what a strange land of wonders the Western States of America would have been! Almost as wonderful as Cassini Land in Mars. But the European builds for himself, as the ancient American tried to fashion natural objects to his own uses; the European having conquered, the American ideal has never had a chance of being carried out on earth."

I saw many wonderful engineering works on Mars—huge canals and causeways, and coasts rounded of their promontories (blown away by explosives)—such as I should think the astronomers of earth, if they have not yet seen them, must surely observe before very long.

ALERIEL

After his first visit to Mars Aleriel returned home to Venus and then continued his travels around the inner part of the solar system visiting Mercury and then approaching the Sun. But being warned not to approach too closely, Aleriel returned to Venus where a Congress is summoned to consider further exploration of space and a return to Mars.

THE CONGRESS

We landed at the City of the North Pole, which is built in a deep valley encircled by colossal mountains from ten to eighteen miles high, and sheltering it from the bitter Arctic blasts. As the Sun does not shine upon it for much of the year (on account partly of the mountain shadows, partly of its being in the Arctic regions), the heat and light are mainly artificial. It happened now, however, to be the Northern summer, and myriads of our countrymen had come from divers lands to see the wonders and beauties of the Arctic regions, and to stay awhile at the City of the North Pole, just as a few adventurous tourists on Earth annually go to see the "Land of the Midnight Sun"—*i.e.,* Norway. With us it is thought pleasant and desirable for every one occasionally to spend a summer in the Arctic regions, and to stay, a few days at least, at the Pole itself. Perhaps the time may come when this will be the case on Earth, but it seems far distant, for—firstly, the sun is farther from your world than from ours of Venus; next, from the tilting of the planet the summer is warmer; and, thirdly, vast progress in command over nature will be required before men can even reach the Poles. I expect it can only be done by perfecting the art of flight, or aeronautics, for the only convenient way of reaching the North or South Pole of either Venus or Earth is by flight.

We descended amid the great ring chain of mountains, down which, in the summer thaw, the cascades were pouring from the glaciers, and we poised our car over the glittering domes and towers of the great City of the North Pole. Then we slowly descended, amid the plaudits of the crowds who welcomed us home.

As we alighted we were welcomed by the thousands of visitors at the Polar city. Joyous was our welcome, and deep our gratitude to Divine Providence, as we descended from the car which had borne us so well through the dangers of our awful, yet glorious, solar journey. We now noticed how it was encrusted with many metals which had fallen on it in the form of metallic rain as we had got near the Sun-spot, and now were crystallised around it in a strange form of metallic efflorescence. Tiny cubes of copper, iron, magnesium, cobalt, were there. The record of our near approach to the Sun was on the car itself.

A congress was summoned, the third day after our arrival, in the assembly-place near the city—a vast amphitheatre enclosed by mountains, and close to a beautiful cascade which in winter was frozen, but now rushed down the mountain crags. The scene in the summer sun was very beautiful as the congress assembled to receive us. Tens of thousands were ranged on the terraces and ledges of the rocks to see us, and to hear what we could relate of our journey to the Sun.

I need not narrate the account of the congress, which was something like the former one, which I have described before. We told all we had seen, and showed the specimens we had collected from Mercury and the solar regions. Then questions were asked, and for several days the congress lasted. At length Azarian, one of the Princes of the City of the Stars, suggested that the work of communicating between world and world of our system, and of studying our sister-worlds by actually visiting them, should be continued, and another journey should be planned. Ezariel was the chief speaker of our party. He assented to the view that now, since we had as mere voyagers visited the worlds around us, and even seen the mighty centre of our system, a more thorough exploration of one or two worlds would be desirable. The two that especially presented themselves to his mind for further inquiry were Mars and the Earth. But he urged that a larger car and a larger party of specialists, who would make a thorough inquiry, were desirable. The difficulty was urged by Axorian, the Prince of the City of the North Pole, that there would be a danger of our being observed and detected both in Mars and on Earth if we went in so large a party. But Ezariel, who had visited, as I told you, both worlds before, parried this serious difficulty by proposing that our party should confine itself to going around the two planets and photographing carefully all the scenery of each, and to land in some remote part of Mars, and on the Earth to rest in the wilds of Central Australia and perhaps in Equatorial Africa, where men would not be likely to find us out, and where we could examine the animal and vegetable life of the Earth, and many other matters of interest, without any fear or risk of interruption or discovery.

This view was accepted by the congress. We each proceeded to our homes, and the great nature-subduer, Ornalion, was entrusted with the construction of a large car for twenty specialists to go through space to Mars and the Earth, to examine in each world the wondrous works of the great Creator. It was provided with powerful magnets and anti-gravitating machinery, and was of the strongest materials. In it a large quantity of specimens, and also all requisite apparatus, could be stored.

THE CANALS OF MARS

I resolved to join the expedition, and in less than a quarter of one of our years I was once more flying through infinite space to the regions of the ruddy world of Mars.

I need not describe our journey thither. The spot we chose to rest on was Hall's Snow Island, as an unfrequented and desolate region, yet not far from the great centres of Martian life. Here we landed by night, and remained two days on one of its lofty peaks, whence we could see part of Copernicus Land, and the Schiaparelli Lake, beyond which Kepler Land shone in rich crimson glory on the horizon.

The sun rose on the ruddy land, shining over the crimson forests, varied by the green seas, which in richest hues adorned a landscape glorious in its gorgeous colourings. On one side the De la Rue Ocean expanded its green surface to the horizon, now rippled by ridges of white foam, now tranquil like a sheet of green glass. Kepler Land on the other side and Copernicus Land spread their crimson expanse to the faint green horizon of the Terby Sea. Along the shore in green lines, here and there, were the great straight canals of Mars, that diffused the waters over the land, and which here stretched to both the Schiaparelli and the Bessel Lakes.

It was arranged that after two days' stay on the snowy peak, which was wellnigh inaccessible to the Martians, the rest of the party should start on an aërial expedition around Mars, and, poised in mid-air at great heights above his atmosphere, should photograph the divers scenes of the planet, and so record all that was to be observed for the philosophers and museums of our world, and that Ulnorion should accompany me on or near the surface of the planet, and that we should be disguised, as nearly as we could, in the Martian costume and aspect, which, in truth, was very difficult, on account of our smaller size.

According to this plan we flew across to the Lagrange peninsula, and thence by the shores of Pratt Bay passed into the interior of Secchi Continent. Here the great system of canals of vast length and width struck our attention. They looked artificial, yet in width were like sounds or straits, but stretched for hundreds of miles, as clear from any undulation or bend as if they had been drawn with a ruler. Their green lines marked the red land, like lines ruled on a music book, varied land with water. On their surfaces were floating islands of the Martians, crowded with houses and factories and towers (like moving cities). On their shores were also vast edifices, where we could see the great machines of the Martians working and moving. Like a huge spider's web they spread over the crimson expanse of land.

From here we resolved to go to where my former Martian guide lived, that by his aid we might both obtain more information about this gorgeous world, and also that Ulnorion might, by his separate report, be able to add to or correct what I had learnt about Mars.

I found without difficulty the home of my former Martian friend and instructor. There it was—the domed house glittering with metal ornaments beneath the ruddy foliage of the forest. I led Ulnorion to the door, and then, noticing one of the windows open, I signed to him to fly in after me. My old friend was there, and was much alarmed at first at the unexpected apparition of two beings from another world, for I had cast off my disguise, so that he might know me. But then recovering himself, he recognised me as his former friend and guest.

"I have returned again to your bright and gorgeous world, as I longed to know more about it. May I have your help to see it again, unknown and unobserved?"

"Welcome!" was the reply. "I often have thought of you and of your bright world, and all you told me."

And then he welcomed us with the Martian rites of greeting, and lighted the sacred fire upon the pillar, and offered us warm food. This we gladly accepted. Ulnorion, I noticed, however, was timid and ill at ease. There is a natural shrinking of all creatures from beings of another world, and so I found Ulnorion and our Martian host shrank from each other instinctively.

But as time went on this lessened. I asked our Martian friend about the events of my past visit, and showed him how I remembered what he had told me. Then I suggested to Ulnorion that he might ask any questions he wished about the ruddy world in which we were, and I would interpret his queries. As I expected, the first question he asked was about the wonderful canals we had recently seen.

"Will you explain to me," said Ulnorion, through me as his interpreter, "those huge canals that, straight as a line, mark several of your continents? They do not seem natural, for nowhere by natural laws are such straight lines formed; nature is ever devious, and tends to undulations, but these look like vast engineering works. Are they such, or do the laws of nature work in this world differently to the way they work in other planets?"

"They are mainly artificial works," said our Martian friend, "though utilising our rivers and lakes. Our command over natural forces has in recent times become very great. So we resolved, for our own convenience, to turn the rivers and lakes into great canals or sounds. It was for the advantage of the country that water and land should be evenly distributed. By machinery and the use of natural forces we were able to correct nature to our own purposes. These straight canals are of great value. Water and land combined produce food, and on the water we can travel with rapidity and comfort from one part of our world to the other. Since we have had no wars we have been able to devote our force to the arts of peace."

"What are those huge floating islands I saw on the canals?" asked Ulnorion.

"They are the floating cities. Instead of staying in one place, it is more convenient to move about. Thus we can live in a perpetual summer, and not merely leave our homes, but take our houses and our gardens with us over the waters from ocean to ocean, from land to land, and draw food both from land and water."

"There is," I said, "on Earth a far-off approach to this moving population in the floating hotels or great steamers of the Mississippi, and, on a very small scale, in the floating population of the little Chinese canals."

"There is another point." said our Martian instructor; "on Earth and in your world of Venus there is no scarcity of water. Our population is great, and our supply of water is not enough. The rains are insufficient. If we depended on nature alone, the inner parts of many of our continents would be desert and want moisture. Now we open them up by these canals, and diffuse water everywhere on the land as is most convenient to us and likely to develop the production of the soil. So land and water brought together produce food. Left to themselves we should have land in one part and sea in the other, and our planet could not then support so much life as it does now."*

* Some very interesting discoveries have recently been made by M. Perrotin about the "canals of Mars," and a map of these extraordinary green straight lines on the red surface of the planet has been constructed by him. They look on it very like the aspect of a railway system on a colossal scale.

The fact was, as he said, the Martians lived mostly on what (to use Earthly language to explain unearthly organisms) you would call aquatic plants. The ruddy vegetation of the land (similar in some points to the food-bearing plants of Earth) is insufficient for the teeming population. But, fortunately, the algæ or sea-plants of Mars are far more nourishing and agreeable than those of Earth. They form an exhaustless store of food, with the huge heaps of edible molluscs (somewhat like your oysters) which fill the Martian seas. But the great ocean-depths are less useful for these aquatic plants and animals than the shallow waters of the huge Martian canals. In ancient times, indeed, the Martians looked to the ocean for supplies of food; but as population increased and also their power of controlling nature, they found it better to construct long shallow seas (which could be drained as required) in which vast oceanic farms could be formed for supplying food. Even on Earth the supply of food by the ocean would be inexhaustible; and perhaps in ages to come, when every land is over-populated, man may be forced as the Martians to establish fish-farms in shallow artificial seas to supplement the food supply.

"There is much wisdom in what you say," I replied. "If Northern Africa or Australia had some such system of canals as this, they would produce much more and suffer less from drought and desert." We issued forth from the house, and mounting on a hill close by, watched the Sun slowly descend over the crimson plain and the vast green network of canals which stretched in all directions at our feet. Our Martian friend named the canals to us and told us where they led.

Thus we conversed until the shadows of evening gathered in; and then Ulnorion and I waited for awhile to watch the dying rays of the Sun shine on the ruddy forest-glades, over which soon shone in the

still sky the two bright evening stars—*i.e.*, Earth with her little satellite
the Moon, and Venus our bright home; and besides these, the two
moons of Mars, Deimos and Phobos. And then, as the constellations
appeared, we returned to the domed house, and under its hospitable
shelter rested for the night.

CANAL LIFE ON MARS

Morning came. The bright sun shone into the metal-adorned dwelling: the same glorious sun as we had known at home, and as you
behold on Earth, to which indeed all Earth life—plants, animals,
men—owes vitality and heat. It shone on the ornate and bright metal
pavement of copper and tin; it shone on the metal walls, and was
reflected upon us.

We arose, and left the dwelling to look on the forest around. There
were the crimson trees in rich splendour, through whose glinting foliage the ruddy rays of the sunlight pierced. There were the rocks rising
over the tall metal dome of the house; there in an opening appeared
the distant green sea and the summit of far-off snowy mountains. Red,
white, and green—all were commingled in that glowing spectacle.

We returned to the house. Our kind but gigantic host welcomed
us on our return, and said to me—

"If you wish to see the canals, the electric boat is at your service.
You may take a long voyage in it, if you like."

"We should indeed," I said. "I wish my companion to see the
great canals of your wonderful world. But how shall we manage
about disguise?"

"I have some garments of our children, which may suit you as
disguises if no one comes near our boat; and if they do, perchance

they may not observe that you are of an order of beings different from ourselves."

So he lifted the portcullis, which served for an inner door, and shortly came forth with our kind hostess, Alehiro, who brought with her the robes of metal scales and glass fibre which her children used. They were beautiful glittering robes, though very different from ours. However, we easily wrapped ourselves in them, and, covering our heads with metallic helms, looked like two Martian children.

A little vessel was floating on the green canal waters, chained to the shore. Our host drew it towards him and entered it. He beckoned to us to do the same. We stepped on board, and lay on the couch which was in the bow. The boat was shaped like a torpedo boat, for throughout the universe the laws of mathematics and mechanics must be the same, and thus the principle of the least possible resistance must be the same, even as far as the attendant worlds of Sirius or Alcyone. Our Martian host touched a brass knob in the bow, and rapidly and silently the boat was propelled upon the green waters.

Forward we swept along the straight reach, with ruddy foliage on either side rising in crimson glories, gorgeous in the sun's light. Here and there amid the red leaves were the glittering metal domes of dwellings. On the shore strange forms of living beings, of shapes unknown to Earth or Venus, might be seen, while others were in the water or flying in the air above. It is true that the types of life are the same throughout the solar system, and thus you, on Earth, may have all the various forms in which it is developed. But still, as there is underlying unity, there is also an infinite diversity in creation. Thus, although the forms of Earth's animal and vegetable life were there, they were all distinct from those you have on Earth. No animal was the same as that you have here, nor even very like it, although in many forms of life the type of some of the animals which you see on Earth; and such as we have with us, could be traced. Then, again, developments of life, such as are very rare on Earth, were here most common; and those which on Earth are small were here gigantic; while, on the other hand, animals which on earth are very common—*e.g.*, the horse, the bull, the sheep, the sparrow, the finch—could not be seen at all, nor any creature like them. Thus the scene before me was one of life and motion, for Mars is made to support life as much as the Earth; but still each and every development of life was distinct from what men see, and the whole scene was like the monstrous imagination of a disordered dream. Still each creature was formed in perfect harmony with its position in creation, and many were very beautiful in glowing colours and in graceful forms.

You need not wonder that in another world the forms of life are different from those on Earth, for is not (even on Earth) marine life distinct from terrestrial, though belonging to the same planet? and even on the land in past ages forms have prevailed and been highly developed, which now are rare and small: *e.g.*, the trilobites of the ancient seas, the silures, the plants of the carboniferous era, the iguanodons, and ichthyosauri, and plesiosauri of secondary ages. These are but Earthly creatures, though of Earth's infancy, and such as man might suppose fitted for another planet. Nay, more, even on Earth at this time are not the flora and fauna of Australia different from those of Europe? How different must be the life on another planet, even though one so like Earth as is Mars!

On we dashed over the green waters embosomed by the crimson forests and fields, till we came to a wide reach, which stretched for eight miles wide, and extended for a thousand miles and more (as our conductor told us) from sea to sea. Its shores were perfectly straight, and it looked like a vast river—like the Mississippi or Amazon on Earth—indeed, no river on Earth in continuous width approaches its size. But it was all the result of the industry and command over nature of the Martians. Rivers had been straightened, lowlands had been submerged, hills had been blown up, whole territories had been altered and changed in aspect, to make that huge canal, or rather submerged land, through which the fertilising waters flowed, to bring moisture and life to the immense submarine fields of vegetation which grew there. Compared to this, the Suez Canal or the greatest ship canals of Earth were but as the little gutters dug by a child for an afternoon's amusement.

Moving on the vast canal, or rather artificial sound, about a mile from us, there was a floating city, resting upon huge pontoons, nearly a mile long, and about a quarter of a mile wide. Each end of the city was narrowed to a point, so its form was not unlike that of a river steamer, only its size as compared with the greatest ocean liners, like the *City of Rome* or the *Oceana*, was as these are to the little ships of your forefathers. The pontoons themselves were enormous vessels, larger than any ship you have on earth. They were bound together in rows, and a pointed one was in the head at each side, acting as a cut-water.

The city was formed like the usual towns of the Martians, with domed houses of bright metal, which glittered in the sun, and in the midst what looked like huge statues, but which, as I imagined, were also the residences or public buildings of the citizens. At each end was a great engine, where it was manifest force was being generated (probably steam, for smoke was issuing from one of them).

"Why do not they build their city on one huge ship? I see it rests on pontoons."

"For fear of accidents. Should a vast ship, capable of supporting such a city as that, meet with an accident—get into shallow water or strike a rock—the loss and risk would be terrible. But now that city has twenty-two pontoons on which to rest. Should any accident befall one of these, it can be removed and replaced by another, which may be obtained in any of the cities on the bank. The city is then uninjured."

"Are those great statues or houses that I see?"

"That lofty statue of a Martian lady is only the representation of a heroine who lived in this floating city of Golonor five hundred years ago. It was in the bad old days, when we had wars in our land. A king of one of the countries the city passed through stopped it, and seized it for ransom, and wanted to enslave the people. They were yielding themselves to slavery, but she roused them to arms, and set herself at their head. They gained the victory, but she was killed. So in her memory they made a statue of her, and put it in the city; not a solid statue, but a hollow one, so that some of her descendants might live in it. They live there to this day."

"In the old war times you speak of, these floating cities must have been exposed to frequent dangers."

"Very true, they were; and this was one of the arguments that were urged against war in the final Peace Congress. They said, even supposing the inhabitants of the land could dwell in peace in their homesteads, those who lived on the seas and rivers were cosmopolites, and ought to be able to go everywhere. Then, again, you see how much of our food is derived from the waters. It was most unjust for those who lived on the shores to claim all the food supplies near them. So we declared all the waters free, and all in them, and thus we made the way to making the land free, and all nations in amity."

"On Earth," I said, "things may tend in this direction. By the law of the nations of Earth the high seas are the property of all, and international law alone rules there. If seas were a chief source of human food, and if, as I see here, a large portion of mankind—men, women, and children—lived upon the sea, we should find something of this state of things. But however have you obtained force to make these vast canals? Have all nations combined?"

"Yes, we have now immense control of nature's forces, as you know. By the action of nature's powers we can mould her to our will. These canals are the works of centuries, wrought by a whole world at peace. The force we once wasted in wars against each other we now use in overcoming nature's obstacles: in sinking land and flooding it with water when we need it; in piercing mountains and moulding them to our purposes; in widening rivers and making them straight. We can do almost what we will with nature, by the kind and loving permission of our Divine Creator, for we are a world at peace and combined, and a thousand millions of Martians with machinery and science at their disposal can, in a few centuries, do almost anything to mould the surface of our planet to our utility."

"But tell me," said my companion, "what is that other huge statue two hundred feet high that I see right in the very centre of the floating city?"

"That is merely the Town Hall, where the citizens assemble for public business. The figure represents the city of Golonor. It is the symbol they know it by from the shore, as it floats from sea to sea."

We soon got ahead of the floating city of Golonor, when another appeared going the opposite way. It was still larger, about a mile and a half long, and had seven immense towers rising from its metal domes.

"How can the inhabitants of these cities get food?" I asked.

"Do you not remember," asked my guide, "that most of our food is floating on the waters, not attached to the land? Those vast aquatic fields offer an almost endless stock of food."

He pointed to the great fields of what were more like huge algae than anything on Earth, the vast marine plants that floated on the canals, some as big as forest trees. Many of the singular changes and variations in tint of Martian seas which even Earth's astronomers have noticed are due to the tinting of the great waters by these vast fields of marine vegetation. As on Earth men and cattle are mainly supported by the grasses and corn, so in Mars it is the aquatic plants in the canals and seas that are the main supports of life. Hence the need for the vast system of irrigation. On Earth the rice plant is the chief marsh plant that provides man with food. Here vast fields and aquatic forests laden with tons of food, transforming the oxygen and carbon of atmosphere and water into food, waved hither and thither in the watery currents, and varied with many tints the green waters.

On we floated in the centre of the stream amidst these submarine forests, passing now in one direction, now in another, the floating cities which slowly and majestically moved through the vast canals.

We had not proceeded above fifty miles before we came to another huge sound—or rather canal, stretching one hundred miles to the north, cutting our canal at right angles. On its waters were two floating cities, and vast forests of vegetation waving in the currents, with their great leaves floating like water-lilies.

Forward we went, and then, some twenty miles on, another canal, with a city built on the shore at the confluence, opened to view. So we went on passing cities and forests, both on sea and land, on this huge masterpiece of the marvellous skill and power of the Martians—an achievement as far superior to any man has yet achieved in this age of steam and iron, as the works of human skill in the nineteenth century are superior to the works of man in the Stone Age.

ALERIEL

THE GREAT SACRIFICE

George C. Wallis

Although many authors portrayed the Martians as benign, both spiritually and technologically advanced, compared to humans, H. G. Wells's The War of the Worlds *changed that image completely. Now the Martians were portrayed as hostile, evil, determined to conquer Earth to save themselves.*

The following story sought to reverse that image, and although a relatively short piece, it is extremely powerful on a cosmic scale. George C. Wallis (1871–1956) is now forgotten to all but a small band of devotees of the early days of science fiction, but he was a regular contributor to both the popular magazines of the late Victorian/Edwardian period and the boys' magazines. Although his output reduced, and he became a cinema manager, he continued to write into the 1940s. The following story first appeared in The London Magazine *for June 1903.*

I. SIGNS IN THE SKY

"IT'S QUEER," SAID HARRISON, RESTING HIS ELBOWS ON THE table meditatively. "The scientific world has been living for years in the comfortable belief that Kepler's and Newton's laws were inviolable, and that predicting the places of the planets at any instant was only a matter of correct calculation—and all at once some of the planets get hundreds of miles out of their track. Either Kepler and Newton were wrong, or something very strange has happened to the poor old Solar System."

We were in Harrison's private observatory waiting for the sky to clear. I lit a cigar carelessly.

"Let's hear the details," I said. "I must confess I've been too busy with other things lately to have time to read up the technical papers. Seems to be a big fuss about things, anyhow."

"Big fuss! I should think so—and there will be a bigger one still if this sort of thing goes on. When the Solar System begins to get behind schedule time, it's serious. It's been going on for over a week now. Only last night Saturn was about a whole degree behind his proper place. Uranus was even more, and as for Neptune we've had to re-discover him. To tell you the truth, Milford, I'm getting a bit scared. According to all long-established mathematical law, any such perturbation of the planetary movements would have a great effect on the orbit of the earth, would perhaps—nay, almost certainly—so upset the balance of the Solar System that it would go to everlasting smash. But the earth hasn't budged an inch out of her way, nor Mars, nor Jupiter—at least, we gave him the benefit of the doubt over the last observation—and here are the outer planets slowing down. Why, with their loss of momentum, they don't fall into the sun, I can't make out. And everything else, so far, seems as per usual. It looks to me as though we were being held back from chaos by a bond that might break at any time. And now you know as much as I do, and I hope you'll get to sleep tomorrow."

"Daresay I shall," I answered. The news did not seem so terrible to me as to Harrison and the other astronomers, who saw its significance with scientific eyes. "The sky looks pretty much the same to us ordinary mortals, and will do to the end, I expect, no matter what extraordinary things are going on. But it's getting clearer. Let's have a peep. What's on view?"

"There are hundreds of telescopes at work now," said Harrison, thoughtfully, unscrewing a cap as he spoke. "We've arranged a plan of campaign between us—a sort of bureau of celestial information—and I'm one of about twenty who have been deputed to watch Mars. If he varies a millimetre from his expected position, I have to wire it to the exchange. He's in the field now, and both moons are just visible. Bend down."

I placed my left, and strongest, eye to the bright dot of light at the end of the long tube, and saw the ruddy planet with its two small moons. I saw the familiar cloudy markings, the well-known snow-patches at the poles, and fancied that I detected, even as I looked, the movement of rapid Phobos—that active little satellite which contrived to get round Mars in less than eight hours. I was very interested at first, as I have always been in telescopic views, but soon grew tired of the constrained position, and made way for Harrison. He was busy with observations and calculations for some time, and at last he looked up with something like a sigh of relief.

"Mars all right, then?"

"Yes. He's exactly where he ought to be. I'll wire to the exchange now, if you don't mind waiting, and see if they have any news of Jupiter."

The clicking of the Morse code was very distinct in the dim observatory, as I bent down and peered through the tube once more. Active little Phobos was at that moment at greatest elongation. I had been looking perhaps a minute when the tiny moon suddenly blazed out with an intense white light. Thus luminous, it lasted several seconds, then it incontinently and utterly disappeared. I gave a startled exclamation, and at the same moment Harrison turned from the telegraph with a scared and puzzled expression:

"It's worse than ever," he said, before I had time to speak. "Jupiter is three minutes of arc behind his place, and the principal asteroids are slowing down. What did you say?"

I told him briefly. He looked eagerly up the tube. The light of a great fear—that fear which was so soon to come into all faces—shone in his eyes.

"Good heavens, Milford, what next? This is no mere cause for wonder, it is something strange and terrible. Some unknown, stupendous influence is at work in the Solar System, and God only knows what will be the end."

Then with a sudden change of manner he bustled round the room, put his paraphernalia back into their place, and said we had better go indoors and get some sleep. He talked wildly, and not a little incoherently, I thought, as we walked up the silent drive and across the lawn. I was not sorry when I found myself dozing off to sleep in bed. There was a sense of practical security between the white sheets. Yet I often thought afterwards of his talk that night as almost prophetic.

For a week things went on as usual. The scientific world was distraught with wonder, and a multiplicity of hypotheses to account

for the action of the outer planets and the burning up and disappearance of Phobos, but the average crowd went about their business
without much concern.

Then the message front Mars came, and theory gave way to fact,
and the popular indifference to a reign of terror that shook the fabric
of civilisation to its base.

II. THE MESSAGE FROM MARS

By what means the Martian intelligences despatched their tiny pro-
jectiles across the abyss of space with such accuracy we shall never
know, nor shall we ever know what those intelligences were like. We
only know that they must have been thousands of years in advance
of us in knowledge and in power, almost god-like in the latter, and
altruistic to a degree which our lower minds cannot comprehend.
We only know that their message came in a number of small, metallic balls, which fell to earth like meteors on the night of August 5th
and the following day.

So accurately timed and speeded were these messengers of the
peril that they fell at nearly regular distances apart, and with such
motion as to bring them to the ground without being fused by the
friction of the atmosphere. Many, no doubt, fell into the seas and
rivers and deserts; many have been found since in all kinds of out-
of-the-way places; but one and all contained similar contents. These
consisted of a tightly rolled drum of a substance not unlike parchment and a few grains of a greyish powder.

Many of these metallic messengers fell into scientific hands on
the morning of the 6th, and the whole world knew their purport on
the 7th. Every telegraph wire carried the dread news; every paper

had articles upon the subject; it was everywhere the chief topic of conversation. One fell into the lane at the back of Harrison's house, and was found accidentally by Harrison himself. We deciphered its meaning together the same afternoon, and wired it to the Press Agencies.

The day before I should have been amused at the idea of any ultra-terrestrial intelligences communicating with us, seeing that we could have no common basis of agreement as to the meaning of signs, but the Martians compelled me to confess my dull wit. The method used was at once simple and convincing.

The first thing that came into view as we unrolled the drum of parchment was a marvellously accurate map of the Solar System, so intricate in detail as to force an exclamation of wonder and praise from Harrison at first sight. On this map Mars was marked with a peculiar sign, resembling a Maltese cross. A number of lines were drawn from Mars to the earth when each were at different points of their orbits—points which Harrison quickly marked with their respective dates—and, on the date on which we had witnessed the disappearance of Phobos, a line was drawn from the surface of Mars to the place of its small satellite, and for the satellite itself was substituted a splash of pale blue colour.

"Then it was the Martians who destroyed Phobos by some terrible projectile or exercise of force?" I cried.

Harrison nodded gravely.

"Yes. Evidently to attract our attention or to make an experiment. But look at this!—look at this! Do you see what it means?"

The unrolled drum now disclosed a map of much larger dimensions, on which the sun and some of the nearer stars were represented by tiny dots. We knew the sun again by the recurrence of the mark attached to it in the former map. Between the star a in Cassiopeia and our own sun, a small cloud of tiny objects (marked with a sign identical with that used to denote the Leonids and other meteor-streams of the Solar System) was shown, whose indicated orbit was directed straight to the sun. This cloud of meteors was marked with two distinctive signs.

"It means, I expect," said I, "that a large cloud of meteors is coming towards us from the direction of Cassiopeia, and so—but don't look scared, man—an extra grand display of celestial fireworks will be a compensation for the disappointment of two Novembers ago!"

My friend pulled himself together with a visible effort, but his voice trembled a little as he said:

"You don't see all I see in this. Do you think the Martians would have taken all this trouble just to warn us of the approach of an ordinary meteor swarm? No—this is a warning of world-peril—so far as I can see, a sentence of death for all humanity."

He paused a moment; then continued, growing calmer gradually:

"You will notice that the orbit of this meteor cloud does not start in Cassiopeia but is prolonged indefinitely beyond. This sug-gests that in order for the Martians to have traced its backward way so far it must be of a size and density unparalleled within our knowledge. Here is the next map conveying that precise informa-tion. Here is the Solar System again, bounded by a circular line; here is the meteor cloud with a circle of the same size drawn *within* it. Here is part of its orbit, marked off with a succession of regular ticks, each tick representing, I think, the distance travelled by the stream in a Martian year. A little calculation will settle that point... Yes, I am right. And here is the last Martian year period marked off into ten minor divisions—they must use the decimal system on Mars—and this tells us that in six weeks from tonight the great stream will be passing our system, scorching us all to death by the heat evolved by the impact of its mass upon the sun. The sun will blaze out like the famous star in Corona Borealis did, and every living thing on earth will be roasted alive! Heaven help us, Milford!"

A half-jesting doubt of the truth of his deductions was upon my lips, but I looked at the maps again and saw that he was right, read thereon the sentence of death in indisputable language. The silent but eloquent dots and lines and marks seemed to dance before my eyes like fantastic figures of fire. I did not speak, and we unrolled the drum of parchment to the end.

III. DAYS OF DESPAIR

The twilight shadows were creeping across the floor of the study when we re-wound the parchment and looked straight into each other's haggard eyes. The further maps and diagrams confirmed and reiterated beyond dispute our worst conjectures, besides being an evident attempt to convey some more information to us—information which, at that time, we completely failed to comprehend.

On a series of Solar maps a great quantity of lines were drawn from Mars to the outer planets, at times and distances easily calculated to be those of the retardations which had so exercised the wonder of the astronomers. That these retardations had been purposely achieved by the Martians, with a definite object in view, we had no room for doubt; that the Martians had solved the problem of the nature and control of gravitation, we were compelled to believe. All the indirect evidence of their existence and intelligence which had been so suddenly thrust upon us, enforced these points.

But what bearing this knowledge, or the knowledge of the coming death, was expected to have upon earthly behaviour, we could not even dimly guess. That something more than a mere warning was intended, we felt sure; what it was, we had no idea.

We found our knowledge and our ignorance alike shared by all the competent students into whose possession the message came. One curious point was noted by all of us, though none then divined its true significance. On the map which represented the meteor stream infringing on the Solar System, the earth, Mars, and the four great outer planets, were shown to be in a direct line between the sun and centre of the great stream.

I parted from Harrison quietly—we felt that ordinary, commonplace sentences were all we dare use just then—and made my way home. It was a clear, warm night, already glowing with faint stars. They seemed to me as still, as steadfast, as prophetic of long endurance, as they have done to man for countless years, though I knew their seeming steadfastness was but a mask of mockery. As I turned the handle of the garden gate I remembered that I was due out that evening, and had no time to spare if I would be punctual. And hitherto I had been punctuality itself where Ethel was concerned. I hurriedly made myself fashionable, and went.

There came an interval in the evening's mirth when Ethel and I found ourselves alone on the balcony we knew so well. The stars were more numerous now, and shone radiantly. A few clouds were creeping up out of the west. The landscape spread out before us down to the river was covered with overlapping shadows. For a few minutes I debated with myself whether or not I should tell Ethel the awful news that would blight for her eyes, as it had done for mine, all the beauty of this quiet scene. If I did not tell her, she would read it in the papers tomorrow.

"Well, Jack," she said at last, breaking the thread of my unpleasant cogitations, "have you turned miserly all at once? 'Silence is golden' you know! It must be something *very* serious to make *you* so solemn!"

"That is true enough"—with the ghost or a smile—"I am frivolous enough, I admit, in a usual way. But 'tis nothing that concerns you—at least—that is, you will hear of it soon enough."

"Hear of what, Jack? I shall not be friends until you tell me all about it whatever it is—that's troubling you."

"I'd better not," I began, weakly: but a moment later I was launched upon the strange recital. I told her the whole story, omitting nothing, and grew marvellously scientific, even eloquently philosophical, with the intensity of my emotion. As I spoke I looked at the stars and the dark landscape, and when I finished and turned to Ethel I found her gaze fixed upon my face with a very curious expression. She took the tidings calmly.

"If this is true, Jack," she said. "I mean, if you and Harrison are not the victims of a dreadful joke—or the originators of one—it will be confirmed by the great scientific men of the world tomorrow or the following day. Then we shall know; until then, let us dismiss the subject. We have heard so many predictions of universal disaster that have come to nothing."

There was no getting the better of Ethel in an argument of this sort, so after a feeble protest I gave way. I even felt a sense of relief in the temporary casting-off of the yoke of terror. "Sufficient unto the day" seemed to me a very good maxim just then. Yet when we parted at the door Ethel grew serious.

"If it *should* be true, Jack," she said, holding my hand lightly, "will you come on and see me as soon as you can? And will you let me see one of these dreadful messages?"

I gave her the required promises readily, a thrill of pleasure running through the sighings of despair, and went home strangely placid. I had been engaged to Ethel for over a year, but until that night I had never known the depth of her love for me. It was strange. I, one of the few sharers of the secret of universal and imminent doom, was glad because a girl, one of the doomed—a mere ephemera who had not seven weeks to live—was more in love with me than I had thought.

But next morning the flood of gloom was upon me again, and upon all who believed.

After a brief call at Harrison's, I was at Ethel's home. It was early, but she met me in the drawing-room, a newspaper in her hand, a pallor on her sweet face.

"It is true, after all," she said.

"Yes," said I, "it's true. And what's the good of anything now? What does anything matter? Only a few weeks, and all the world, and you, and I, will be wiped out of existence as thoroughly as wrong figures on a schoolboy's slate."

"Yes, but our duties and our love remain the same, Jack. Whether we die tomorrow or fifty years hence does not matter at all. Whether we live well *now*, whether we love well *now*, matters everything. It is only weak souls who are slaves to time. You know the lines:

We should count time by heart-throbs, not by hours,
    By feelings, not by figures on a dial."

"Of course you are right, Ethel," I said, gloomily, "but I am a mere, prosaic, modern man, unable, I fear, to soar to the heights of your transcendentalism. There is something unspeakably terrible to me in the thought of what is coming—that in seven weeks from now the world will be a scorched and lifeless ember; that all that men have

striven after, and achieved and hoped for through countless generations, will be utterly wasted and lost."

"It is terrible to me, too, Jack, but we must not let it overmaster
us. We must work. There will be plenty to do for all who can keep
cool heads, and we shall face the end better if we do not anticipate it."

She spoke bravely, firing with enthusiasm. I felt a little cheered
for the moment, but once out in the street again despair settled over
me the deeper. And as the days wore on and the awful truth—confirmed by another corroborative message from Mars—gradually
percolated through the meshes of ignorance and doubt, reaching
to the lowest substratum of society and to the most remote corners
of the earth, that despair settled over most men. But for the almost
automatic instinct of law and order that upheld the Governments,
and the heroism that the peril called forth from many natures such as
Ethel's, civilisation would have gone to ruin long before the fatal day.

Who that was not forced would work against his will, with that
dread shadow ever creeping nearer? Who would save, who respect
any law but the law of strength, who paint, or write, or speak, or
strive for fame or honour when in six weeks all must die?

The first days of the dread suspense have well been called the
days of desolation. Many went mad in them, many died of fright or
by self-destruction, many made fortunes at which their neighbours
laughed, many lost their all and lived on charity, caring nothing. But
many were mentally sober yet, and worked on.

IV. A CLEFT IN THE CLOUDS

At the end of the first week mankind was divided into three factions—those who believed in the approaching catastrophe and were

afraid; those who believed and were not afraid; and those who did not believe. The latter faction was a very small one, although it included some clever men. They spoke and wrote eloquently and scoffingly of antecedent improbabilities, universal experience, illusions, gigantic hoaxes, and the like. Their jests fell on heedless ears. One faction was too terrified to reason, to refute, to reprove; the other was too feverishly intent upon the daily work that casts out fear. And some, gay and reckless, were too busy making the most, in a frivolous sense, of the short time that remained to them.

You heard many grim jokes as you went along the streets. You saw men, for once, in their true colours. The churches and chapels and mission rooms were crowded nightly with fervent and trembling audiences, listening now to the preacher with an attention before unknown. And now the preacher had a theme that appealed to all. As in the days of old, he pointed his perorations with a fiery moral, this time drawing from science his picture of the end of the world. The drum of the Salvation Army rolled incessantly in the streets, and at nearly every corner and crossing you heard the cries of modern Solomon Eagles: "Repent, repent, ere it be too late, generation of sinners!" Faces blanched with terror as the once unheeded words fell on their ears: "The earth shall be melted with fervent heat and the heavens be rolled together like a scroll." And on the other hand you heard the calm, dispassionate reasonings of the Rationalists and Determinists. Their arguments penetrated the fever heat of fear as icicles of impersonal logic. They strove to drive home the lesson that here was one more proof of the fact that the inexorable workings of Nature give no sanction to man's anthropomorphic imaging of the Unknowable God.

The air was full of strange theories and queer suggestions. The intellect of all humanity was at work on the one absorbing problem.

Up at Harrison's one evening, whither I had taken Ethel to see the Martian messages, we were talking of these things.

"Have you heard Schiaparelli's latest?" enquired Harrison, picking up a copy of the *British Mechanic* and glancing at a paragraph. "It's a daring idea, but has its merits. He calculates the sweep of the meteoric orbit from the portion shown to us on the Martian maps, and together with that, and the rate at which the stream is travelling, deduces the conclusion that it completes a circuit once in 20,000,000 of our years. That being so, the meteors must have passed through our system and enriched and superheated the sun 20,000,000 years ago, and at similar periods for who knows how far back? And you know Kelvin's estimate of the sun's present age—20,000,000 years. If Schiaparelli is right, the sun is constantly cooling and yet continually being revived by the impact of this immense stream of matter. This also suggests an argument in favour of the meteoritic origin of the Solar System, as against the old nebular hypothesis."

"It is a clever thought," said Ethel, "but then, you know, Kelvin's estimate is not a proved fact—it was seriously questioned by Proctor—and the ascertaining of a 20,000,000-year orbit is a very delicate matter indeed."

"Yes," said Harrison. "And another thing. The theory requires a very large body at or near the centre of the alleged orbit, and no visible star happens to be there. Of course, there may be one of the dark, burnt-out suns in that position—and equally, of course, there may not."

"Just so," said I. "And after all, it does not matter, because we shall never know."

"Of course not," said Harrison, gravely. "But if Professor Belmont's idea is right, *that* will matter a great deal."

"And that is—?"

"That the Martians intend to ward off the catastrophe by some means," my friend replied. "I will read you Belmont's summing-up from the *Scientific American*: 'That the Martians intended to convey to us more than the mere fact of the approach of the meteor-stream, no one who has seen the messages doubts. That this some-thing more is an intimation that they will endeavour to prevent the disaster, seems to me equally beyond dispute. We know that they are retarding the outer planets—and now the earth and Venus and Mars itself—so as to bring all the planets in a right line between the centre of the sun and the centre of the meteor-stream at the time it will pass through and around the Solar System. On the map which conveys this information we find lines drawn from Mars to the outer planets, each line marked with a sign, and terminating in a sign, identical with the signs on the map marking the destruction of Phobos. The one spectroscopic observation of that destruction which we possess shows that a mass of pure hydrogen of immense volume was suddenly fired. This cannot have been sent from Mars; we can only account for it by supposing that the Martians—who, we know, can control gravitation—know the nature of the primeval element out of which all our so-called elements are formed, and can transmute these "elements" at their will; that, in fact, by means incomprehensible to us, they dissolved the whole mass of Phobos into incandescent hydrogen.

'The conclusion seems forced upon one that at the instant of impact they will similarly dissolve Neptune, Uranus, Saturn, and Jupiter, thus opposing the central portion of the meteor-stream with a succession of flaming hydrogen shields, in passing through which the meteors will be fused, and dissipated into cosmic dust. That the grains of grey powder in the Martian messages were intended for us to prove their accuracy with, seems convincingly shown by the fearful explosions which have taken place in the laboratories, because after each explosion the presence of a large body of hydrogen has been detected in the vicinity.

'Thus much appears certain. It is too daring to go further and affirm that the last map of the series suggests the possible self-destruction of Mars (and of the earth also, we being supposed to have learned the nature of the grey powder) should the hydrogenising of the outer planets prove insufficient? With the Martian message before me, I affirm that such is my belief.'"

"Feasible, is it not?" added Harrison.

"Quite," said I, "except the last suggestion. That seems too terrible, unless we suppose the Martians to have reached such a pitch of intelligence as to feel no repugnance at the idea of a world-suicide."

"May there not be another explanation?" asked Ethel, quietly. "It is evident that they are aware intelligences exist here. May not their intentional destruction of their own planet make the last flame-shield necessary to save *us* from death? May it not indicate a contemplated act of supreme self-sacrifice on the part of a race—a world?"

We sat still awhile, silently digesting the strange, new thought. Then Harrison cried:

"That shall be in all the leading papers tomorrow!"

V. THE FLASHES OF FLAME

Some other pen than mine must write the full story of those days of waiting, those days of drawn and agonised suspense. I lived my life in a very narrow sphere. Excepting at the house where I lodged, Ethel's and Harrison's, I spoke to very few people. Yet what I saw and read impressed upon me so vivid and terrible a picture of a world under sentence of death, gone mad with fear, that even now it colours all my dreams with a nameless horror.

But for the hint of hope conveyed in Belmont's theory and Ethel's now famous suggestion, I believe that mankind would have gone mad *en masse*, wrecked every institution of society that makes for order, and reverted to barbarism. As it was, the strain of alternate hope and fear showed itself in all faces, in all words, in all acts. Politics and business, peace and war, love and sport, travel and invention, all sank into sudden insignificance. Towards the end of the last week of security all supplies except the staples of life fell off alarmingly, even at panic prices. No one travelled except those who must, or those who hurried home from distant places. The cry of every human heart was for the presence of those dear to him in the last, dreaded hours.

The churches throughout the world announced that they would hold services with open doors on the last day, and two-thirds of the literature that poured from the world's printing presses consisted of sermons, exhortations, warnings, and words of supposed comfort put forth on behalf of the various religions which sway humanity. The Buddhist spoke resignedly of the peace of Nirvana (for even to India's millions the truth had reached); the Moslem, kneeling barefooted in the mosque, grew fervent over the joys of Paradise; the Catholic told his beads and prayed to the Holy Mother; the Protestant foresaw the nearness of the Second Coming; the Theist and Rationalist, with ideas broadened by the great conception of the vastness and unity and incomprehensibility of Nature, preached only courage and calmness, pleading that men should act a man's part even in the darkest hour, no matter whether a further lease of mortal life, or glory inconceivable, or death eternal, awaited all.

And there were some who rushed into more violent excesses of frivolity, debauchery and crime than even Rome knew in her most degenerate days. The lower class of theatres and music halls were filled nightly with reckless crowds; and despite the efforts of the military and police, forcible robberies and other worse deeds were enacted daily in the dark corners of great cities and on desolate country roads.

Fortunately the great mass of the people, especially in the stolid, English-speaking countries, contained themselves admirably, neither evincing any spirit of superhuman heroism nor of sub-human despair. The sky was black enough, no doubt, but plenty of time for "the panic of wild affright" when the storm burst. There was yet a gleam of hope shining.

The moment of contact between the meteor-stream and Neptune arrived at last. For some nights previously we had fine displays of shooting stars—the advance guard of the great group—which struck fresh terror into the minds of the ignorant, and now was the time to verify Belmont's hypothesis. Harrison and I were alone in the observatory once more, waiting in the small hours for the sign that should confirm what we both believed.

Harrison was at the eye-piece; I was wondering why, on so clear a night, we had seen fewer meteors than on the two previous evenings. Suddenly my friend uttered an exclamation of relief and seized my arm.

"Look—quick! It is true! The Martians are at work!"

I glanced through the dark tube, and saw where the tiny point of Neptune should have shone, a small cloud of intensely vivid light—the light of incandescent hydrogen. Belmont's reading of the Martian message was correct; the intelligences that inhabited the ruddy planet, superior to us in intellect and in power, were fighting the great peril. Knowing by means we cannot even guess that the earth held intelligences also, they had warned us of the peril and of their attempt to avert it. The thought, although familiar enough now, came home to me with fresh force, with an almost staggering greatness—was almost too large for a human brain to grasp, otherwise than as a wildly-impossible dream. Yet it was true.

I moved aside for Harrison to look once more, but in a little over ten minutes the cloud dimmed and disappeared. How many millions of meteors had been fused into cosmic dust in their headlong rush through that shield of flaming hydrogen? How many millions came after them, with shape and motion unimpaired? Flow many millions?—how many trillions of trillions!

We busied ourselves with the telegraph as the cloud vanished, sending and receiving news. We learnt that the spectroscope showed the flame of Neptune's destruction to be the flame of almost pure hydrogen, and that it was of immense volume. News of the destruction of Uranus came from the European observatories some days later, with the determination of the speed of the great meteor-stream and the fixing of the dates when it would reach the earth and the sun respectively. Saturn's annihilation was invisible everywhere, owing to heavy clouds, but the hydrogenising of the mighty mass of Jupiter was visible to the naked eye. To Harrison and me, sweeping the sky with the telescope, the sight was one never to be forgotten.

A straggling meteor shot through the field of view a moment prior to the predicted time, and the luminous trail in its wake had scarcely vanished when the huge globe of the giant planet seemed to melt into nothingness before our gaze. A moment's blank. Then, in place of the round orb, a swiftly expanding cloud of flame shone, glowing as with the sustained blast of a furnace, shooting out fierce red tongues of fire round all its jagged and increasing circumference, glittering with a thousand points of yet intenser flame, as though riddled through and through with a torrent of stars.

The cloud of flame endured for more than half-an-hour, and in every second of that time it was swallowing in its capacious maw myriads upon myriads of groups of those restless, hurrying enemies of ours, fusing them with the furnace heat of friction into harmless dust. The grey dawn stole across the sky shortly after the cloud became invisible. We felt a thrill of hope now that we were sure those Martian intelligences were fighting so bravely for us and for themselves. Yet whether we were saved we did not know. The peril was not yet past. The stress of suspense was not yet over.

VI. THE SUPREME SACRIFICE

It was late in the afternoon, and the whole sky was growing dull with the approach of twilight, when Ethel and I walked together to my friend's house. She could not rest at home, she said, waiting to know the end, and I was more than willing that she should be with me in the moment when the nature of that end should be known for good and all. After that supreme moment, whether the verdict was life or death, I had promised to return home with her. In the last hours we would be together.

On our way we met and passed many people. Their faces reflected all the shades of fear, from dim doubt to wild terror. Some walked defiantly, some furtively, some with affected unconcern, but we did not see one face that betokened real carelessness or suggested real composure. One group we passed at the corner of a street were indeed singing and praying and preaching loudly, and called to us to join them, but the scared expression in their eyes—red with want of sleep, with long and anxious vigils at bedroom windows, repeated studies of the dangerous sky—belied the complacency they professed and offered. Sadly shaking off the nervous hands that one zealot laid upon us, we hurried on.

Harrison and his wife greeted us briefly but sincerely, and the four of us went straight to the garden seat near the open door of the observatory. If the calculations of the astronomers were correct, we should receive news of the great issue from Greenwich in a quarter of an hour. As Greenwich time is about five hours in advance of American Eastern time, we should have to wait that period for a distinct observation of Mars ourselves. As the minutes were counted off and the telegraph instrument gave no sign, the tension drew its cords tightly around us.

Save for a few drifting clouds, the sky was dark and clear and cold; the air was still; the whole world about us seemed plunged into waiting silence. We were each loth to break the spell of that hush, and sat apart, busy with our own thoughts. I remember that I was thinking something like this: The Martians, besides having control of gravitation, must have means of knowing the total amount of matter in the meteor cloud. Knowing that, and how much of it they have destroyed already, they will know whether what yet remains is sufficient to raise the sun's heat beyond the point fatal to life. They must also know if the hydrogenising of their own planet would avert the calamity, and so save the earth and the inner planets. If Mars is hydrogenised, it will mean that such is the case; if he is not, it will mean that even Martian intelligence is beaten and that only universal death remains. I also remember wondering whether any of the Martians would try to escape from the ruin of their world and come to earth, as Wells's Martians did.

I was roused from my reverie by Harrison shutting his chronometer with a snap. The time had expired and the wire had not spoken. Mars yet existed.

"We will wait a little longer," said Ethel, very quietly, but with pale face. "The calculations may be in error or the sky cloudy in Europe. Until we have seen Mars with our own eyes we will not go home. And it may be that the danger is really past—that the meteors have already been reduced in number below the danger point."

"That might be so, but I do not think the Martians, knowing the approximate mass of the meteors, would have sent us any message in that case. For my part I go further than Belmont now. I believe that they foresaw the need of self-sacrifice and contemplated it from the first, only sending us the message to suggest the same self-destruction to us, in the event of their calculations proving in error or the hydrogen shields not fusing sufficient of the meteors. The balance of mass between death and life for us may be—I think it is—very fine now, and we may yet see what we want. They may be delaying their own destruction because of a concentration of the meteors in the tail of the stream. We will wait, as Miss Holroyd suggests, until we have seen Mars himself."

We waited, and the sky darkened swiftly. An hour later a brilliant meteor shot across the sky. After a short interval it was followed by another, and they by others, until the heavens seemed riven by myriads of lances of fire.

"The meteors—the harbingers of death!" cried Ethel, her hands locked in silent prayer. We looked at each other for a few moments, then back at the sky. It held us fascinated. The meteors—evidently a portion of the great stream which had escaped the hydrogen shields—came scattering to right and left from that point on the horizon where Mars would rise. East and west, north and south, they spread; the sky was full of their brief shillings. It has been said by those who remember the great Leonid showers of 1866–7, that those displays were almost as nothing compared with the terribly grand vision of a hurricane of stars that blazed through the heavens on that never-to-be-forgotten night of fate.

The number of the meteors was simply incalculable, and as their radiant point rose slowly to the horizon, the light of their intense incandescence grew hurtful to our weary eyes. Sheer exhaustion of the optic nerve drove us into the house, and the calm of an abnormal excitement bade us to the supper table. Then, after a short rest, back to the observatory. The meteor storm still swept in fiery violence through the silent sky.

The hours passed. Now voicing what scraps of forlorn hope we could find, and now relapsing into a stillness that seemed prophetic of the world as it would be in the lifeless days to come, we four sat in the observatory, waiting for a glimpse of Mars. Once or twice I went to the doorway and looked out across the quiet garden, thick and dense with the night shadows, illuminated only by the pulsing light of the meteor-riven heavens. The trees stood mysteriously grey and still, not a twig moved, nor a leaf upon the evergreens of the hedge. Away over the dim housetop, outlined as the horizon of the falling stars, the old Park Hill rose, a smudge of indistinguishable darkness, with one solitary house-light betokening the presence of humanity upon its desolate slope.

As I stood in the doorway the last time, thinking of time and space, and life and death and destiny, and love that is greater than all, yet ephemeral as those tiny bodies that were lighting the sky with their evanescent radiance—thoughts that one can *think*, but can neither write nor speak—Ethel touched me on the arm. She then drew me within, dosing the door softly after me.

"You will catch cold, Jack," she said. "And as the sky is clear of clouds, and the number of the meteors is diminishing, we shall soon have Mars in the field of the telescope."

I laughed, rather bitterly. With a grim sense of incongruous humour, I remarked that there had never been a finer chance of ignoring the laws of health, especially with regard to chills, as we should all, no doubt, he hot enough soon. Ethel put her hand over my mouth without answering, and I sat down. I shall never forget her calm courage in those nerve-straining hours.

Then Harrison slowly swung the tube round and adjusted the eyepiece according to calculation, and for a few minutes peered at the field of view. In silence his wife and then Ethel succeeded him at the instrument; in silence I, too, received upon my optic nerve those waves of ruddy light, which, having traversed forty-million miles of vibrant ether, told me Mars yet lived. Mars lived—the meteor stream was then too vast for even Martian intelligence to reduce to impotence. Mars lived—and therefore it and Earth, with the minor planets that yet remained to the relentless sun, must on the morrow die. Was this, then, the end of all—the Purpose of the Ages?...

At that moment I heard, though faintly, the sound of feet on the road outside, then voices pitched in the key of despair, then a woman's choking sob. All suddenly the horror of it struck me as it had never done before. With a sharp cry I left the telescope and staggered to a chair, and out of the dim shadows under the galvanised dome my imagination fashioned a vision of the World's Death.

I saw the countless meteors still shooting, incandescent, through the air, and knew that when one fell to earth in dust ten billion billion more sped on towards the all-compelling, all-consuming, superheated sun. I saw fierce spots on his golden disc, and new red-flaming prominences around his rim, as though, insatiate, he reached out greedy arms towards the stricken planets. I saw his colour change to a fiercer red, and felt the scorching flood of his heat grow more and more intense, from tropical dawns to noons in which no men could live, save in dungeons and cellars and caves. I watched the temperate zone, fast followed by the tropic as that was pursued by the *burning zone,* recede to north and south, even to the shuddering Poles. I saw the Alpine hills grow moist, and the late snow run over and down them in warm, black torrents; saw the glaciers sweat and slip and slide, and, melting as they slid, descend with roar and ruin into flooded valleys. I saw grass go brown, and drop in dust where it did not burn. I saw the sea bubble and boil, and rise in clouds of scalding steam.

Finally, I beheld a charred and blackened earth—a world in which there was no life, neither of man nor beast, nor creeping nor flying thing, nor tree nor herb of any kind—a world of heat and darkness and utter desolation.

And then the vision passed; it could not have lasted many seconds. All was still and cold in the observatory. Ethel was looking at me, but not curiously. Harrison and his wife were looking at each other. Feeling that I must do something, that inaction would be dangerous, I once more put my eye to the telescope. I had not been watching Mars for twenty seconds when the ruddy planet melted away into the sky around him, showing again swiftly as a vast, expanding cloud of flame, shotted through and through with a myriad points of yet more vivid fire. A minute longer I remained at the tube, to make sure my eyes had not deceived me; then I told the others.

The cloud of consuming hydrogen lasted long enough for all of us to see it several times. After it faded, and whilst we three talked wildly and gladly, like doomed prisoners suddenly set free, Harrison's lingers were busy with the telegraph.

It was true, after all; quite true. Mars had died so that the earth *could* live. Those unknown intelligences who had warned us of the peril had made the last supreme sacrifice to avert the full fury of the great assault. It is a thought that even yet passes human comprehension, yet it is true—that a world has sacrificed itself for a world, a race of intelligent beings has blotted itself out of existence in order that another and less-intellectual race might live.

I need only add that the meteor display continued one night more and then ceased abruptly; that the approaching winter was very mild and the succeeding summer almost tropical: that the earth is now the largest planet of the Solar System; and that I married Ethel within the month.

THE FORGOTTEN MAN OF SPACE

P. Schuyler Miller

When science fiction developed as a distinct genre in the American pulp magazines from 1926 onwards, it was soon engulfed by the lowest common denominator of crude adventure fiction, and the blaster-and-ray-gun style of "space opera", as it came to be called, took over. Hugo Gernsback, who had given the name of science fiction to the genre, was mortified at the excesses that were occurring and, in 1931, with his new editor David Lasser, he encouraged his writers to avoid the basic "man versus monster, rescues maiden" plot that had emerged, and concentrate on the realism of scientific development and space exploration. A number of writers responded: Laurence Manning, Nathan Schachner, Edmond Hamilton and, in particular, P. Schuyler Miller (1912–1974).

By training a research chemist, by passion an amateur archaeologist and by vocation a writer and critic, Miller had been fascinated by the wonders of science and history in all its forms since his teenage years, and had sold his first stories to Gernsback when he was eighteen. Miller enjoyed both the exotic and the realistic, giving his stories a powerful atmosphere. One of his early works, 'The Titan'—which is told from the viewpoint of a Martian and shows the failings of the decadent Martian lifestyle, had been rejected by the magazines because of its harsh realism and sexual implications. That story saw a partial publication in 1934 but was not published complete until 1952, twenty years after it was written. Thankfully the following story did not have to wait for decades and was published in the April 1933 Wonder Stories. It considers the fragile ecology of Mars and how it needs to be protected.

IN THE SHAFT IT WAS PITCH-BLACK BUT FOR THE GLOW OF RADIUM in the rock—low-grade stuff that they couldn't afford to take out—and the white beam of the torch. Here in the shaft there was enough dust to show the beam. Outside, the clear desert air was almost dustless and the beam of a torch was almost invisible, save on the darkest nights.

It was hot and stuffy in the heavy lead-lined suit. Now that the mine was gutted there probably wasn't enough radium left to harm him, but it was wise to play safe. The first prospectors had paid for their carelessness—paid horribly with their lives. Cramer shuddered. That wasn't so long ago!

He turned and went back up the long, slanting tunnel toward the spot of daylight that marked the entrance. Gronfeld was wrong for once. The electroscope wasn't down here at all. As a matter of fact, he, Cramer, had taken it up to the hut when it showed that the lode was played out. If Graham had brought it back again as Gronfeld claimed, he probably knew where it was and was keeping quiet out of spite.

Cramer frowned. When they started out, three long Martian years ago, there had been a tie stronger than lust of profit binding them together. Then Gronfeld had found the lode and it turned out to be fabulously rich. There were millions for all of them. They had lost it once—one of Graham's blasts opened a lateral seam that had them fooled for a while. But just as they were ready to give up and cash in on what they had, Cramer had found the main lode. There was no mistake about it now, though. The mine was gutted—empty. And they were rich for life!

That earlier camaraderie had died out after they struck the claim. Gronfeld and Graham had hung together longest. They were a lot older than he and had different tastes, But of late their gruff monosyllables had grown harsher and shorter and their tempers testier. They seemed suspicious of each other. Neither one could go out without having the other trailing along, watching him like a hawk.

They checked and rechecked each gram of the rich ore with—what seemed to Cramer—childish exactness. As if in that huge fortune a gram or half a gram made any difference! They were dealing in millions—not tens and hundreds! After all, though, they were getting along in years and they'd led a pretty tough life. You had to make allowances.

He stopped at the mouth of the shaft to squirm out of his suit. Instinctively he turned to where the locker should be, then laughed aloud. No more of that! This was just a hole in the rock now. The suit went in the ship and, in a few minutes, they would be thundering across the desert to Lanak and the canals—and then home. Home! Ah! Earth would be good after six years in this barren hell!

He stood looking out over the fantastic, tumbled badlands that reached away in red confusion to the horizon. Horizons were near on Mars, even in the great sea plains, and the clear air made them seem nearer. Without some kind of rocket-ship, no man could go into those eroded red wastes and live. None but a giant.

There had been giants in the first days of men on Mars—men who had gone out into thé desert and lived and, after years had returned to die. They had made beasts of themselves—brutes living from hand to mouth, stalking the weird half-reptilian creatures that roamed to gorges, finding water in secret places and drinking blood when there was no water. It was a killing life, but they lived it.

Thanks to the rockets that was all over. Even the poorest desert-rat could afford a tiny ship with water tanks and storage for a pay-load. Down there at the foot of the slope was the hut. Beyond, around the spur, would be the ship, hot silver in the sun, waiting for him. Gronfeld must have found the 'scope by now—probably Graham had remembered and told him. They'd be impatient, waiting for him to get back. Then up and away into the black skies, and all the misery of those six long years would be gone and forgotten. Forgotten! As if a man could ever forget in the desert!

There was new life in his stride as he went up over the worn red rock of the hillside toward the place where the ship was. No need to go by way of the hut. Its rude walls of heaped talus were deserted and its smoke-hole gaped empty. He was done with that and all like it! Straight over the spur and down to the ship—that was the way. And then—home!

His wiry arms drew him up to the knife-edge of broken strata that edged the cliff. Anticipation was tingling like fire in his veins. It was great to stand here alone, high above everything, and then to look up into the black sky and let your eyes drop slowly down—down to the horizon-down to the red desert—down to the sculptured hills with their spidery gullies—down at last to the silvery ship nestling under the cliff! He closed his eyes. Up now, and open them to the hard sky, and now down—down—down—

The ship was gone!

*   *   *

Forgotten. Oh, but it was bitter! It was on old story in the desert—one partner too many when there was a rich pay lode—one who could be conveniently "forgotten" until it no longer mattered. No one could prove anything when the desert was done with him. There was no one to care.

He had the hut, and it was cold and empty, without fuel and without food. A few empty cans on the stone slab that had been their table, a shrinking stain of dirty water on the sanded floor—no more.

He had the mine, and it was empty, a rifled seam in the cliffside with its pale glow of wealth fading away. A cluttered heap of rock from the last blast, after the electroscope had showed that the lode had petered out, a dribble of black ore-dust on the floor of the tunnel where a can had leaked, thin echoes clattering along the walls—no more.

He had one feeble hope of life—no more.

There was no water at the mine. While they were scraping feverishly at the side of the hill, wondering what they had found, what the ship carried was enough. When black millions stared at them from the red rock they knew that it would be but a drop in the gallons they must have. They had to find water and they must have food.

They found water and food beyond the horizon—in the riddled, cavernous limestone that marks the buried streams and icecaves of the Martian desert. They found the sprawling brown vines and fat pods of that nameless plant that has preserved the lives of more men than history can ever know. And for three long Martian years—years twice as long as those of Earth—they had lived on water and Martian peas.

In an hour the ship had gone and returned with its tanks heavy with water. Half an hour to fill them—it meant at least a hundred earthly miles, doubled and trebled by the tortuous gorges that lay between. It meant ten days at the least.

Most of those days would be waterless and all of them would be without food.

There was water in the mine-shaft—a single can. They had forgotten that.

Slinging it over his back in a twist of dried vine, Cramer went down past the squat red hut into the red desert. The sun was slanting down from the zenith and the long shadows were creeping out from beneath the rocks.

Cramer lay flat on his blistered face in the red sand close under the edge of an angular spur of sandstone. Ten suns had climbed ponderously to the zenith and wavered down. Ten cruel nights had frozen the blood in his veins as ten burning days had boiled it. Ten days he remembered, five of them made horrible by the thirst that was drying up his skin, shrivelling his flesh, clogging his mouth and throat with his blackened tongue and plugging his nostrils with caustic dust. Five days fusing together, merging into a red warped blur of pain and heat and thirst, riddled with crazy visions, wracked with cruel memories—five days of hell.

Only fate knew how many more there had been.

It was day now. Cramer's mind was very clear—crystal-clear and keen. Everything stood out in his brain sharp and distinct and hard, as though he were feeling them with his fingers or with his swollen tongue. Every little nerve in all his body vibrated with pain and every muscle was withered by his thirst.

Thirst burned in him like a great never-ending fire licking up through his throat and mouth and nostrils into his brain. It was like a torrent of little ants, desert ants, sand-ants, swarming over his helpless body and tearing at it with venomed mandibles—a flood of many little units merging into one, yet all distinct. Every little pain in all his tortured body was a unit of the great red thirst-pain—every one distinct and clear in his brain. He could count them, if counting had not ceased to exist, if all meaning had not been swallowed up by the avid little pains that were part of the great pain that had become his body.

There was a picture in the back of his eyes, against the retinas. He could feel it there. It had lain there motionless, for as long as he could remember since his brain had become clear. He could not change it, for the muscles of his eyes were dry and paralysed by the little pains.

It was a picture of cliffs. Red cliffs rising up out of a tumble of broken rock into the black sky. Pink cliffs, cooler and whiter than the crimson sand that lapped hungrily at their base. Gray cliffs, dusted over with red dust and permeated with red. Limestone cliffs laid down in unremembered centuries in the depths of an unremembered sea. Bodies of set-things, pulpy and white, showering down out of the cool green gloom and through the slow ages being pressed and twisted and broken into cliffs, high cliffs fed with the red dust of sleeping iron—red marble cliffs cut into fantasy, hollowed with caves.

He examined the part of the picture that had to do with caves. They were peppered all over the face of the rock and crowded under its tilting time-eaten ledges. The cliff was rotten with them, big and little, black mottled against red, dark and cool and moist in the bright desert. They ran back and down into the rock and at the bottom there were slender rivers running in the dark, and long lakes arched over with shadows. In one of them stood dripping columns of sweet coolness—of ice—of life!

He knew the caves. He had come before, in the ship, with Gronfeld or with Graham. He knew the caves. There was life there—the flowing life that had been in his veins, that the sun and red desert had sucked out—in the blurred, waterless days before his brain had become clear, and he was lying here. There was water there. There was water!

In the desert there was death.

The hard, clear, bright picture in the back of his brain was blurring over with a sort of red-black veil, like clotting hot blood pouring down over his open eyes. The shadows of the caves were melting into the shadows of the cliffs. The cliffs were swimming in redness, melting into it, swirling fantastically in a vortex of swift, undulant motion. The desert and the cliffs and the cool caves of the cliffs and the hard black sky were all eddying into one, into a great red stain against his retinas, into a vast red madness in his brain—all swallowed up by the thirst-pain that had become a huge red Thing eating—eating—eating—

The red swirl melted mercifully into darkness.

There were dreams in the darkness. Not sight-dreams—not red visions—but sound-dreams. Little sibilant shufflings in the sands. Little clickings on the rock. Little excited whisperings and breath-hissings. And then there were touch-dreams. Little gentle fingers pushing through the pain. Little swinging motions, short and hurried and breathless. And then coolness. And then no dreams.

Cramer woke to the cool vision of myriads of eyes. They were round, eyes, big and phosphorescently green in the darkness. They had narrow pupils that pulsed and fluctuated as they stared at him, widening slits of black against milky yellow-green.

The agony of thirst was fading. Moisture was in the air and in the cool stone on which he lay. Moisture was dripping musically on crystal, its sound singing in his ears. Moisture was trickling through his broken lips, over his swollen tongue, into his thirst-seared throat. Moisture was soaking into his parched skin and into the muscles under it, and into his hungering vitals. The eyes were giving him life.

He moved, painfully. The eyes receded and their pupils became fine lines, fear-lines. The trickle of moisture through his lips slobbered and stopped. Eagerly he ran his tongue over the stain of water on his chin. Pain made him draw it back. A thin whimper whispered in his throat, and from the darkness a whisper answered, like the mewing of kittens very far away. The eyes came closer.

Two of the eyes were just above him, very close. There was a greyness beyond the dark. Against it was the rounded silhouette behind the eyes—a small round head with great fan-like ears—a small, stout body—thin arms. There were hands and there was something in the hands. It approached him. The trickle of water began again and the other eyes came close to him, beside him. There were soft, deft touches of little fingers on his hot flesh. There was the caress of cool water. He raised his hand. His finger-tips touched fur, soft and warm, fur that flinched and then steadied. Sleek muscles moved under the fur. Blood pounded.

Cramer drifted into sleep.

Many times Cramer woke to the grey dark and the slow trickle of water on his burning body. Once he ate something soft and rather tasteless that woke a gnawing hunger in his vitals, but after a little that subsided into the dull throb of the thirst-pain that was being washed out of his soul. He slept again.

When he woke the clearness had come back into his brain. It was a soft clearness, like deep water, not hard and brilliant as it had been in the desert. He saw things gently and his body responded drowsily to what he saw. He moved his hand, and it stirred lazily, as through water, with a sort of voluptuous dull ache throbbing through it as the muscles contracted. He let it fall again and rolled his head toward the greyness.

The dark arched above him and the greyness was a soft blur against it. A thin column of water dropped down out of it to spatter on unseen ledges and spray his body with its delicious coolness.

Far up where the grey began, as though at the end of a long shaft of pale mist, was a spot of bright white. There was a pink flush against it—a sort of glare reflected from some invisible source very far above. That white stain was digging into his memory. He closed his eyes and let his mind drift back in the blackness. Then suddenly he knew.

He was in the ice-caves.

He had been here before. The picture came to him—the great cave above, opening under the overhang of the cliff, its mouth always in shadow—the green-white ice welling out of the crannies of the rock, glistening with moisture, reflecting the flush of the desert—the little rivulet of clear water dropping into blackness. He had gone down, far down, on a rope of twisted vines. He had seen the ice as a pale white blink at the end of a shaft of grey and felt the mist wafting up from far below. But he had not found the bottom.

Now, as he opened his eyes again, it seemed to him that he could make out the shape of the cavern where he lay.

It was a great hollow dome, sheer-walled, cut away by eddying water. There were dark spots along the base of its walls—tunnels, leading down. One of them was grey. And the eyes had disappeared.

He rolled over on his face and drew his legs up under him, stiffening his arms. He rose on all fours, then tottered back on his knees, wavering dizzily. The nausea passed and he put out an exploring hand. There was a low rock quite close to him. With a heave he was on his feet.

The cavern was suddenly much smaller than he remembered it. The roof swooped at him and the walls rushed in. Only the shaft of greyness stretched endlessly up, unchanged. It was as though he had been a little flat thing of two eyes and a brain, whereas now he was a six-foot mass of flesh and bone, a man.

The idea started a little feathery tickling at the bottom of his brain. It was funny! He laughed a great roaring, echoing laugh that rocked thunderously about him.

Abruptly there was a sudden wave of motion. The grey tunnel went flickeringly black. There was the click of tiny claws hurrying on stone. There were the kittenish mewings, alarmed and plaintive. There were the eyes again.

They swirled about him in the dark. There were shapes that he could not make out, moving swiftly. The narrow pupils were dilated—questioning. The hurrying forms pressed closed. Little hard hands pushed at his calves and knees. Clusters of paired eyes hovered about his thighs. Tottering precariously above them, he shuffled forward.

There was a large tunnel that twisted steeply upward, too tortuous for any light to filter through to the inner, cavern. When they saw that he went willingly, the little creatures ceased their pushing and pattered ahead through the dark, leading the way. At a fork in the passage they crowded into the false path, staring silently up at him. Then light came suddenly around a hairpin bend in the tunnel and he saw them.

They were like rabbits. That was his first thought They had small, blunt heads with huge round ears, and red-brown, furry bodies. Their hind legs were much like those of an earthly rabbit or squirrel, shaped for agility and speed, but their feet were like monkeys' feet and their fore-limbs were to all intents and purposes arms—human arms—with tiny furry hands and blunt nails. They had no tails.

If their hands were human, their faces were elfin. There were the great glowing eyes, slightly protruding, and there were stubby noses, soft and flat like rabbits' noses. Their mouths were round and pursed with square white teeth. They seemed to wear a perpetual grimace of whimsical amazement. A "whimace," Cramer called it, thinking smilingly of his "Alice in Wonderland" with its aptly coined words. The light-coloured tufts of fur above the big round eyes helped to make their faces elfishly ridiculous. Cramer never forgot that first impression of scores of tiny furry fairies scuttling about on squattering legs, waving their furry hands in excited gesture.

He looked down. At the base of the cliff, crowded into the narrow band of shadow that lay between the sheer rock and the desert, were hundreds of the little creatures, staring, expectantly up. Thy were waiting for something—for someone. He wondered if it were he.

Then he saw something that made him gape. The little beasts stood erect on their bent hind legs, like a rabbit or a squirrel on its haunches. That was a natural enough posture in animals of the type that they seemed to represent. But they were not animals!

Slung over their shoulders were little fibre bags, woven out of the tough bark of the vines that swarmed over the bottom of the cliff!

He stared down at those that surrounded him. They too had bags—were shouldering them from a pile in a nearby cave-mouth. Five of them came struggling out of the depths of a crevice, dragging something huge and unwieldy. Then and there Cramer lost his last doubts as to the intelligence of these creatures of the desert.

They had woven a bag for him!

He examined it closely before he followed them down the sheer face of the rock to where the main group waited. It was like burlap, though coarser, woven crudely out of twisted strands of bark. It was crammed with fat pods of the big brown Martian desert-pea that grew so profusely under the cliffs, and in a sort of insulating blanket of heavy leaves was a spongy fungus-growth, its fine pores saturated with water. Cramer realised that his long trek through the red desert had not ended.

The sun was low and they travelled in the shadows of the cliff until it merged with the red sands. Then strung out in a straggling caravan they headed out into the desert. From his place at the rear of the long line, Cramer watched their tiny rounded forms bobbing far ahead against the dunes. They moved with an elastic loping hop, very much like the rabbits they resembled, but with their sacks they seemed to him more like a caravan of gnomes, packing a fabulous treasure across a coral sea.

With night they came together into a compact group with Cramer at the centre. They could see in the dark as well or better than in the glare of day, but they realised that he must be guided and chose their pace accordingly. When day came and the sun glared at them over the edge of the desert, they turned aside into a labyrinth of gorges where there were crannies and burrows and a shadowed shelter large enough for him.

They ate little and drank less. Cramer realised the necessity of that. Because of his stumbling presence the distance covered by their night-marches had been cut by more than half. They were on half-rations, yet they did not desert him or try to hurry him. These little beast-creatures showed more consideration than most men.

Six days of travel brought them out of the desert into rock country again. Their water was almost gone, but more than half of the food remained. What did it mean? Why had they started on this tedious trek across the desert face of Mars? Why did they carry a burden so much greater than they needed? It puzzled him.

He could see that they were growing uneasy. They were behind schedule, and it seemed to make a difference—a big difference. He sensed impatience and a shade of regret growing in the big round eyes that stared up at him in the dark. And he resolved to do something about it.

At evening of the sixth day they were assembling in the lee of a crumbling bluff, waiting to take up the night's march. Cramer hauled himself out of the nook in which he had been sleeping and beckoned to his neighbour, a large male with a broad black line down his back.

With the little creature at his heels, he strode over to where the leader of the caravan was assembling his followers. Squatting in the sand before them, he pointed off in the direction in which they were going, then to the waiting throng. He moved aside, out of the line of march, taking his black-backed friend with him, and made an imperious gesture of dismissal. Then he waited.

He had to do it again before they realised what he meant. Then he saw understanding dawn on the little leader. A flurry of excited mewing ran over the crowd of watching creatures. The leader seemed to be conferring with those nearest him. Next two of the older males separated from the group and came over to where Cramer sat with the black-striped one. There was a piping whistle from the leader and the line got under way, loping over the loose sand at a speed at least twice as great as he could make. With his three guides, Cramer followed as fast as he could manage.

Three nights later they reached their goal. They had cut through a wilderness of rotted sandstone, its tortuous gorges heaped with sand and strewn with talus from the tottering crags that lined them. Cramer's sense of direction long since had been lost, but the three who guided him seemed to be certain of the way. About midnight they reached a sheer wall of red-ribbed white rock—the only white rock Cramer had seen on Mars. A dark line split it from top to bottom, a great fault in the planet's crust. A foot or less of space separated the sheer walls. Into it his little guides vanished. With a moment's hesitation he followed.

He had to sidle along like a crab, dragging his pack after him. He had to twist his feet around and fit them into crevices that threatened to seize them and hold them forever. He had to inch his way up fifty feet and more to where the crevice widened enough to let him through, or squirm along on his side through a mere rabbit-hole with three pairs of eyes peering anxiously out of the dark. Finally, lame and sore in every muscle, he reached the end, and tumbled head-long out on the ledge that ended the fault.

Ages ago a meteor had crashed into the centre of a limestone butte, throwing up a shattered, weirdly broken wall of rock-wreckage and filling the bowl of the resultant crater with rock-dust finer than fine sand. The force of the impact had split the plateau along an old fault-line, opening the crevice which was its single exit to the outer world. Here in the hidden crater was the secret sanctuary of the little red-brown rabbit-men.

They were busy now—furiously busy. The—floor of the crater swarmed with them, crouching close over the arid soil, scratching and prodding, shuffling queerly. Cramer could not see what they were doing, but they reminded him of a flock of hens pecking and scratching for grain.

His simile was poor. They were sowing, not reaping. A sort of insane frenzy seemed to have possessed every individual of the tribe. Piled in confusion against the walls of the crater were the dry stalks of a previous harvest. They looked queer—blighted. They had lost the sere red-brownness of the normal vines. A black dry-rot stained them, a powdery dust was eating them away. Many were contorted by huge knots and boles. Something had gone very wrong with that last harvest. It was that something that had sent the males of the tribe hundreds of miles across the arid face of Mars to find new seed. It was that something that had brought them to him and saved him from the terrible hunger of the red sands.

From the vantage-point of a cave-mouth, high on the wall of the crater, Cramer watched the planting. With their strong, nailed feet the males threw out the powdery rock-dust in long straight furrows. Behind them came their mates, strewing the seed with skillful hands. A sudden thrust of their stubby thumbs shot the peas from their pods—a double shuffle of agile feet covered them. At intervals of a few inches were buried large chunks of the porous water-holding fungus. Water was the greatest problem of the little half-human people—was, in fact, the greatest problem of any thinking race that would try to conquer the dying planet—but they seemed to have solved it in a way all their own.

Cramer learned more of that fantastic, frenzied ceremony of planting in the years that followed—ten long Martian years in which he came more and more to be one of the desert folk—the Maee, as his rude tongue translated their mewing call. They had a language of a few simple words, supplemented by signs and shrill expletive cries and whistles—emotion-sounds. They had a rude social order with a chief-leader and a nobility of the older and wiser males. In a sense they were monogamists, although with each recurring spring there was a mating ceremony in which many of the younger creatures took new mates and discarded old ones. Few of the older members of the tribe participated, squatting in their dark cave-mouths beside the mates they had chosen for life and staring owlishly down at the weaving, darting shadows on the crater floor.

They had no fire—no tools—and so far as Cramer could discover, no religion or superstition. They were animal, and yet they were not animals. They twisted bark into cord and wove it into bags, but they knew nothing of cloth and wore no clothes or adornments. They planted the desert peas and, in the long dry fall, reaped their harvest, but there was no use of plough or spade. Their sole implements were their feet and their clever hands.

The peas were the only food they had. Each harvest was heaped high in the dry, cool cave they had allotted to Cramer. Here they came when they were hungry and took what they needed. Cramer could never discover their system of rationing, yet system there must have been. As if by instinct each creature took what was proper and no more. In the beginning Cramer had thought to make their life easier by applying his human intelligence to the apportionment of the food under his care. There was never any need for that intelligence.

They lived to eat and they ate to live. So it seemed to Cramer. Whatever pleasures they might have, besides the annual ceremony of mating, meant nothing to him. Their psychology was not his. Superficially he became one of them, sharing in their simple work and feeding from the common store, but never in all the years he was with them did he really see into their minds. He was never really sure that there were minds for him to see.

Always he returned to the puzzle of the planting. He learned other facts, saw other things that helped a little to interpret the meanings that he could not see, but the real problem never changed. It was not a question of water. He had soon realised that. In some of the deeper caverns there were springs with water enough to keep them alive but none to spare. Once a year, over a range of about ten days, the underground sources were replenished by the melting polar ice, thousands of miles away. In those ten days they must, plant—must sow their seed with its accompanying sponges of water. What moisture it gave was enough to sprout the peas.

With uncanny speed the young plants thrust their rootlets deep into the powdery soil, far down to the buried watercourses. By the time the fungi had rotted away and given up the last of their absorbed moisture, the desert-bred peas had reached a supply of their own. By that time, too, a second planting had become impossible. There was no longer water to spare for it.

That explained much—the impatience of the little creatures as time passed, when their straggling caravan was still far from home, the extra seed that they had carried, the importance of the planting ceremony to their simple lives. It did not explain why they had trekked hundreds of miles across a waterless desert for that seed. It did not explain how they had come to find him.

As the barren seasons rolled past, Cramer lost all count of time. He was a machine—an automaton—feeding, watching, dully wondering. He saw that that first harvest was incredibly rich. The stout brown vines were covered with swollen, heavy pods. The thick leaves grew huge and had a metallic sheen. The ordinarily minute blossoms grew into gigantic purple blooms that flooded the crater and the caves with a cloying, suffocating perfume. At harvesting Cramer had to find another cave. The granary in which he had been living was filled to overflowing.

The second year the purple flowers were smaller and their perfume less powerful. Some of the vines died and on others the leaflets were stunted and withered. Most of the peas were still enormously larger than any Cramer had ever seen, but there were a few, commonest near the centre of the crater where the land was lowest, in which the pods were small and many of the peas shrivelled and were dwarfed.

Year by year he watched the blight spread and the harvest dwindle. There was still food enough for the little colony, for those rich, early harvests supplied food for more than two years as well as seed for the planting. But there would not be enough for long. All of the peas were dwarfed now, and most of them were black and glossy as the leaves had been. Then in the fifth year a black stain appeared on the vines nearest the centre of the crater and spread swiftly.

A powdery black dust consumed leaves and stalks and withered the roots. The peas were small and hard and black, with a bitter metallic taste. They would not sprout. That year, when the floods came and the water rose in the deepest caverns, half the tribe gathered for the trek across the desert in search of new seed. Cramer went with them.

When there was water enough to saturate their sponges, they went. Cramer's eyes had long since adapted themselves to the life of darkness that he led and there was no delay because of him. In three days they covered the distance to the water-caves where they had found him ten earthly years before. For a single day they rested, filling their sacks with seed and replenishing their water. In three more days they were back at the crater. The water had subsided, but the females and young had stored away great quantities of the spongy fungus, saturated with water, in readiness for the planting. It was cool in the lower caves, but the water evaporated rapidly into the thin air. The year when he had come the caravan had returned barely in time. Another day or two and there would not have been enough water. That year many would have died.

The Martian years! On Earth that time would foe almost doubled. Cramer's name had long since been forgotten in the home-world that he had loved. Among the Maee he was taken for granted—was almost one of their own kind. Then for a second time he went with the seed-seekers.

They came up out of the desert to the long, low line of red cliffs, pale rose in the starlight. A great wave of heartsickness rose in Cramer's throat as he stood there under the towering wall of rock, staring out across the sands to that horizon which hid the hillside where he had been "forgotten." Above him a great star glowed softly white among the steel points of the constellations—Earth—his home.

Crouched there at the mouth of his cave, the horizon lightening with the sunrise, he remembered Earth and men.

The Maee were weirdly manlike, but they were not men. Every day he discovered new humanity with them, but he could not forget the animal beneath. He longed for the heave of sullen seas against granite cliffs with the wind swirling in his ears and the scent of the pines in his nostrils. He longed for the lingering, fading tints of evening and the slow flush of dawn. He longed for the beauty of the moon, cheese-white against a bowl of cobalt, diamond-studded. He longed for blue days when the sky-lanes were strewn with cloud-castles and for the softness of a night in which the stars were not hard, bright, watching eyes. But most of all, he longed for men.

The Maee had a language, but he could not speak it or understand. They had a life of their own, a society, but he was alien to it. In the long red days when the Maee slept and the sun shimmered over the brown vines, he would sit and stare into emptiness, dreaming of the sound of a human voice, longing for human friendship, hungering for all the complex trivialities that go to make up human life. Men were somewhere there beyond the sands and the contorted crags. He was a man! But men never came.

He turned away from the sudden glare of the sunrise and went into the cave. Ice glimmered in the gloom. He went toward it, touched it. It was cool and soothing to his feverish skin. He could close his eyes and remember the coolness of Earth—cool moss under the green arch of the forest—cool shadows across the hillsides—cool streams among majestic peaks—cool flight in the spangled darkness above the clouds. He could still remember. It was all he had now.

He let his fingers trail along the smooth surface of the ice. A little thrill ran up from them through his arms, knotting the muscles. He stiffened. He felt the sharp edge of a fresh cut in the ice.

Men had been here!

By daylight it was plain. Men had come often, had come recently. They would come again. Or—would they?

All through the day he sat thinking. It was hard to think now, after all the years. He was old now. And there was no answer. The Maee could not help him—could not understand. He could stay, hoping against hope that men would come, living each endless day twice over, lying, sleepless through the interminable night, wasting slowly away. He could go with them, and never know. In the end he decided to go.

But he must be sure! He must not let them come and go without him! There must be a way! Laboriously, wakening the long-buried memories of a discarded life, he scratched his message in the thin sand that formed the floor of the cave. Then he went with the Maee.

They came! Day after day he clambered to the top of the cliff to watch, and one day they came! They were a steel-bright speck over the desert, glittering against the sky. They were an oval gem, tailed with fire. They were a smooth-flanked craft of steel, hurtling through the skies. They checked the vessel settled slowly to the plateau. The side of the little ship swung open.

Men came!

There were two, young prospectors as he had been. He was lean and dry and old, a withered skeleton with a grizzled beard. His voice was strange, even in his own ears. He had not heard it for very long. He saw them smiling, nudging each other as he babbled out his crazy, jumbled mass of words—all that had happened—all that he had seen—all that he had learned of the Maee—everything—anything—anything so long as it was speech, so long as they would listen. The old man was cracked—he knew—but they were men. They were men! Tears were in his old eyes after twenty earthly years.

They gave him men's food and men's drink—canned meat and cold coffee out of cans—but it was better than the tasteless peas and the metallic, glowing water of the Maee. They put clothes on him and listened when he told them about the crater and the caves and the planting. They asked questions—polite, kind questions. They were being kind—kind to a cracked old man—kind because they were men—his breed—men! After twenty years, there were other men!

He listened to what they told him, eagerly, hungrily. They told him about Earth—about wars—Europe all one nation—the yellow peoples growing strong and bold—they told him about Mars of the canals—Lanak—civilisation—new laws and new governments, and the new ways they had of mining, getting every last milligram out of the rock. "Soaking up the glow" they called it.

He showed them the crater and the caves and the Maee. The Maee were strange—timid. They squatted in the cave-mouths, watching. Their eyes shone out of the deep darkness. They moved away when he approached even the old black-backed one—even his old friend. They were strange. But it didn't matter! He didn't care!

He showed them the things that he knew—the granary—the water-caves. He gave them food, peas from the granary—all they wanted. They filled their ship with food and took water, plenty of water from the caves.

They were interested in caves, especially in those that ran back under the crater. He was glad. He showed them all he knew—the place where the fungus grew and the tunnels beyond where there was light—caves too small for any but the Maee to enter. He had wanted to go in and explore, many years ago when he was still young. The tunnels widened beyond. But he was too big. These were men—clever, intelligent men! Eagerly he watched them drill and set their explosives. The Maee watched too, from the dark—myriads of round eyes watching from the dark. He ran with the other men when it was time, but the Maee did not run. They sat and watched from the dark till the glare came, and the noise.

The black-striped one was killed. Others died, too—others he had known for a very long time. The gases got some of them, and then there was the concussion and the falling rock. The fungus-beds were buried by the rock that fell. But the men took the dead Maee away to their little ship and came back with torches and instruments to explore the caves beneath the crater.

He did not go. Somehow, he did not want to go where the Maee had died. The years had made him different from other men, more like the beasts, like the Maee. He saw different things and thought differently. But they went, trampling over the fallen rock, and when they returned there was a queer hard luster in their eyes.

They were men. They took him with them—away from the crater and the caves—home! The Maee watched them go, silently, from the cave-mouths. Myriads of green eyes glowing in the dark. He lay far back in the tail of the little ship, near the rockets, among the great piles of pods. The men were talking, whispering together, up forward in the control-cubby. He lay and listened to their voices. A half glow of contentment enveloped him. He was a man again!

The big man was talking now. The big man was Barron and the young one was Galt. Barron had a harsh voice, slurred and coarse. It was like Graham's voice, years ago. Cramer didn't like it.

"It's lousy with the stuff!" Barron grated.

"Yeah," Galt agreed to everything Barron said.

"The's metals too—platinum and that. I made tests. It was the big meteor brought em' in."

"Think you can get it?" Galt sounded a little sceptical.

"Sure!" Barron didn't like being doubted. "You seen the scope. Kicked clean off the scale, didn't it? You seen the little chunk from the blast—big as a house and just a little piece at that."

Gal's young voice was awed—sort of reverent.

"Gosh!" he murmured. "It's like heaven, findin' it like that! Like a dream. Millions for the both of us, and then Lanak and the canals and home. Earth!"

Barron was talking on—details—practicality. He was no milksop, "dreamin' about home!" "We can blast down through from the top, right in the middle where it's lowest. We'll save time that way, and there's no chance of shiftin' the water. We got water there, and food, just for the takin', and we don't want to lose it. By jinks, kid, we got it soft! Millions for the both of us!"

Galt's voice sounded a little dubious. "What food do you mean? Won't blasting like that kill the peas?"

The big man roared with laughter. "Peas! Who wants the lousy driedup swill? We got meat, kid—just for th' takin'! Rabbits. Thousands of 'em. Fill up that big crack with a couple good blasts and they're there till we're done with th' place. We'll eat meat, kid."

Galt peered back over his shoulder. The old man was lying still—sleeping maybe. Crazy old duffer! Living half his life over millions and never knowing it. Gibbering about rabbits like they were men, and about peas.

"What about the old fellow?" Galt asked.

Barron leered knowingly. "Him? The's nobody knows about him but us and nobody that cares a cuss. We can forget him."

Forget!

Both men turned at the sound. The old man was trying to stand up. The acceleration pushed him back. He hunched forward on his knees. He was by the fuel-chambers, where the outlets bulged into the ship. He was laughing—crazy, screaming laughter.

Ah! He was opening the air valves!

*   *   *

Over the red desert a bright speck blossomed into a great white puff of flame. After a little a sound came, thin and very far away, like the bursting of a rock.

A plume of fire streaked slowly down across the sky and vanished into the upflung chaos of the bad-lands. A fountain of light shot up where it fell, bright with specks of burning metal. Another sound came, deeper, the thin echo of a mighty roar.

The Maee were watching from the crack in the plateau that was the only entrance to their secret haven. In the dark their eyes were great and round—myriads of green eyes, watching from the dark. Somehow they understood what he who had lived among them had done for them.

A MARTIAN ODYSSEY

Stanley G. Weinbaum

It is interesting how from time to time certain stories capture the public imagination and rapidly pass into legend, so that even if that story may later seem dated by contemporary standards it nevertheless still stimulates a rosy glow in the memories of long-time readers of science fiction. Such was the case with 'A Martian Odyssey'. It marked the author's debut in the science-fiction magazines and was an instant success. H. P. Lovecraft remarked what a pleasure it was "that someone had at last escaped the sickening hackneyedness in which 99.99% of all pulp interplanetary stuff is engulfed".

In 'A Martian Odyssey' (Wonder Stories, July 1934) Stanley G. Weinbaum (1902–1935) introduced a whole new world of ecology for Mars. Until then most authors had concentrated on humans or humanoid Martians, with little concern for the planet's other creatures. Weinbaum did the opposite. He described a wide menagerie of creatures, each ideally suited to their place in the Martian world. Alas Weinbaum's writing career was cut short after eighteen months by lung cancer, yet in that brief period he produced another twenty or so stories, many, even though rather dated now, still of classic status. No other writer has burst on to the field with such incandescence, only to pass too quickly into legend.

J ARVIS STRETCHED HIMSELF AS LUXURIOUSLY AS HE COULD IN the cramped general quarters of the *Ares*.

"Air you can breathe!" he exulted. "It feels as thick as soup after the thin stuff out there!" He nodded at the Martian landscape stretching flat and desolate in the light of the nearer moon, beyond the glass of the port.

The other three stared at him sympathetically—Putz, the engineer, Leroy, the biologist, and Harrison the astronomer and captain of the expedition. Dick Jarvis, of course, was chemist of the famous crew, the *Ares* expedition, first human beings to set foot on the mysterious neighbour of the earth, the planet Mars. This, of course, was in the old days, less than twenty years after the mad American Doheny perfected the atomic blast at the cost of his life, and only a decade after the equally mad Cardoza rode on it to the moon. They were true pioneers, these four of the *Ares*. Except for a half-dozen moon expeditions and the ill-fated de Lancey flight aimed at the seductive orb of Venus, they were the first men to feel other gravity than earth's, and certainly the first successful crew to leave the earth-moon system. And they deserved that success when one considers the difficulties and discomforts—the months spent in acclimatization chambers back on earth, learning to breathe air as tenuous as that of Mars, the challenging of the void in the tiny rocket driven by the cranky reaction motors of the twenty-first century, and mostly the facing of an absolutely unknown world.

Jarvis stretched again and fingered the raw and peeling tip of his frost-bitten nose. He sighed again contentedly.

"Well," exploded Harrison abruptly, "are we going to hear what happened? You set out all shipshape in an auxiliary rocket, we don't get a peep for ten days, and finally Putz here picks you out of a lunatic ant-heap with a freak ostrich as your pal! Spill it, man!"

"'Speel'?" queried Leroy perplexedly. "Speel what?"

"He means '*spiel*'," explained Putz soberly. "It iss to tell."

Jarvis met Harrison's amused glance without the shadow of a smile. "That's right, Karl," he said in grave agreement with Putz. "*Ich spiel es!*" He grunted comfortably and began.

"According to orders," he said, "I watched Karl here take off toward the North, and then I got into my flying sweat-box and headed South. You'll remember, Cap—we had orders not to land, but just scout about for points of interest. I set the two cameras clicking and buzzed along, riding pretty high—about two thousand feet—for a couple of reasons. First, it gave the cameras a greater field, and second, the under-jets travel so far in this half-vacuum they call air here that they stir up dust if you move low."

"We know all that from Putz," grunted Harrison. "I wish you'd saved the films, though. They'd have paid the cost of this junket; remember how the public mobbed the first moon pictures?"

"The films are safe," retorted Jarvis. "Well," he resumed, "as I said, I buzzed along at a pretty good clip; just as we figured, the wings haven't much lift in this air at less than a hundred miles per hour, and even then I had to use the under-jets.

"So, with the speed and the altitude and the blurring caused by the under-jets, the seeing wasn't any too good. I could see enough, though, to distinguish that what I sailed over was just more of this grey plain that we'd been examining the whole week since our land-ing—same blobby growths and same eternal carpet of crawling little plant-animals, or biopods, as Leroy calls them. So I sailed along, calling back my position every hour as instructed, and not knowing whether you heard me."

"I did!" snapped Harrison.

"A hundred and fifty miles south," continued Jarvis imperturbably, "the surface changed to a sort of low plateau, nothing but desert and orange-tinted sand. I figured that we were right in our guess, then, and this grey plain we dropped on was really the Mare Cimmerium which would make my orange desert the region called Xanthus. If I were right, I ought to hit another grey plain, the Mare Chronium in another couple of hundred miles, and then another orange desert, Thyle I or II. And so I did."

"Putz verified our position a week and a half ago!" grumbled the captain. "Let's get to the point."

"Coming!" remarked Jarvis. "Twenty miles into Thyle—believe it or not—I crossed a canal!"

"Putz photographed a hundred! Let's hear something new!"

"And did he also see a city?"

"Twenty of 'em, if you call those heaps of mud cities!"

"Well," observed Jarvis, "from here on I'll be telling a few things Putz didn't see!" He rubbed his tingling nose, and continued. "I knew that I had sixteen hours of daylight at this season, so eight hours— eight hundred miles—from here, I decided to turn back. I was still over Thyle, whether I or II I'm not sure, not more than twenty-five miles into it. And right there, Putz's pet motor quit!"

"Qvit? How?" Putz was solicitous.

"The atomic blast got weak. I started losing altitude right away, and suddenly there I was with a thump right in the middle of Thyle! Smashed my nose on the window, too!" He rubbed the injured member ruefully.

"Did you maybe try vashing der combustion chamber mit acid

sulphuric?" inquired Putz. "Sometimes der lead giffs a secondary radiation—"

"Naw!" said Jarvis disgustedly. "I wouldn't try that, of course—not more than ten times! Besides, the bump flattened the landing gear and busted off the under-jets. Suppose I got the thing working—what then? Ten miles with the blast coming right out of the bottom and I'd have melted the floor from under me!" He rubbed his nose again. "Lucky for me a pound only weighs seven ounces here, or I'd have been mashed flat!"

"I could have fixed!" ejaculated the engineer. "I bet it vas not serious."

"Probably not," agreed Jarvis sarcastically. "Only it wouldn't fly. Nothing serious, but I had my choice of waiting to be picked up or trying to walk back—eight hundred miles, and perhaps twenty days before we had to leave! Forty miles a day! Well," he concluded, "I chose to walk. Just as much chance of being picked up, and it kept me busy."

"We'd have found you," said Harrison.

"No doubt. Anyway, I rigged up a harness from some seat straps, and put the water tank on my back, took a cartridge belt and revolver, and some iron rations, and started out."

"Water tank!" exclaimed the little biologist, Leroy. "She weigh one-quarter ton!"

"Wasn't full. Weighed about two hundred and fifty pounds earth-weight, which is eighty-five here. Then, besides, my own personal two hundred and ten pounds is only seventy on Mars, so, tank and all, I grossed a hundred and fifty-five, or fifty-five pounds less than my everyday earth-weight. I figured on that when I undertook the forty-mile daily stroll. Oh—of course I took a thermo-skin sleeping bag for these wintry Martian nights.

—

"Off I went, bouncing along pretty quickly. Eight hours of daylight meant twenty miles or more. It got tiresome, of course—plugging along over a soft sand desert with nothing to see, not even Leroy's crawling biopods. But an hour or so brought me to the canal—just a dry ditch about four hundred feet wide, and straight as a railroad on its own company map.

"There'd been water in it sometime, though. The ditch was covered with what looked like a nice green lawn. Only, as I approached, the lawn moved out of my way!"

"Eh?" said Leroy.

"Yeah; it was a relative of your biopods. I caught one—a little grass-like blade about as long as my finger, with two thin, stemmy legs."

"He is where?" Leroy was eager.

"He is let go! I had to move, so I ploughed along with the walking grass opening in front and closing behind. And then I was out on the orange desert of Thyle again.

"I plugged doggedly along, cussing the sand that made going so tiresome, and, incidentally, cussing that cranky motor of yours, Karl. It was just before twilight that I reached the edge of Thyle, and looked down over the grey Mare Chronium. And I knew there was seventy-five miles of *that* to be walked over, and then a couple of hundred miles of that Xanthus desert, and about as much more Mare Cimmerium. Was I pleased? I started cussing you fellows for not picking me up!"

"We were trying, you sap!" said Harrison.

"That didn't help. Well, I figured I might as well use what was left of daylight in getting down the cliff that bounded Thyle. I found an easy place, and down I went. Mare Chronium was just the same sort of place as this—crazy leafless plants and a bunch of crawlers; I gave it a glance and hauled out my sleeping bag. Up to that time, you know, I hadn't seen anything worth worrying about on this half-dead world—nothing dangerous, that is."

"Did you?" queried Harrison.

"*Did* I! You'll hear about it when I come to it. Well, I was just about to turn in when suddenly I heard the wildest sort of shenanigans!"

"Vot iss shenanigans?" inquired Putz.

"He say, '*Je ne sais quoi*'," explained Leroy. "It is to say, 'I don't know what'."

"That's right," agreed Jarvis. "I didn't know what, so I sneaked over to find out. There was a racket like a flock of crows eating a bunch of canaries—whistles, cackles, caws, trills, and what have you. I rounded a clump of stumps, and there was Tweel!"

"Tweel?" said Harrison, and "Tveel?" said Leroy and Putz.

"That freak ostrich," explained the narrator. "At least, Tweel is as near as I can pronounce it without sputtering. He called it something like 'Trrrweerrlll'."

"What was he doing?" asked the Captain.

"He was being eaten! And squealing, of course, as any one would."

"Eaten! By what?"

"I found out later. All I could see then was a bunch of black ropy arms tangled around what looked like, as Putz described it to you, an ostrich. I wasn't going to interfere, naturally; if both creatures were dangerous, I'd have one less to worry about.

"But the bird-like thing was putting up a good battle, dealing vicious blows with an eighteen-inch beak, between screeches. And besides, I caught a glimpse or two of what was on the end of those arms!" Jarvis shuddered. "But the clincher was when I noticed a little black bag or case hung about the neck of the bird-thing! It was intelligent! That or tame, I assumed. Anyway, it clinched my decision. I pulled out my automatic and fired into what I could see of its antagonist.

"There was a flurry of tentacles and a spurt of black corruption, and then the thing, with a disgusting sucking noise, pulled itself and its arms into a hole in the ground. The other let out a series of clacks, staggered around on legs about as thick as golf sticks, and turned suddenly to face me. I held my weapon ready, and the two of us stared at each other.

"The Martian wasn't a bird, really. It wasn't even bird-like, except just at first glance. It had a beak all right, and a few feathery appendages, but the beak wasn't really a beak. It was somewhat flexible; I could see the tip bend slowly from side to side; it was almost like a cross between a beak and a trunk. It had four-toed feet, and four fingered things—hands, you'd have to call them, and a little roundish body, and a long neck ending in a tiny head—and that beak. It stood an inch or so taller than I, and—well, Putz saw it!"

The engineer nodded. "Yah! I saw!"

II. TWEEL OF MARS

Jarvis continued. "So—we stared at each other. Finally the creature went into a series of clackings and twitterings and held out its hands toward me, empty. I took that as a gesture of friendship."

"Perhaps," suggested Harrison, "it looked at that nose of yours and thought you were its brother!"

"Huh! You can be funny without talking! Anyway, I put up my gun and said, 'Aw, don't mention it,' or something of the sort, and the thing came over and we were pals.

"By that time, the sun was pretty low and I knew that I'd better build a fire or get into my thermo-skin. I decided on the fire. I picked a spot at the base of the Thyle cliff, where the rock could reflect a little heat on my back. I started breaking off chunks of this desiccated Martian vegetation, and my companion caught the idea and brought in an armful. I reached for a match, but the Martian fished into his pouch and brought out something that looked like a glowing coal; one touch of it, and the fire was blazing—and you all know what a job we have starting a fire in this atmosphere!

"And that bag of his!" continued the narrator. "That was a manu-factured article, my friends; press an end and she popped open—press the middle, and she sealed so perfectly you couldn't see the line. Better than zippers.

"Well, we stared at the fire a while and I decided to attempt some sort of communication with the Martian. I pointed at myself and said 'Dick'; he caught the drift immediately, stretched a bony claw at me and repeated 'Tick.' Then I pointed at him, and he gave that whistle I called Tweel; I can't imitate his accent. Things were going smoothly; to emphasise the names. I repeated 'Dick,' and then, pointing at him, 'Tweel.'

"There we stuck! He gave some clacks that sounded negative, and said something like 'P-p-p-proot.' And that was just the beginning; I was always 'Tick,' but as for him—part of the time he was 'Tweel,' and part of the time he was 'P-p-p-proot,' and part of the time he was sixteen other noises!

"We just couldn't connect! I tried 'rock,' and I tried 'star,' and 'tree,' and 'fire,' and Lord knows what else, and try as I would, I couldn't get a single word! Nothing was the same for two successive minutes, and if that's a language, I'm an alchemist! Finally I gave it up and called him Tweel, and that seemed to do.

"But Tweel hung on to some of my words. He remembered a couple of them, which I suppose is a great achievement if you're used to a language you have to make up as you go along. But I couldn't get the hang of his talk; either I missed some subtle point or we just didn't *think* alike—and I rather believe the latter view.

"I've other reasons for believing that. After a while I gave up the language business, and tried mathematics. I scratched two plus two equals four on the ground, and demonstrated it with pebbles. Again Tweel caught the idea, and informed me that three plus three equals six. Once more we seemed to be getting somewhere.

"So, knowing that Tweel had at least a grammar school education, I drew a circle for the sun, pointing first at it, and then at the last glow of the sun. Then I sketched in Mercury, and Venus, and Mother Earth, and Mars, and finally, pointing to Mars, I swept my hand around in a sort of inclusive gesture to indicate that Mars was our current environment. I was working up to putting over the idea that my home was on the earth.

"Tweel understood my diagram all right. He poked his beak at it, and with a great deal of trilling and clucking, he added Deimos and Phobos to Mars, and then sketched in the earth's moon!

"Do you see what that proves? It proves that Tweel's race uses telescopes—that they're civilised!"

"Does not!" snapped Harrison. "The moon is visible from here as a fifth magnitude star. They could see its revolution with the naked eye."

"The moon, yes!" said Jarvis. "You've missed my point. Mercury isn't visible! And Tweel knew of Mercury because he placed the Moon at the *third* planet, not the second. If he didn't know Mercury, he'd put the earth second, and Mars third, instead of fourth! See?"

"Humph!" said Harrison.

"Anyway," proceeded Jarvis, "I went on with my lesson. Things were going smoothly, and it looked as if I could put the idea over. I pointed at the earth on my diagram, and then at myself, and then, to clinch it, I pointed to myself and then to the earth itself shining bright green almost at the zenith.

"Tweel set up such an excited clacking that I was certain he understood. He jumped up and down, and suddenly he pointed at himself and then at the sky, and then at himself and at the sky again. He pointed at his middle and then at Arcturus, at his head and then at Spica, at his feet and then at half a dozen stars, while I just gaped at him. Then, all of a sudden, he gave a tremendous leap. Man, what a hop! He shot straight up into the starlight, seventy-five feet if an inch! I saw him silhouetted against the sky, saw him turn and come down at me head first, and land smack on his beak like a javelin! There he stuck square in the centre of my sun-circle in the sand—a bull's-eye!"

"Nuts!" observed the captain. "Plain nuts!"

"That's what I thought, too! I just stared at him open-mouthed while he pulled his head out of the sand and stood up. Then I figured he'd missed my point, and I went through the whole blamed rigmarole again, and it ended the same way, with Tweel on his nose in the middle of my picture!"

"Maybe it's a religious rite," suggested Harrison.

"Maybe," said Jarvis dubiously. "Well, there we were. We could exchange ideas up to a certain point, and then—blooey! Something in us was different, unrelated; I don't doubt that Tweel thought me just as screwy as I thought him. Our minds simply looked at the world from different viewpoints, and perhaps his viewpoint is as true as ours. But—we couldn't get together, that's all. Yet, in spite of all difficulties, I *liked* Tweel, and I have a queer certainty that he liked me."

—

"Nuts!" repeated the captain. "Just daffy!"

"Yeah? Wait and see. A couple of times I've thought that perhaps we—" He paused, and then resumed his narrative. "Anyway, I finally gave it up, and got into my thermo-skin to sleep. The fire hadn't kept me any too warm, but that damn sleeping bag did. Got stuffy five minutes after I closed myself in. I opened it a little and bingo! Some eighty-below-zero air hit my nose, and that's when I got this pleasant little frostbite to add to the bump I acquired during the crash of my rocket.

"I don't know what Tweel made of my sleeping. He sat around, but when I woke up, he was gone. I'd just crawled out of my bag, though, when I heard some twittering, and there he came, sailing down from that three-story Thyle cliff to alight on his beak beside me. I pointed to myself and toward the north, and he pointed at himself and toward the south, but when I loaded up and started away, he came along.

"Man, how he travelled!—a hundred and fifty feet at a jump, sailing through the air stretched out like a spear, and landing on his beak. He seemed surprised at my plodding, but after a few moments he fell in beside me, only every few minutes he'd go into one of his leaps, and stick his nose into the sand a block ahead of me. Then he'd come shooting back at me; it kept me nervous at first to see that beak of his coming at me like a spear, but he always ended in the sand at my side.

"So the two of us plugged along across the Mare Chronium. Same sort of place as this—same crazy plants and same little green biopods growing in the sand, or crawling out of your way. We talked—not that we understood each other, you know, but just for company. I sang songs, and I suspect Tweel did too; at least, some of his trillings and twitterings had a subtle sort of rhythm.

"Then, for variety, Tweel would display his smattering of English words. He'd point to an outcropping and say 'rock,' and point to a pebble and say it again; or he'd touch my arm and say 'Tick,' and then repeat it. He seemed terrifically amused that the same word meant the same thing twice in succession, or that the same word could apply to two different objects. It set me wondering if perhaps his language wasn't like the primitive speech of some earth people—you know, Captain, like the Negritoes, for instance, who haven't any generic words. No word for food or water or man—words for good food and bad food, or rain water and sea water, or strong man and weak man—but no names for general classes. They're too primitive to understand that rain water and sea water are just different aspects of the same thing. But that wasn't the case with Tweel; it was just that we were somehow mysteriously different—our minds were alien to each other. And yet—we *liked* each other!"

"Looney, that's all," remarked Harrison. "That's why you two were so fond of each other."

"Well, I like *you!*" countered Jarvis wickedly. "Anyway," he resumed, "don't get the idea that there was anything screwy about Tweel. In fact, I'm not so sure but that he couldn't teach our highly praised human intelligence a trick or two. Oh, he wasn't an intellectual superman. I guess; but don't overlook the point that he managed to understand a little of my mental workings, and I never even got a glimmering of his."

"Because he didn't have any!" suggested the captain, while Putz and Leroy blinked attentively.

"You can judge of that when I'm through," said Jarvis. "Well, we plugged along across the Mare Chronium all that day, and all the next. Mare Chronium—Sea of Time! Say, I was willing to agree with Schiaparelli's name by the end of that march! Just that grey, endless plain of weird plants, and never a sign of any other life. It was so monotonous that I was even glad to see the desert of Xanthus toward the evening of the second day.

"I was fair worn out, but Tweel seemed as fresh as ever, for all I never saw him drink or eat. I think he could have crossed the Mare Chronium in a couple of hours with those block-long nose dives of his, but he stuck along with me. I offered him some water once or twice; he took the cup from me and sucked the liquid into his beak, and then carefully squirted it all back into the cup and gravely returned it.

"Just as we sighted Xanthus, or the cliffs that bounded it, one of those nasty sand clouds blew along, not as bad as the one we had here, but mean to travel against. I pulled the transparent flap of my thermo-skin bag across my face and managed pretty well, and I noticed that Tweel used some feathery appendages growing like a moustache at the base of his beak to cover his nostrils, and some similar fuzz to shield his eyes."

"He is desert creature!" ejaculated the little biologist, Leroy.

"Huh? Why?"

"He drink no water—he is adapt' for sand storm—"

"Proves nothing! There's not enough water to waste anywhere on this desiccated pill called Mars. We'd call all of it desert on earth, you know." He paused. "Anyway, after the sand storm blew over, a little wind kept blowing in our faces, not strong enough to stir the sand. But suddenly things came drifting along from the Xanthus cliffs—small, transparent spheres, for all the world like glass tennis balls! But light—they were almost light enough to float even in this thin air—empty, too; at least, I cracked open a couple and nothing came out but a bad smell. I asked Tweel about them, but all he said was 'No, no, no,' which I took to mean that he knew nothing about them. So they went bouncing by like tumbleweeds, or like soap bubbles, and we plugged on toward Xanthus. Tweel pointed at one of the crystal balls once and said 'rock,' but I was too tired to argue with him. Later I discovered what he meant.

"We came to the bottom of the Xanthus cliffs finally, when there wasn't much daylight left. I decided to sleep on the plateau if possible; anything dangerous, I reasoned, would be more likely to prowl through the vegetation of the Mare Chronium than the sand of Xanthus. Not that I'd seen a single sign of menace, except the rope-armed black thing that had trapped Tweel, and apparently that didn't prowl at all, but lured its victims within reach. It couldn't lure me while I slept, especially as Tweel didn't seem to sleep at all, but simply sat patiently around all night. I wondered how the creature had managed to trap Tweel, but there wasn't any way of asking him. I found that out too, later; it's devilish!

"However, we were ambling around the base of the Xanthus barrier looking for an easy spot to climb. At least, I was. Tweel could have leaped it easily, for the cliffs were lower than Thyle—perhaps sixty feet. I found a place and started up, swearing at the water tank strapped to my back—it didn't bother me except when climbing—and suddenly I heard a sound that I thought I recognised!

"You know how deceptive sounds are in this thin air. A shot sounds like the pop of a cork. But this sound was the drone of a rocket, and sure enough, there went our second auxiliary about ten miles to westward, between me and the sunset!"

"Vas me!" said Putz. "I hunt for you."

"Yeah; I knew that, but what good did it do me? I hung on to the cliff and yelled and waved with one hand. Tweel saw it too, and set up a trilling and twittering, leaping to the top of the barrier and then high into the air. And while I watched, the machine droned on into the shadows to the south.

"I scrambled to the top of the cliff. Tweel was still pointing and trilling excitedly, shooting up toward the sky and coming down head-on to stick upside down on his beak in the sand. I pointed toward the south and at myself, and he said, 'Yes—Yes—Yes'; but somehow I gathered that he thought the flying thing was a relative of mine, probably a parent. Perhaps I did his intellect an injustice; I think now that I did.

"I was bitterly disappointed by the failure to attract attention. I pulled out my thermo-skin bag and crawled into it, as the night chill was already apparent. Tweel stuck his beak into the sand and drew up his legs and arms and looked for all the world like one of those leafless shrubs out there. I think he stayed that way all night."

"Protective mimicry!" ejaculated Leroy. "See? He is desert creature!"

III. THE PYRAMID BEING

"In the morning," resumed Jarvis, "we started off again. We hadn't gone a hundred yards into Xanthus when I saw something queer! This is one thing Putz didn't photograph, I'll wager!

"There was a line of little pyramids—tiny ones, not more than six inches high, stretching across Xanthus as far as I could see! Little buildings made of pygmy bricks, they were, hollow inside and truncated, or at least broken at the top and empty. I pointed at them and said 'What?' to Tweel, but he gave some negative twitters to indicate, I suppose, that he didn't know. So off we went, following the row of pyramids because they ran north, and I was going north.

"Man, we trailed that line for hours! After a while, I noticed another queer thing: they were getting larger. Same number of bricks in each one, but the bricks were larger.

"By noon they were shoulder high. I looked into a couple—all just the same, broken at the top and empty. I examined a brick or two as well; they were silica, and old as creation itself!"

"How you know?" asked Leroy.

"They were weathered—edges rounded. Silica doesn't weather easily even on earth, and in this climate—!"

"How old you think?"

"Fifty thousand—a hundred thousand years. How can I tell? The little ones we saw in the morning were older—perhaps ten times as old. Crumbling. How old would that make *them*? Half a million years? Who knows?" Jarvis paused a moment. "Well," he resumed, "we followed the line. Tweel pointed at them and said 'rock' once or twice, but he'd done that many times before. Besides, he was more or less right about these.

"I tried questioning him. I pointed at a pyramid and asked 'People?' and indicated the two of us. He set up a negative sort of clucking and said, 'No, no, no. No one-one-two. No two-two-four,' meanwhile rubbing his stomach. I just stared at him and he went through the business again. 'No one-one-two. No two-two-four.' I just gaped at him."

"That proves it!" exclaimed Harrison. "Nuts!"

"You think so?" queried Jarvis sardonically. "Well, I figured it out different! 'No one-one-two!' You don't get it, of course, do you?"

"Nope—nor do you!"

"I think I do! Tweel was using the few English words he knew to put over a very complex idea. What, let me ask, does mathematics make you think of?"

"Why—of astronomy. Or—or logic!"

"That's it! 'No one-one-two!' Tweel was telling me that the builders of the pyramids weren't people!—or that they weren't intelligent, that they weren't reasoning creatures! Get it?"

"Huh! I'll be damned!"

"You probably will."

"Why," put in Leroy, "he rub his belly?"

"Why? Because, my dear biologist, that's where his brains were! Not in his tiny head—in his middle!"

"*C'est impossible!*"

"Not on Mars, it isn't! This flora and fauna aren't earthly; your bio-pods prove that!" Jarvis grinned and took up his narrative. "Anyway, we plugged along across Xanthus and in about the middle of the afternoon, something else queer happened. The pyramids ended."

"Ended!"

"Yeah; the queer part was that the last one—and now they were ten-footers—was capped! See? Whatever built it was still inside; we'd trailed 'em from their half-million-year-old origin to the present.

"Tweel and I both noticed it about the same time. I yanked out my automatic (I had a clip of Boland explosive bullets in it) and Tweel, quick as a sleight-of-hand trick, snapped a queer little glass revolver out of his bag. It was much like our weapons, except that the grip was larger to accommodate his four-taloned hand. And we held our weapons ready while we sneaked up along the lines of empty pyramids.

"Tweel saw the movement first. The top tiers of bricks were heaving, shaking, and suddenly slid down the sides with a thin crash. And then—something—something was coming out!

"A long, silver-grey arm appeared, dragging after it an armoured body. Armoured, I mean, with scales, silver-grey and dull-shining.

The arm heaved the body out of the hole; the beast crashed to the sand.

"It was a nondescript creature—body like a big grey cask, arm and a sort of mouth-hole at one end; stiff, pointed tail at the other—and that's all. No other limbs, no eyes, ears, nose—nothing! The thing dragged itself a few yards, inserted its pointed tail in the sand, pushed itself upright, and just sat.

"Tweel and I watched it for ten minutes before it moved. Then, with a creaking and rustling like—oh, like crumpling stiff paper—its arm moved to the mouth-hole and out came a brick! The arm placed the brick carefully on the ground, and the thing was still again.

"Another ten minutes—another brick. Just one of Nature's brick-layers. I was about ready to slip away and move on when Tweel pointed at the thing and said 'rock'! I went 'huh?' and he said it again. Then, to the accompaniment of some of his trilling, he said, 'No—no—,' and gave two or three whistling breaths.

"Well, I got his meaning, for a wonder! I said, 'No breath?' and demonstrated the word. Tweel was ecstatic; he said, 'Yes, yes, yes! No, no, no breet!' Then he gave a leap and sailed out to land on his nose about one pace from the monster!

"I was startled, you can imagine! The arm was going up for a brick, and I expected to see Tweel caught and mangled, but—nothing happened! Tweel pounded on the creature, and the arm took the brick and placed it neatly beside the first. Tweel rapped on its body again, and said 'rock,' and I got up nerve enough to take a look myself.

"Tweel was right again. The creature *was* rock, and it didn't breathe!"

"How you know?" snapped Leroy, his black eyes blazing interest.

"Because I'm a chemist. The beast was made of silica! There must have been pure silicon in the sand, and it lived on that. Get it? We, and Tweel, and those plants out there, and even the biopods are *carbon* life; this thing lived by a different set of chemical reactions. It was silicon life!"

"*La vie silicieuse!*" shouted Leroy. "I have suspect, and now it is proof! I must go see! *Il faut que je—*"

"All right! All right!" said Jarvis. "You can go see. Anyhow, there the thing was, alive and yet not alive, moving every ten minutes, and then only to remove a brick. Those bricks were its waste matter. See, Frenchy? We're carbon, and our waste is carbon dioxide, and this thing is silicon, and *its* waste is silicon dioxide—silica. But silica is a solid, hence the bricks. And it built itself in, and when it was covered, it moved over to a fresh place to start over. No wonder it creaked! A living creature half a million years old!"

"How you know how old?" Leroy was frantic.

"We trailed its pyramids from the beginning, didn't we? If this weren't the original pyramid builder, the series would have ended somewhere before we found him, wouldn't it?—ended and started over with the small ones. That's simple enough, isn't it?

"But he reproduces, or tries to. Before the third brick came out, there was a little rustle and out popped a whole stream of those little crystal balls. They're his spores, or eggs, or seeds—call 'em what you want. They went bouncing by across Xanthus just as they'd bounced by us back in the Mare Chronium. I've a hunch how they work, too— this is for your information, Leroy. I think the crystal shell of silica is no more than a protective covering, like an eggshell, and that the active principle is the smell inside. It's some sort of gas that attacks silicon, and if the shell is broken near a supply of that element, some reaction starts that ultimately develops into a beast like that one."

"You should try!" exclaimed the little Frenchman. "We must break one to see!"

"Yeah? Well, I did. I smashed a couple against the sand. Would you like to come back in about ten thousand years to see if I planted some pyramid monsters? You'd most likely be able to tell by that time!" Jarvis paused and drew a deep breath. "Lord! That queer creature! Do you picture it? Blind, deaf, nerveless, brainless—just a mechanism, and yet—immortal! Bound to go on making bricks, building pyramids, as long as silicon and oxygen exist, and even afterwards it'll just stop. It won't be dead. If the accidents of a million years bring it its food again, there it'll be, ready to run again, while brains and civilisations are part of the past. A queer beast—yet I met a stranger one!"

"If you did, it must have been in your dreams!" growled Harrison.

"You're right!" said Jarvis soberly. "In a way, you're right. The dream-beast! That's the best name for it—and it's the most fiendish, terrifying creation one could imagine! More dangerous than a lion, more insidious than a snake!"

"Tell me!" begged Leroy. "I must go see!"

"Not *this* devil!" He paused again. "Well," he resumed, "Tweel and I left the pyramid creature and ploughed along through Xanthus. I was tired and a little disheartened by Putz's failure to pick me up, and Tweel's trilling got on my nerves, as did his flying nosedives. So I just strode along without a word, hour after hour across that monotonous desert.

"Toward mid-afternoon we came in sight of a low dark line on the horizon. I knew what it was. It was a canal; I'd crossed it in the rocket and it meant that we were just one-third of the way across Xanthus. Pleasant thought, wasn't it? And still, I was keeping up to schedule.

"We approached the canal slowly; I remembered that this one was bordered by a wide fringe of vegetation and that Mud-heap City was on it."

IV. THE DREAM-BEAST

"I was tired, as I said. I kept thinking of a good hot meal, and then from that I jumped to reflections of how nice and home-like even Borneo would seem after this crazy planet, and from that, to thoughts of little old New York, and then to thinking about a girl I know there—Fancy Long. Know her?"

"'Vision entertainer,'" said Harrison. "I've tuned her in. Nice blonde—dances and sings on the *Yerba Mate* hour."

"That's her," said Jarvis ungrammatically. "I know her pretty well—just friends, get me?—though she came down to see us off in the *Ares*. Well, I was thinking about her, feeling pretty lonesome, and all the time we were approaching that line of rubbery plants.

"And then—I said, 'What 'n hell!' and stared. And there she was—Fancy Long, standing plain as day under one of those crack-brained trees, and smiling and waving just the way I remembered her when we left!"

"Now you're nuts, too!" observed the captain.

"Boy, I almost agreed with you! I stared and pinched myself and closed my eyes and then stared again—and every time, there was Fancy Long smiling and waving! Tweel saw something, too; he was trilling and clucking away, but I scarcely heard him. I was bounding toward her over the sand, too amazed even to ask myself questions.

"I wasn't twenty feet from her when Tweel caught me with one of his flying leaps. He grabbed my arm, yelling, 'No—no—no!' in his squeaky voice. I tried to shake him off—he was as light as if he were built of bamboo—but he dug his claws in and yelled. And finally some sort of sanity returned to me and I stopped less than ten feet from her. There she stood, looking as solid as Putz's head!"

"Vot?" said the engineer.

"She smiled and waved, and waved and smiled, and I stood there dumb as Leroy, while Tweel squeaked and chattered. I *knew* it couldn't be real, yet—there she was!

"Finally I said, 'Fancy! Fancy Long!' She just kept on smiling and waving, but looking as real as if I hadn't left her thirty-seven million miles away.

"Tweel had his glass pistol out, pointing it at her. I grabbed his arm, but he tried to push me away. He pointed at her and said, 'No breet! No breet!,' and I understood that he meant that the Fancy Long thing wasn't alive. Man, my head was whirling!

"Still, it gave me the jitters to see him pointing his weapon at her. I don't know why I stood there watching him take careful aim, but I did. Then he squeezed the handle of his weapon; there was a little puff of steam, and Fancy Long was gone! And in her place was one of those writhing, black, rope-armed horrors like the one I'd saved Tweel from!

"The dream-beast! I stood there dizzy, watching it die while Tweel trilled and whistled. Finally he touched my arm, pointed at the twisting thing, and said, 'You one-one-two, he one-one-two.' After he'd repeated it eight or ten times, I got it. Do any of you?"

"*O'ui!*" shrilled Leroy. "*Moi—je le comprends!* He mean you think of something, the beast he know, and you see it! *Un chien*—a hungry dog, he would see the big bone with meat! Or smell it—not?"

"Right!" said Jarvis. "The dream-beast uses its victim's longings and desires to trap its prey. The bird at nesting season would see its mate, the fox, prowling for its own prey, would see a helpless rabbit!"

"How he do?" queried Leroy.

"How do I know? How does a snake back on earth charm a bird into its very jaws? And aren't there deep-sea fish that lure their victims into their mouths? Lord!" Jarvis shuddered. "Do you see how insidious the monster is? We're warned now—but henceforth we can't trust even our eyes. You might see me—I might see one of you—and back of it may be nothing but another of those black horrors!"

"How'd your friend know?" asked the captain abruptly.

"Tweel? I wonder! Perhaps he was thinking of something that couldn't possibly have interested me, and when I started to run, he realised that I saw something different and was warned. Or perhaps the dream-beast can only project a single vision, and Tweel saw what I saw—or nothing. I couldn't ask him. But it's just another proof that his intelligence is equal to ours or greater."

"He's daffy, I tell you!" said Harrison. "What makes you think his intellect ranks with the human?"

"Plenty of things! First, the pyramid-beast. He hadn't seen one before; he said as much. Yet he recognised it as a dead-alive automaton of silicon."

"He could have heard of it," objected Harrison. "He lives around here, you know."

"Well, how about the language? I couldn't pick up a single idea of his and he learned six or seven words of mine. And do you realise what complex ideas he put over with no more than those six or seven words? The pyramid-monster—the dream-beast! In a single phrase he told me that one was a harmless automaton and the other a deadly hypnotist. What about that?"

"Huh!" said the captain.

"*Huh* if you wish! Could you have done it knowing only six words of English? Could you go even further, as Tweel did, and tell me that another creature was of a sort of intelligence so different from ours that understanding was impossible—even more impossible than that between Tweel and me?"

"Eh? What was that?"

"Later. The point I'm making is that Tweel and his race are worthy of our friendship. Somewhere on Mars—and you'll find I'm right—is a civilisation and culture equal to ours, and maybe more than equal. And communication is possible between them and us; Tweel proves that. It may take years of patient trial, for their minds are alien, but less alien than the next minds we encountered—if they *are* minds."

"The next ones? What next ones?"

"The people of the mud cities along the canals." Jarvis frowned, then resumed his narrative. "I thought the dream-beast and the silicon-monster were the strangest beings conceivable, but I was wrong. These creatures are still more alien, less understandable than either and far less comprehensible than Tweel, with whom friendship is possible, and even, by patience and concentration, the exchange of ideas.

"Well," he continued, "we left the dream-beast dying, dragging itself back into its hole, and we moved toward the canal. There was a carpet of that queer walking-grass scampering out of our way, and when we reached the bank, there was a yellow trickle of water flowing. The mound city I'd noticed from the rocket was a mile or so to the right and I was curious enough to want to take a look at it.

"It had seemed deserted from my previous glimpse of it, and if any creatures were lurking in it—well, Tweel and I were both armed.

And by the way, that crystal weapon of Tweel's was an interesting device; I took a look at it after the dream-beast episode. It fired a little glass splinter, poisoned, I suppose, and I guess it held at least a hundred of 'em to a load. The propellant was steam—just plain steam!"

"Shteam!" echoed Putz. "From vot come shteam?"

"From water, of course! You could see the water through the transparent handle, and about a gill of another liquid, thick and yellowish. When Tweel squeezed the handle—there was no trigger—a drop of water and a drop of the yellow stuff squirted into the firing chamber, and the water vaporised—pop!—like that. It's not so difficult; I think we could develop the same principle. Concentrated sulphuric acid will heat water almost to boiling, and so will quicklime, and there's potassium and sodium—

"Of course, his weapon hadn't the range of mine, but it wasn't so bad in this thin air, and it *did* hold as many shots as a cowboy's gun in a Western movie. It was effective, too, at least against Martian life; I tried it out, aiming at one of the crazy plants, and darned if the plant didn't wither up and fall apart! That's why I think the glass splinters were poisoned.

"Anyway, we trudged along toward the mud-heap city and I began to wonder whether the city builders dug the canals. I pointed to the city and then at the canal, and Tweed said 'No—no—no!' and gestured toward the south. I took it to mean that some other race had created the canal system, perhaps Tweel's people. I don't know; maybe there's still another intelligent race on the planet, or a dozen others. Mars is a queer little world."

V. THE BARREL-PEOPLE

"A hundred yards from the city we crossed a sort of road—just a hard-packed mud trail, and then, all of a sudden, along came one of the mound builders!

"Man, talk about fantastic beings! It looked rather like a barrel trotting along on four legs with four other arms or tentacles. It had no head, just body and members and a row of eyes completely around it. The top end of the barrel-body was a diaphragm stretched as tight as a drum head, and that was all. It was pushing a little coppery cart and tore right past us like the proverbial bat out of Hell. It didn't even notice us, although I thought the eyes on my side shifted a little as it passed.

"A moment later another came along, pushing another empty cart. Same thing—it just scooted past us. Well, I wasn't going to be ignored by a bunch of barrels playing train, so when the third one approached, I planted myself in the way—ready to jump, of course, if the thing didn't stop.

"But it did. It stopped and set up a sort of drumming from the diaphragm on top. And I held out both hands and said mildly, 'We are friends!' And what do you suppose the thing did?"

"Said, 'Pleased to meet you,' I'll bet!" suggested Harrison.

"I couldn't have been more surprised if it had! It drummed on its diaphragm, and then suddenly boomed out, 'We are v-r-r-riends!' and gave its pushcart a vicious poke at me! I jumped aside, and away it went while I stared dumbly after it.

"A minute later another one came hurrying along. This one didn't pause, but simply drummed out, 'We are v-r-r-riends!' and scurried by. How did it learn the phrase? Were all of the creatures in some sort of communication with each other? Were they all parts of some central organism? I don't know, though I think Tweel does.

"Anyway, the creatures went sailing past us, every one greeting us with the same statement. It got to be funny; I never thought to find so many friends on this God-forsaken ball! Finally I made a puzzled gesture to Tweel; I guess he understood, for he said, 'One-one-two—yes!—two-two-four—no!' Get it?"

"Sure," said Harrison. "It's a Martian nursery rhyme."

"Yeah! Well, I was getting used to Tweel's symbolism, and I figured it out this way. 'One-one-two—yes!' The creatures were intelligent. 'Two-two-four—no!' Their intelligence was not of our order, but something different and beyond the logic of two and two is four. Maybe I missed his meaning. Perhaps he meant that their minds were of low degree, able to figure out the simple things—'One-one-two—yes!'—but not more difficult things—'Two-two-four—no!' But I think from what we saw later that he meant the other.

"After a few moments, the creatures came rushing back—first one, then another. Their pushcarts were full of stones, sand, chunks of rubbery plants, and such rubbish as that. They droned out their friendly greeting, which didn't really sound so friendly, and dashed on. The third one I assumed to be my first acquaintance and I decided to have another chat with him. I stepped into his path again and waited.

"Up he came, booming out his 'We are v-r-r-riends' and stopped. I looked at him; four or five of his eyes looked at me. He tried his password again and gave a shove on his cart, but I stood firm. And then the—the dashed creature reached out one of his arms, and two finger-like nippers tweaked my nose!"

"Haw!" roared Harrison. "Maybe the things have a sense of beauty!"

"Laugh!" grumbled Jarvis. "I'd already had a nasty bump and a mean frostbite on that nose. Anyway, I yelled 'Ouch!' and jumped aside and the creature dashed away; but from then on, their greeting was 'We are v-r-r-riends! Ouch!' Queer beasts!

"Tweel and I followed the road squarely up to the nearest mound. The creatures were coming and going, paying us not the slightest attention, fetching their loads of rubbish. The road simply dived into an opening, and slanted down like an old mine, and in and out darted the barrel-people, greeting us with their eternal phrase.

"I looked in; there was a light somewhere below, and I was curious to see it. It didn't look like a flame or torch, you understand, but more like a civilised light, and I thought that I might get some clue as to the creatures' development. So in I went and Tweel tagged along, not without a few trills and twitters, however.

"The light was curious; it sputtered and flared like an old arc light, but came from a single black rod set in the wall of the corridor. It was electric, beyond doubt. The creatures were fairly civilised, apparently.

"Then I saw another light shining on something that glittered and I went on to look at that, but it was only a heap of shiny sand. I turned toward the entrance to leave, and the Devil take me if it wasn't gone!

"I suppose the corridor had curved, or I'd stepped into a side passage. Anyway, I walked back in the direction I thought we'd come, and all I saw was more dimlit corridor. The place was a labyrinth! There was nothing but twisting passages running every way, lit by occasional lights, and now and then a creature running by, sometimes with a pushcart, sometimes without.

"Well, I wasn't much worried at first. Tweel and I had only come a few steps from the entrance. But every move we made after that seemed to get us in deeper. Finally I tried following one of the creatures with an empty cart, thinking that he'd be going out for his rubbish, but he ran around aimlessly, into one passage and out another. When he started dashing around a pillar like one of these Japanese waltzing mice, I gave up, dumped my water tank on the floor, and sat down.

"Tweel was as lost as I. I pointed up and he said 'No—no—no!' in a sort of helpless trill. And we couldn't get any help from the natives; they paid us no attention at all, except to assure us they were friends—ouch!

"Lord! I don't know how many hours or days we wandered around there! I slept twice from sheer exhaustion; Tweel never seemed to need sleep. We tried following only the upward corridors, but they'd run uphill a ways and then curve downwards. The temperature in that damned ant hill was constant; you couldn't tell night from day and after my first sleep I didn't know whether I'd slept one hour or thirteen, so I couldn't tell from my watch whether it was midnight or noon.

"We saw plenty of strange things. There were machines running in some of the corridors, but they didn't seem to be doing anything— just wheels turning. And several times I saw two barrel-beasts with a little one growing between them, joined to both."

"Parthenogenesis!" exulted Leroy. "Parthenogenesis by budding—like *les tu-lipes!*"

"If you say so, Frenchy," agreed Jarvis. "The things never noticed us at all, except, as I say, to greet us with 'We are v-r-r-riends! Ouch!' They seemed to have no home-life of any sort, but just scurried around with their pushcarts, bringing in rubbish. And finally I discovered what they did with it.

"We'd had a little luck with a corridor, one that slanted upwards for a great distance. I was feeling that we ought to be close to the surface when suddenly the passage debouched into a domed chamber, the only one we'd seen. And man!—I felt like dancing when I saw what looked like daylight through a crevice in the roof.

"There was a—a sort of machine in the chamber, just an enormous wheel that turned slowly, and one of the creatures was in the act of dumping his rubbish below it. The wheel ground it with a crunch—sand, stones, plants, all into powder that sifted away somewhere. While we watched, others filed in, repeating the process, and that seemed to be all. No rhyme nor reason to the whole thing—but that's characteristic of this crazy planet. And there was another fact that's almost too bizarre to believe.

"One of the creatures, having dumped his load, pushed his cart aside with a crash and calmly shoved himself under the wheel! I watched him crushed, too stupefied to make a sound, and a moment later, another followed him! They were perfectly methodical about it, too; one of the cartless creatures took the abandoned pushcart.

"Tweel didn't seem surprised; I pointed out the next suicide to him, and he just gave the most human-like shrug imaginable, as much as to say, 'What can I do about it?' He must have known more or less about these creatures.

"Then I saw something else. There was something beyond the wheel, something shining on a sort of low pedestal. I walked over; there was a little crystal about the size of an egg, fluorescing to beat Tophet. The light from it stung my hands and face, almost like a static discharge, and then I noticed another funny thing. Remember that wart I had on my left thumb? Look!" Jarvis extended his hand. "It dried up and fell off—just like that! And my abused nose—say, the pain went out of it like magic! The thing had the property of hard X-rays or gamma radiations, only more so; it destroyed diseased tissue and left healthy tissue unharmed!

"I was thinking what a present *that'd* be to take back to Mother Earth when a lot of racket interrupted. We dashed back to the other side of the wheel in time to see one of the pushcarts ground up. Some suicide had been careless, it seems.

"Then suddenly the creatures were booming and drumming all around us and their noise was decidedly menacing. A crowd of them advanced toward us; we backed out of what I thought was the passage we'd entered by, and they came rumbling after us, some pushing carts and some not. Crazy brutes! There was a whole chorus of 'We are v-r-r-riends! Ouch!' I didn't like the 'ouch'; it was rather suggestive.

"Tweel had his glass gun out and I dumped my water tank for greater freedom and got mine. We backed up the corridor with the barrel-beasts following—about twenty of them. Queer thing—the ones coming in with loaded carts moved past us inches away without a sign.

"Tweel must have noticed that. Suddenly, he snatched out that glowing coal cigar-lighter of his and touched a cart-load of plant limbs. Puff! The whole load was burning—and the crazy beast pushing it went right along without a change of pace! It created some disturbance among our 'V-r-r-riends,' however—and then I noticed the smoke eddying and swirling past us, and sure enough, there was the entrance!

"I grabbed Tweel and out we dashed and after us our twenty pursuers. The daylight felt like Heaven, though I saw at first glance that the sun was all but set, and that was bad, since I couldn't live outside my thermo-skin bag in a Martian night—at least, without a fire.

"And things got worse in a hurry. They cornered us in an angle between two mounds, and there we stood. I hadn't fired nor had

Tweel; there wasn't any use in irritating the brutes. They stopped a little distance away and began their booming about friendship and ouches.

"Then things got still worse! A barrel-brute came out with a pushcart and they all grabbed into it and came out with handfuls of foot-long copper darts—sharp-looking ones—and all of a sudden one sailed past my ear—zing! And it was shoot or die then.

"We were doing pretty well for a while. We picked off the ones next to the pushcart and managed to keep the darts at a minimum, but suddenly there was a thunderous booming of 'v-r-r-riends' and 'ouches,' and a whole army of 'em came out of their hole.

"Man! We were through and I knew it! Then I realised that Tweel wasn't. He could have leaped the mound behind us as easily as not. He was staying for me!

"Say, I could have cried if there'd been time! I'd liked Tweel from the first, but whether I'd have had gratitude to do what he was doing—suppose I *had* saved him from the first dream-beast—he'd done as much for me, hadn't he? I grabbed his arm, and said 'Tweel,' and pointed up, and he understood. He said, 'No—no—no, Tick!' and popped away with his glass pistol.

"What could I do? I'd be a goner anyway when the sun set, but I couldn't explain that to him. I said, 'Thanks, Tweel. You're a man!' and felt that I wasn't paying him any compliment at all. A man! There are mighty few men who'd do that.

"So I went 'bang' with my gun and Tweel went 'puff' with his, and the barrels were throwing darts and getting ready to rush us, and booming about being friends. I had given up hope. Then suddenly an angel dropped right down from Heaven in the shape of Putz, with his under-jets blasting the barrels into very small pieces!

"Wow! I let out a yell and dashed for the rocket; Putz opened the door and in I went, laughing and crying and shouting! It was a moment or so before I remembered Tweel; I looked around in time to see him rising in one of his nosedives over the mound and away.

"I had a devil of a job arguing Putz into following! By the time we got the rocket aloft, darkness was down; you know how it comes here—like turning off a light. We sailed out over the desert and put down once or twice. I yelled 'Tweel!' and yelled it a hundred times, I guess. We couldn't find him; he could travel like the wind and all I got—or else I imagined it—was a faint trilling twittering drifting out of the south. He'd gone, and damn it! I wish—I wish he hadn't!"

The four men of the *Ares* were silent—even the sardonic Harrison. At last little Leroy broke the stillness.

"I should like to see," he murmured.

"Yeah," said Harrison. "And the wart-cure. Too bad you missed that; it might be the cancer cure they've been hunting for a century and a half."

"Oh, that!" muttered Jarvis gloomily. "That's what started the fight!" He drew a glistening object from his pocket.

"Here it is."

YLLA

Ray Bradbury

Ray Bradbury was an incurable romantic with a talent for word play. In just a few words his stories would conjure visions, be they exotic, in the vastness of space, or chilling, in the depths of the dark, or inspiring, in the distant future. Often his stories are pure poetry, none more so than those that make up the episodic collection The Martian Chronicles *(1950). Bradbury admitted that his delight in reading the Martian stories by Edgar Rice Burroughs proved a strong influence. "*The Martian Chronicles *would never have happened otherwise," he later recalled. But whereas Burroughs went for action-packed adventure, Bradbury's stories were more reflective, more evocative, more mindful. The earliest of the series to be published is actually the last story in the book: 'The Million-Year Picnic' (1946), in which a family leave Earth to make Mars their home, but its final line—which I won't reveal here—wraps up the entire book perfectly. Throughout the book we follow waves of refugees from Earth, escaping the threat of a nuclear war, and trying to settle on Mars, but at the outset, in the following story, Bradbury considers how the Martians view their coming in an episode every bit as relevant to our attitude to refugees today as it was seventy years ago.*

THEY HAD A HOUSE OF CRYSTAL PILLARS ON THE PLANET MARS by the edge of an empty sea, and every morning you could see Mrs. K eating the golden fruits that grew from the crystal walls, or cleaning the house with handfuls of magnetic dust which, taking all dirt with it, blew away on the hot wind. Afternoons, when the fossil sea was warm and motionless, and the wine trees stood stiff in the yard, and the little distant Martian bone town was all enclosed, and no one drifted out their doors, you could see Mr. K himself in his room, reading from a metal book with raised hieroglyphs over which he brushed his hand, as one might play a harp. And from the book, as his fingers stroked, a voice sang, a soft ancient voice, which told tales of when the sea was red steam on the shore and ancient men had carried clouds of metal insects and electric spiders into battle.

Mr. and Mrs. K had lived by the dead sea for twenty years, and their ancestors had lived in the same house, which turned and followed the sun, flower-like, for ten centuries.

Mr. and Mrs. K were not old. They had the fair, brownish skin of the true Martian, the yellow coin eyes, the soft musical voices. Once they had liked painting pictures with chemical fire, swimming in the canals in the seasons when the wine trees filled them with green liquors, and talking into the dawn together by the blue phosphorous portraits in the speaking room.

They were not happy now.

This morning Mrs. K stood between the pillars, listening to the desert sands heat, melt into yellow wax, and seemingly run on the horizon.

Something was going to happen.

She waited.

She watched the blue sky of Mars as if it might at any moment grip in on itself, contract, and expel a shining miracle down upon the sand.

Nothing happened.

Tired of waiting, she walked through the misting pillars. A gentle rain sprang from the fluted pillar tops, cooling the scorched air, falling gently on her. On hot days it was like walking in a creek. The floors of the house glittered with cool streams. In the distance she heard her husband playing his book steadily, his fingers never tired of the old songs. Quietly she wished he might one day again spend as much time holding and touching her like a little harp as he did his incredible books.

But no. She shook her head, an imperceptible, forgiving shrug. Her eyelids closed softly down upon her golden eyes. Marriage made people old and familiar, while still young.

She lay back in a chair that moved to take her shape even as she moved. She closed her eyes tightly and nervously.

The dream occurred.

Her brown fingers trembled, came up, grasped at the air. A moment later she sat up, startled, gasping.

She glanced about swiftly, as if expecting someone there before her. She seemed disappointed; the space between the pillars was empty.

Her husband appeared in a triangular door. "Did you call?" he asked irritably.

"No!" she cried.

"I thought I heard you cry out."

"Did I? I was almost asleep and had a dream!"

"In the daytime? You don't often do that."

She sat as if struck in the face by the dream. "How strange, how very strange," she murmured. "The dream."

"Oh?" He evidently wished to return to his book.

"I dreamed about a man."

"A man?"

"A tall man, six feet one inch tall."

"How absurd; a giant, a misshapen giant."

"Somehow"—she tried the words—"he looked all right. In spite of being tall. And he had—oh, I know you'll think it silly—he had *blue* eyes!"

"Blue eyes! Gods!" cried Mr. K. "What'll you dream next? I suppose he had *black hair*!"

"How did you *guess*?" She was excited.

"I picked the most unlikely colour," he replied coldly.

"Well, black it was!" she cried. "And he had a very white skin; oh, he was *most* unusual! He was dressed in a strange uniform and he came down out of the sky and spoke pleasantly to me." She smiled.

"Out of the sky; what nonsense!"

"He came in a metal thing that glittered in the sun," she remembered. She closed her eyes to shape it again. "I dreamed there was the sky and something sparkled like a coin thrown into the air, and suddenly it grew large and fell down softly to land, a long silver craft, round and alien. And a door opened in the side of the silver object and this tall man stepped out."

"If you worked harder you wouldn't have these silly dreams."

"I rather enjoyed it," she replied, lying back. "I never suspected myself of such an imagination. Black hair, blue eyes, and white skin! What a strange man, and yet—quite handsome."

"Wishful thinking."

"You're unkind. I didn't think him up on purpose; he just came in my mind while I drowsed. It wasn't like a dream. It was so unexpected and different. He looked at me and he said, 'I've come from the third planet in my ship. My name is Nathaniel York—'"

"A stupid name; it's no name at all," objected the husband.

"Of course it's stupid, because it's a dream," she explained softly. "And he said, 'This is the first trip across space. There are only two of us in our ship, myself and my friend Bert.'"

"*Another* stupid name."

"And he said, 'We're from a city on *Earth*; that's the name of our planet,'" continued Mrs. K. "That's what he said. 'Earth' was the name he spoke. And he used another language. Somehow I understood him. With my mind. Telepathy, I suppose."

Mr. K turned away. She stopped him with a word. "Yll?" she called quietly. "Do you ever wonder if—well, if there *are* people living on the third planet?"

"The third planet is incapable of supporting life," stated the husband patiently. "Our scientists have said there's far too much oxygen in their atmosphere."

"But wouldn't it be fascinating if there *were* people? And they travelled through space in some sort of ship?"

"Really, Ylla, you know how I hate this emotional wailing. Let's get on with our work."

It was late in the day when she began singing the song as she moved among the whispering pillars of rain. She sang it over and over again.

"What's that song?" snapped her husband at last, walking in to sit at the fire table.

"I don't know." She looked up, surprised at herself. She put her hand to her mouth, unbelieving. The sun was setting. The house was closing itself in, like a giant flower, with the passing of light. A wind blew among the pillars; the fire table bubbled its fierce pool of silver lava. The wind stirred her russet hair, crooning softly in her ears. She stood silently looking out into the great sallow distances of sea bottom, as if recalling something, her yellow eyes soft and moist. "Drink to me only with thine eyes, and I will pledge with mine," she sang, softly, quietly, slowly. "Or leave a kiss but in the cup, and I'll not look for wine." She hummed now, moving her hands in the wind ever so lightly, her eyes shut. She finished the song.

It was very beautiful.

"Never heard that song before. Did you compose it?" he inquired, his eyes sharp.

"No. Yes. No, I don't know, really!" She hesitated wildly. "I don't even know what the words are; they're another language!"

"What language?"

She dropped portions of meat numbly into the simmering lava. "I don't know." She drew the meat forth a moment later, cooked, served on a plate for him. "It's just a crazy thing I made up, I guess. I don't know why."

He said nothing. He watched her drown meats in the hissing fire pool. The sun was gone. Slowly, slowly the night came in to fill the room, swallowing the pillars and both of them, like a dark wine poured to the ceiling. Only the silver lava's glow lit their faces.

She hummed the strange song again.

Instantly he leaped from his chair and stalked angrily from the room.

Later, in isolation, he finished supper.

When he arose he stretched, glanced at her, and suggested, yawning, "Let's take the flame birds to town tonight to see an entertainment."

"You don't *mean* it?" she said. "Are you feeling well?"

"What's so strange about that?"

"But we haven't gone for an entertainment in six months!"

"I think it's a good idea."

"Suddenly you're so solicitous," she said.

"Don't talk that way," he replied peevishly. "Do you or do you not want to go?"

She looked out at the pale desert. The twin white moons were rising. Cool water ran softly about her toes. She began to tremble just the least bit. She wanted very much to sit quietly here, soundless, not moving until this thing occurred, this thing expected all day, this thing that could not occur but might. A drift of song brushed through her mind.

"I—"

"Do you good," he urged. "Come along now."

"I'm tired," she said. "Some other night."

"Here's your scarf." He handed her a phial. "We haven't gone anywhere in months."

"Except you, twice a week to Xi City." She wouldn't look at him.

"Business," he said.

"Oh?" She whispered to herself.

From the phial a liquid poured, turned to blue mist, settled about her neck, quivering.

The flame birds waited, like a bed of coals, glowing on the cool smooth sands. The white canopy ballooned on the night wind, flapping softly, tied by a thousand green ribbons to the birds.

Ylla laid herself back in the canopy and, at a word from her husband, the birds leaped, burning, towards the dark sky. The ribbons tautened, the canopy lifted. The sand slid whining under; the blue hills drifted by, drifted by, leaving their home behind, the raining pillars, the caged flowers, the singing books, the whispering floor creeks. She did not look at her husband. She heard him crying out to the birds as they rose higher, like ten thousand hot sparkles, so many red-yellow fireworks in the heavens, tugging the canopy like a flower petal, burning through the wind.

She didn't watch the dead, ancient bone-chess cities slide under, or the old canals filled with emptiness and dreams. Past dry rivers and dry lakes they flew, like a shadow of the moon, like a torch burning.

She watched only the sky.

The husband spoke.

She watched the sky.

"Did you hear what I said?"

"What?"

He exhaled. "You might pay attention."

"I was thinking."

"I never thought you were a nature-lover, but you're certainly interested in the sky tonight," he said.

"It's very beautiful."

"I was figuring," said the husband slowly. "I thought I'd call Hulle tonight. I'd like to talk to him about us spending some time, oh, only a week or so, in the Blue Mountains. It's just an idea—"

"The Blue Mountains!" She held to the canopy rim with one hand, turning swiftly towards him.

"Oh, it's just a suggestion."

"When do you want to go?" she asked, trembling.

"I thought we might leave tomorrow morning. You know, an early start and all that," he said very casually.

"But we *never* go this early in the year!"

"Just this once, I thought—" He smiled. "Do us good to get away. Some peace and quiet. You know. You haven't anything *else* planned? We'll go, won't we?"

She took a breath, waited, and then replied, "No."

"What?" His cry startled the birds. The canopy jerked.

"No," she said firmly. "It's settled. I won't go."

He looked at her. They did not speak after that. She turned away.

The birds flew on, ten thousand firebrands down the wind.

In the dawn the sun, through the crystal pillars, melted the fog that supported Ylla as she slept. All night she had hung above the floor, buoyed by the soft carpeting of mist that poured from the walls when she lay down to rest. All night she had slept on this silent river, like a boat upon a soundless tide. Now the fog burned away, the mist level lowered until she was deposited upon the shore of wakening.

She opened her eyes.

Her husband stood over her. He looked as if he had stood there for hours, watching. She did not know why, but she could not look him in the face.

"You've been dreaming again!" he said. "You spoke out and kept me awake. I *really* think you should see a doctor."

"I'll be all right."

"You talked a lot in your sleep!"

"Did I?" She started up.

Dawn was cold in the room. A grey light filled her as she lay there.

"What was your dream?"

She had to think a moment to remember. "The ship. It came from the sky again, landed, and the tall man stepped out and talked with me, telling me little jokes, laughing, and it was pleasant."

Mr. K touched a pillar. Founts of warm water leaped up, steaming; the chill vanished from the room. Mr. K's face was impassive.

"And then," she said, "this man, who said his strange name was Nathaniel York, told me I was beautiful and—and kissed me."

"Ha!" cried the husband, turning violently away, his jaw working.

"It's only a dream." She was amused.

"Keep your silly, feminine dreams to yourself!"

"You're acting like a child." She lapsed back upon the few remaining remnants of chemical mist. After a moment she laughed softly. "I thought of some *more* of the dream," she confessed.

"Well, what is it, what *is* it?" he shouted.

"Yll, you're so bad-tempered."

"Tell me!" he demanded. "You can't keep secrets from me!" His face was dark and rigid as he stood over her.

"I've never seen you this way," she replied, half shocked, half entertained. "All that happened was this Nathaniel York person told me—well, he told me that he'd take me away into his ship, into the sky with him, and take me back to his planet with him. It's really quite ridiculous."

"Ridiculous, is it!" he almost screamed. "You should have heard yourself, fawning on him, talking to him, singing with him, oh gods, all night; you should have *heard* yourself!"

"Yll!"

"When's he landing? Where's he coming down with his damned ship?"

"Yll, lower your voice."

"Voice be damned!" He bent stiffly over her. "And *in* this dream"—he seized her wrist—"didn't the ship land over in Green Valley, *didn't* it? Answer me!"

"Why, yes—"

"And it landed this afternoon, didn't it?" he kept at her.

"Yes, yes, I think so, yes, but only in a dream!"

"Well"—he flung her hand away stiffly—"it's good you're truthful! I heard every word you said in your sleep. You mentioned the valley and the time." Breathing hard, he walked between the pillars like a man blinded by a lightning bolt. Slowly his breath returned. She watched him as if he were quite insane. She arose finally and went to him. "Yll," she whispered.

"I'm all right."

"You're sick."

"No." He forced a tired smile. "Just childish. Forgive me, darling." He gave her a rough pat. "Too much work lately. I'm sorry. I think I'll lie down awhile—"

"You were so excited."

"I'm all right now. Fine." He exhaled. "Let's forget it. Say, I heard a joke about Uel yesterday, I meant to tell you. What do you say you fix breakfast, I'll tell the joke, and let's not talk about all this."

"It was only a dream."

"Of course." He kissed her cheek mechanically. "Only a dream."

At noon the sun was high and hot and the hills shimmered in the light.

"Aren't you going to town?" asked Ylla.

"Town?" He raised his brows faintly.

"This is the day you *always* go." She adjusted a flower-cage on its pedestal. The flowers stirred, opening their hungry yellow mouths.

He closed his book. "No. It's too hot, and it's late."

"Oh." She finished her task and moved towards the door. "Well, I'll be back soon."

"Wait a minute! Where are you going?"

She was in the door swiftly. "Over to Pao's. She invited me!"

"Today?"

"I haven't seen her in a long time. It's only a little way."

"Over in Green Valley, isn't it?"

"Yes, just a walk, not far, I thought I'd—" She hurried.

"I'm sorry, really sorry," he said, running to fetch her back, looking very concerned about his forgetfulness. "It slipped my mind. I invited Dr. Nlle out this afternoon."

"Dr. Nlle!" She edged toward the door.

He caught her elbow and drew her steadily in. "Yes."

"But Pao—"

"Pao can wait, Ylla. We must entertain Nlle."

"Just for a few minutes—"

"No, Ylla."

"No?"

He shook his head. "No. Besides, it's a terribly long walk to Pao's. All the way over through Green Valley and then past the big canal and down, isn't it? And it'll be very, very hot, and Dr. Nlle would be delighted to see you. Well?"

She did not answer. She wanted to break and run. She wanted to cry out. But she only sat in the chair, turning her fingers over slowly, staring at them expressionlessly, trapped.

"Ylla?" he murmured. "You *will* be here, won't you?"

"Yes," she said after a long time. "I'll be here."

"All afternoon?"

Her voice was dull. "All afternoon."

Late in the day Dr. Nlle had not put in an appearance. Ylla's husband did not seem overly surprised. When it was quite late he murmured something, went to a closet, and drew forth an evil weapon, a long yellowish tube ending in a bellows and a trigger. He turned, and upon his face was a mask, hammered from silver metal, expressionless, the mask that he always wore when he wished to hide his feelings, the mask which curved and hollowed so exquisitely to his thin cheeks and chin and brow. The mask glinted, and he held the evil weapon in his hands, considering it. It hummed constantly, an insect hum. From it hordes of golden bees could be flung out with a high shriek. Golden, horrid bees that stung, poisoned, and fell lifeless, like seeds on the sand.

"Where are you going?" she asked.

"What?" He listened to the bellows, to the evil hum. "If Dr. Nlle is late, I'll be damned if I'll wait. I'm going out to hunt a bit. I'll be back. You be sure to stay right here now, won't you?" The silver mask glimmered.

"Yes."

"And tell Dr. Nlle I'll return. Just hunting."

The triangular door closed. His footsteps faded down the hill.

She watched him walking through the sunlight until he was gone. Then she resumed her tasks with the magnetic dusts and the new fruits to be plucked from the crystal walls. She worked with energy and dispatch, but on occasion a numbness took hold of her and she caught herself singing that odd and memorable song and looking out beyond the crystal pillars at the sky.

She held her breath and stood very still, waiting.

It was coming nearer.

At any moment it might happen.

It was like those days when you heard a thunderstorm coming and there was the waiting silence and then the faintest pressure of the atmosphere as the climate blew over the land in shifts and shadows and vapours. And the change pressed at your ears and you were suspended in the waiting time of the coming storm. You began to tremble. The sky was stained and coloured; the clouds were thickened; the mountains took on an iron taint. The caged flowers blew with faint sighs of warning. You felt your hair stir softly. Somewhere in the house the voice-clock sang, "Time, time, time, time…" ever so gently, no more than water tapping on velvet.

And then the storm. The electric illumination, the engulfments of dark wash and sounding black fell down, shutting in, forever.

That's how it was now. A storm gathered, yet the sky was clear. Lightning was expected, yet there was no cloud.

Ylla moved through the breathless summer-house. Lightning would strike from the sky any instant; there would be a thunderclap, a boil of smoke, a silence, footsteps on the path, a rap on the crystalline door, and her *running* to answer…

Crazy Ylla! she scoffed. Why think these wild things with your idle mind?

And then it happened.

There was a warmth as of a great fire passing in the air. A whirling, rushing sound. A gleam in the sky, of metal.

Ylla cried out.

Running through the pillars, she flung wide a door. She faced the hills. But by this time there was nothing.

She was about to race down the hill when she stopped herself. She was supposed to stay here, go nowhere. The doctor was coming to visit, and her husband would be angry if she ran off.

She waited in the door, breathing rapidly, her hand out.

She strained to see over towards Green Valley, but saw nothing.

Silly woman. She went inside. You and your imagination, she thought. That was nothing but a bird, a leaf, the wind, or a fish in the canal. Sit down. Rest.

She sat down.

A shot sounded.

Very clearly, sharply, the sound of the evil insect weapon.

Her body jerked with it.

It came from a long way off. One shot. The swift humming distant bees. One shot. And then a second shot, precise and cold, and far away.

Her body winced again and for some reason she started up, screaming, and screaming, and never wanting to stop screaming. She ran violently through the house and once more threw wide the door.

The echoes were dying away, away.

Gone.

She waited in the yard, her face pale, for five minutes.

Finally, with slow steps, her head down, she wandered about the pillared rooms, laying her hand to things, her lips quivering, until finally she sat alone in the darkening wine-room, waiting. She began to wipe an amber glass with the hem of her scarf.

And then, from far off, the sound of footsteps crunching on the thin, small rocks.

She rose up to stand in the centre of the quiet room. The glass fell from her fingers, smashing to bits.

The footsteps hesitated outside the door.

Should she speak? Should she cry out, "Come in, oh, come in"? She went forward a few paces.

The footsteps walked up the ramp. A hand twisted the door latch. She smiled at the door.

The door opened. She stopped smiling.

It was her husband. His silver mask glowed dully.

He entered the room and looked at her for only a moment. Then he snapped the weapon bellows open, cracked out two dead bees, heard them spat on the floor as they fell, stepped on them, and placed the empty bellows-gun in the corner of the room as Ylla bent down and tried, over and over, with no success, to pick up the pieces of the shattered glass. "What were you doing?" she asked.

"Nothing," he said with his back turned. He removed the mask.

"But the gun—I heard you fire it. Twice."

"Just hunting. Once in a while you like to hunt. Did Dr. Nlle arrive?"

"No."

"Wait a minute." He snapped his fingers disgustedly. "Why, I remember now. He was supposed to visit us *tomorrow* afternoon. How stupid of me."

They sat down to eat. She looked at her food and did not move her hands. "What's wrong?" he asked, not looking up from dipping his meat in the bubbling lava.

"I don't know. I'm not hungry," she said.

"Why not?"

"I don't know; I'm just not."

The wind was rising across the sky; the sun was going down. The room was small and suddenly cold.

"I've been trying to remember," she said in the silent room, across from her cold, erect, golden-eyed husband.

"Remember what?" He sipped his wine.

"That song. That fine and beautiful song." She closed her eyes and hummed, but it was not the song. "I've forgotten it. And, somehow, I don't want to forget it. It's something I want always to remember." She moved her hands as if the rhythm might help her to remember all of it. Then she lay back in her chair. "I can't remember." She began to cry.

"Why are you crying?" he asked.

"I don't know, I don't know, but I can't help it. I'm sad and I don't know why, I cry and I don't know why, but I'm crying."

Her head was in her hands; her shoulders moved again and again.

"You'll be all right tomorrow," he said.

She did not look up at him; she looked only at the empty desert and the very bright stars coming out now on the black sky, and far away there was a sound of wind rising and canal waters stirring cold in the long canals. She shut her eyes, trembling.

"Yes," she said. "I'll be all right tomorrow."

MEASURELESS TO MAN

Marion Zimmer Bradley

Despite the developments in science fiction set on Mars during the 1930s, the passion for the planetary romance established by Edgar Rice Burroughs did not fade. If anything, it increased. After A Princess of Mars *had appeared in book form in 1917, Burroughs wrote seven more Martian novels, with the last,* The Synthetic Men of Mars, *serialised in 1939 and published in book form in 1940. There were a few other, shorter stories in the series, some written by his son, but the Martian well had more or less run dry by the end of the 1930s. There was no shortage of imitators, though many, like Otis Adelbert Kline and Ralph Milne Farley, lacked the inventiveness of Burroughs and simply followed the formula. At least Robert E. Howard brought some independent thinking to his stories, though* Almuric, *serialised in 1939, is his only true planetary romance. He soon carved his own edifice with his heroic fantasy stories, especially those featuring Conan the Barbarian.*

The mantle of the thinking-person's writer of planetary romance was soon taken up: first by Leigh Brackett, who had been an avid reader of Burroughs since she was seven, and then by Marion Zimmer Bradley (1930–1999), who had in turn been an avid reader of Brackett's work. In fact she felt she had a close affinity with Brackett, commenting that 'our mental computers were programmed similarly'.

Bradley is probably best known for her long-running series of novels set on the planet Darkover, starting with The Sword of Aldones *(1962), a world on the fringe of a Galactic Empire which resists attempts to be fully incorporated and retains an independence through the increasing use of psi powers, almost akin to magic. Bradley was always more of a fantasy rather than science-fiction enthusiast, and she came to the attention of the wider world with her best-selling Arthurian novel* The Mists of Avalon *(1982) and its sequels.*

Before Bradley developed the Darkover series she experimented with other settings, blending science with fantastic imagery, most notably in the following story, 'Measureless to Man' (also known as 'The Dark Intruder'), first published in 1962. It has much sympathy with the works of both Leigh Brackett and Ray Bradbury in overlapping the present-day image of Mars with a more ancient, fantastic one.

ANDREW SLAYTON SNAPPED THE DUSTY LEATHER NOTEBOOK shut, and tossed it into his blanket roll. He stood up, ducking to avoid the ridgepole of the tent—Andrew, who had grown up on low-gravity Mars, was just over seven feet tall—and stood up, his head a little bent, looking at the other men who shared this miniature outpost against the greatest desert ever known to man.

The flaps of the tent were tightly pegged against the fierce and unpredictable sandstorms of the Martian night. In the glow of a portable electric lamp, the four roughnecks who would do the actual digging squatted around an up-ended packing box, intent on tonight's instalment of their perpetual poker game.

A dark oblong in the corner of the tent rose and fell with regular snores. John Reade, temporary leader of this expedition, was not young, and the day's work had been exhausting.

The men glanced up from their cards as Slayton approached them. "Want to sit in, kid?" Mike Fairbanks asked, "Kater's losing his shirt. We could use a new dealer."

"No, thanks. Not tonight."

Fat Kater shook with laughter, and jeered "The kid'ud rather read about Kingslander's men, and how they all went nuts and shot each other up!"

Spade Hansen flung down his cards, with a gesture of annoyance. "That's nothing to joke about, Kater." He lowered his gruff voice. "Find anything in the logs, Andy?"

Andrew squatted, elbows on thighs, beside the big foreman. "Nothing but what we know already, Spade. It beats me. As near as I can figure out, Jack Norton's expedition—he only had ten men—was washed up inside a week. Their rations are still cached over there. And, according to Kingslander's notebook, his outfit went the same way. They reached here safely, made camp, did a little exploring—they found the bodies of Norton's men and buried them—then, one by one, they all went insane and shot each other. Twenty men—and within ten days, they were just twenty—corpses."

"Pleasant prospect," Kater glowered, slapping down his cards on the improvised table and scowling as Rick Webber raked in the pot. "What about us?"

Rick Webber meticulously stacked his winnings and scaled his cards at Hensen. "Quit your worrying. Third time lucky—maybe we'll get through, all right."

"And maybe we won't," Fairbanks grunted, raking the cards together and shuffling them with huge fists, "You know what they call this outfit back in Mount Denver? *Reade's Folly.*"

"I'd hate to tell you what they called the first men who actually tried *living* on Mars," said a sleepy, pleasant voice from the corner, and John Reade thrust up his shock of white hair. "But we're here." The old man turned to Andrew. "Wasn't there even a clue in the logs, some notion of what might have happened to them?"

Andrew swivelled to face him. "Not a word, sir. Kingslander kept the log himself until he was shot, then one of his men—Ford Benton—kept it. The last couple of pages are the most awful gibberish—not even in English. Look for yourself—he was obviously out of his head for days." Andrew unfolded his long legs, hauled up a corner of the tent flap, and stood, staring morosely across the dark wasteland of rocks and bare bushes, toward the looming mass of Xanadu.

Xanadu. Not the Xanadu of Coleridge's poem, but—to the half-forgotten space drifter who discovered the place thirty years ago—a reasonable facsimile. It was a cloistered nun of a city, hidden behind a wide skirt of the most impassable mountains on Mars. And the city was more impassable than the mountains. No human being had ever entered it—yet.

They'd tried. Two expeditions, twelve years apart, had vanished without trace, without explanation other than the dusty notebook Andrew had unearthed, today, from the rotted shreds of a skeleton's clothing.

Archaeological expeditions, on Mars, all start the same way. You argue, wheedle, beg, borrow and steal until you have the necessary authority and a little less than the necessary funds. Earth, torn with internecine wars and slammed down under currency restrictions, does not send much money to Mars at any time. All but the barest lifeline of supplies was choked off when it was finally verified that Mars had no heavy metals, very little worth mining. The chronically bankrupt Geographical Society had abandoned Mars even before Xanadu was discovered. The thronging ruins of Venus, the strange surviving culture of subterranean men on Titan, the odd temples of the inner moons of Jupiter, are more rewarding than the desert barrens of Mars and its inaccessible Xanadu—the solitary remnant of a Martian society which must have vanished before mankind, on Earth, had discovered fire.

For all practical purposes, Mars is a military frontier, patrolled by the U.N. to keep any one country from using it as a base for developing secret weapons. It's also a good place to test new atomic engines, since there isn't much of a fallout problem and no worry about a large population getting fallout jitters. John Reade, retired Major in the Space Service, had good military contacts, and had managed to get a clearance for the third—only the third—attempt to conquer Xanadu.

Private expeditions on Mars are simple to the point of being primitive. No private citizen or foundation could possibly pay freight charges for machinery to Mars. Private citizens travel on foot, taking with them only what they can carry on their backs. Besides, no one could take a car, a plane or a rocketship over the mountains and still find a safe place to land. Pack animals are out of the question: horses and burros cannot adapt to the thin air—thicker than pre-space theorists had dared to hope, but still pretty thin and dogs and chimpanzees, which can, aren't much good for pack-work. The Geographic Society is still debating about importing yaks and llamas from high-altitude Peru and Tibet; meanwhile, it's a good thing that gravity on Mars is low enough to permit tremendous packloads of necessities.

The prime necessity is good lungs and a sackful of guts, while you scramble, scratch and curse your way over the mountains. Then a long, open valley, treacherously lined with needles of rock, and Xanadu lying—the bait in the mouth of the trap—at the top.

And then—what?

Kater and Hansen and the rest were grumbling over the cards again. "This place is jinxed," Mike complained, turning up a deuce, "We'll be lucky if we get a cent out of it. Now if we were working on Venus—but Mars, nyaah! Even if we find something, which I doubt, and live to tell about it—who cares?"

"Yeah," Spade muttered. "Reade, how much did you spend for dynamite to blast the walls?"

"You didn't pay for it," Reade said cheerfully.

Andrew stooped, shrugging on his leather jacket; thumbed the inside heating-units. "I'm going for a walk."

"Alone?" Reade asked sharply.

"Sure, unless someone wants to come along," Andrew said, then suddenly understood. He pulled his pistol from his pocket, and handed it, butt-first, to Reade. "Sorry, I should have remembered. This is about where the shooting started, with the others."

Reade laughed, but he didn't return the gun.

"Don't go too far."

*   *   *

It was one of the rare, clear nights which sometimes did penance for the usual sandstorms. Andrew drew down the tent flap behind him, walked away into the darkness. At his foot he felt a little scurrying, stooped, and caught up one of the blunt-nosed sand-mice. It squirmed on his palm, kicking hard with all six puny legs; then felt the comforting heat of his hand and yeep-yeeped with pleasure; he walked on, idly scratching the scaly little beast.

The two small moons were high overhead, and there was a purplish, shimmery light over the valley, with its grotesque floor of rock spires, fuzzed between with blackish patches of prickle-bushes—*spinosa martis*—matted in a close tangle between each little peak.

Downwind he heard the long screaming of a banshee; then he saw it, running blindly, a huge bird with its head down between trailing, functionless wings. Andrew held his breath and stood still. The banshees had no intelligence to speak of, but by some peculiar tropism, they would rush toward anything that moved; the very heat of his body might attract them, and their huge clawed feet could disembowel a man at one stroke. And he had no pistol!

This one failed to sense him; it ran, trailing its wings and screaming eerily, like a cloaked girl, blindly into the dusk. Andrew let out his breath violently in relief. Suddenly he realised that he was not sure just which way the tent lay. He turned, crowding against one of the rock-spires. A little hollow gleamed pallidly in the moonlight. He remembered climbing a rise; he must have come this way—

He slid down roughly, a trailing pricker raking his hand. The sand-mouse leaped from his palm with a squeal and scuffled away. Andrew, sucking his bleeding palm, looked up and saw the walls of Xanadu lifting serried edges just over his head. How could he possibly have come so near in just a few minutes? Everything looked different—

He spun around, trying to scramble up the way he had come. He fell. His head struck rock, and the universe went dark,

"Take it easy." John Reade's voice sounded disembodied over his head, "Just lie still. You've got a bad bump, Andy." He opened his eyes to the glare of stars and a bitter wind on his face. Reade caught at his hand as he moved it exploringly toward his face. "Let it alone, the bleeding's stopped. What happened? The banshee get you?"

"No, I fell. I lost my way, and I must have hit my head." Andrew let his eyes fall shut again. "I'm sorry, sir; I know you told us not to go near the city alone. But I didn't realise I'd come so close."

Kendo frowned and leaned closer. "Lost your *way*? What are you talking about? I followed you—brought your pistol. I was afraid you'd meet a banshee. You hadn't gone two hundred yards from the tent, Andy. When I caught up with you, you were stumbling around, and then you rolled down on the ground into that little hollow. You kept muttering *No, no, no*—I thought the banshee had got you."

Andrew pushed himself upright. "I don't think so, sir. I looked up and saw the city right over my head. That's what made me fall. That's when it started,"

"When *what* started?"

"I—don't know." Andrew put up his hand to rub his forehand, whining as he touched the bruise. Suddenly he asked, "John, did you ever wonder what the old Martians—the ones who built Xanadu—called the place?"

"Who hasn't?" The old man nodded, impatiently. "I guess we'll never know, though. That's a fool question to ask me right now!"

"It's something I felt," Andrew said, groping for words. "When I got up, after I stumbled, everything looked different. It was like seeing double; one part was just rocks, and bushes, and ruins, and the other part was—well, it wasn't like anything I'd ever seen before. I felt—" he hesitated, searching for words to define something strange, then said with an air of surprise, "*Homesick*. Yes, that's it. And the most awful—desolation. The way I'd feel, I guess, if I went back to Mount Denver and found it burned down flat, And then for just a second I knew what the city was called, and why it was dead, and why we couldn't get into it, and why the other men went crazy. And it scared me, and I started to run—and that's when I slipped, and hit my head."

Reade's worried face relaxed in a grin.

"Rubbish! The bump on your head mixed up your time-sense a little, that's all. Your hallucination, or whatever it was, came *after* the bump, not before."

"No," Andrew said quietly, but with absolute conviction. "I wasn't hurt that bad, John."

Reade's face changed; held concern again. "All right," he said gently, "Tell me what you think you know."

Andrew dropped his face in his hands. "Whatever it was, it's gone! The bump knocked it right out of head. I remember that I knew—" he raised a drawn face, "but I can't remember what!"

Reade put his hand on the younger man's shoulder. "Let's get back to the tent, Andy, I'm freezing out here. Look, son, the whole thing is just your mind working overtime from that bump you got. Or—"

Andrew said bitterly "You think I'm going crazy."

"I didn't say that, son. Come on. We can talk it over in the morning." He hoisted Andrew to his feet. "I told Spade that if we weren't back in half an hour, he'd better come looking for us."

The men looked up from their cards, staring at the blood on Andrew's face, but the set of Reade's mouth silenced any comments. Andrew didn't want to talk. He quickly shucked jacket and trousers, crawled into his sleeping bag, thumbed the heat-unit and immediately fell asleep.

*   *   *

When he woke, the tent was empty. Wondering why he had been allowed to sleep—Spade usually meted out rough treatment to blanket-huggers—Andrew dressed quickly, gulped a mug of the bitter coffee that stood on the hot-box, and went out to look for the others.

He had to walk some distance to find them. Armed with shovels, the four roughnecks were digging up the thorny prickle-bushes near the hollow where Andrew had fallen, while Reade, in the lee of a rock, was scowling over the fine print of an Army manual of Martio-biology.

"Sorry I overslept, John. Where do I go to work?"

"You don't. I've got another job for you." Reade turned to bark a command at Fairbanks. "Careful with the damned plant! I told you to wear gloves! Now get them on, and don't touch those things with your bare hands." He glanced back at Andrew. "I had an idea overnight," he said. "What do we really know about *spinosa martis*? And this doesn't quite look like the species that grows around Mount Denver. I think maybe this variety gives off some kind of gas—or poison." He pointed at the long scratch on Andrew's hand. "Your trouble started after you grabbed one of them. You know, there's locoweed on Earth that drives cattle crazy—mushrooms and other plants that secrete hallucinogens. If these things give off some sort of volatile mist, it could have dispersed in that little hollow down there—there wasn't much wind last night."

"What shall I do?" he asked.

"I'd rather not discuss that here. Come on, I'll walk back to the tent with you." He scrambled stiffly to his feet. "I want you to go back to Mount Denver, Andy."

Andrew stopped; turned to Reade accusingly.

"You *do* think I've gone crazy!"

Reade shook his head. "I just think you'll be better off in Mount Denver. I've got a job for you there—one man would have to go, anyhow, ami you've had one—well, call it a hallucination—already. If it's a poison, the stuff might be cumulative. We may just wind up having to wear gas masks." He put a hand on the thick leather of Andrew's jacket sleeve. "I know how you feel about this place, Andy. But personal feelings aren't important in this kind of work."

"John—" half hesitant, Andrew looked back at him, "I had an idea overnight, too."

"Let's hear it."

"It sounds crazy, I guess," Andrew said diffidently, "but it just came to me. Suppose the old Martians were beings without bodies—discarnate intelligences? And they're trying to make contact with us? Men aren't used to that kind of contact, and it drives them insane."

Reade scowled. "Ingenious," he admitted, "as a theory, but there's a hole in it. If they're discarnate, how did they build—" he jerked his thumb at the squat, fortress-like mass of Xanadu behind them.

"I don't know, sir. I don't know how the drive units of a spaceship work, either. But I'm here." He looked up. "I think one of them was trying to get in touch with me, last night. And maybe if I was trying, too—maybe if I understood, and tried to open my mind to it, too—"

Reade looked disturbed. "Andy, do you realise what you're suggesting? Suppose this is all your imagination—"

"It isn't, John."

"Wait, now. Just suppose, for a minute; try to see it my way."

"Well?" Andrew was impatient.

"By trying to 'open your mind', as you put it, you'd just be surrendering your sane consciousness to a brooding insanity. The human mind is pretty complex, son. About nine-tenths of your brain is dark, shadowy, all animal instinct. Only the conscious fraction can evaluate—use logic. The balance between the two is pretty tricky at best. I wouldn't fool around with it, if I were you. Listen, Andy, I know you were born on Mars, I know how you feel. You feel at home here, don't you?"

"Yes, but that doesn't mean—"

"You resent men like Spade and Kater, coming here for the money that's in it, don't you?"

"Not really. Well, yes, but—"

"There was a Mars-born kid with Kingslander, Andy. Remember the log? He was the first to go. In a place like this, imagination is worse than smallpox. You're the focal point where trouble would start, if it started. That's why I picked men like Spade and Kater— insensitive, unimaginative—for the first groundwork here. I've had my eye on you from the beginning, Andy, and you reacted just about the way I expected. I'm sorry, but you'll have to go."

Andrew clenched his fists in his pocket, speaking drymouthed. "But if I was right—wouldn't it be easier for them to contact someone like me? Won't you try to see it *my* way?" He made a final, hopeless appeal. "Won't you let me stay? I *know* I'm safe here—I know they won't hurt me, whatever happens to the others. Take my gun if you want to—keep me in handcuffs, even—but don't send me back!"

Reade's voice was flat and final. "If I had any doubts, I wouldn't have them after that. Every word you say is just making it worse. Leave while you still can, Andy."

Andrew gave up. "All right. I'll start back now, if you insist."

"I do." Reade turned away and hurried back toward the crew, and Andrew went into the tent and started packing rations in his blanket-roll for the march. The pack was clumsy, but not a tenth as heavy as the load he'd packed on the way up here. He jerked the straps angrily tight, hoisted the roll to his shoulder, and went out.

Reade was waiting for him. He had Andrew's pistol.

"You'll need this." He gave it to him; hauled out his notebook and stabbed a finger at the sketchy map he had drawn on their way over the mountains. "You've got your compass? Okay, look; this is the place where our route crossed the mail-car track from Mount Denver to the South Encampment. If you camp there for a few hours, you can hitch a ride on the mail-car—there's one every other day—into Mount Denver. When you get there, look up Montray. He's getting the expedition together back there." Reade tore the leaf from his notebook, scribbling the address on the back. Andrew lifted an eyebrow; he knew Reade had planned the expedition in two sections, to prevent the possibility that they, too, would vanish without even a search-party sent after them.

"He won't have things ready, of course, but tell him to hurry it up, and give him all the help you can. Tell him what we're up against."

"You mean what you're up against. Are you sure you can trust me to run your errands in Mount Denver?"

"Don't be so grim about it," Reade said gently. "I know you want to stay, but I'm only doing my duty the way I see it. I have to think of everybody, not just you—or myself." He gripped Andrew's shoulder. "If things turn out all right, you can come back when they're all under control. Good luck, Andy,"

"And if they don't?" Andrew asked, but Reade had turned away.

*   *   *

It had been a rough day. Andrew sat with his back against a boulder, watching the sun drop swiftly toward the reddish range of rock he had climbed that afternoon. Around him the night wind was beginning to build up, but he had found a sheltered spot between two boulders; and in his heated sleeping-bag, could spend a comfortable night even at sixty-below temperatures.

He thought ahead while he chewed the tasteless Marbeef—Reade had outfitted the expedition with Space Service surplus—and swallowed hot coffee made from ice painstakingly scraped from the rocks. It had taken Reade, and five men, four days to cross the ridge. Travelling light, Andrew hoped to do it in three. The distance was less than thirty miles by air, but the only practicable trail wound in and out over ninety miles, mostly perpendicular. If a bad sandstorm built up, he might not make it at all, but anyone who spent more than one season on Mars took that kind of risk for granted.

The sun dropped, and all at once the sky was ablaze with stars. Andrew swallowed the last of his coffee, looking up to pick out the Heavenly Twins on the horizon—the topaz glimmer of Venus, the blue star-sapphire that was Earth. Andrew had lived on Earth for a few years in his teens, and hated it; the thick moist air, the dragging feel of too much gravity. The close-packed cities nauseated him with their smell of smoke and grease and human sweat. Mars air was thin and cold and scentless. His parents had hated Mars the same way he had hated Earth—they were biologists in the Xenozoology division, long since transferred to Venus. He had never felt quite at home anywhere, except for the few days he had spent at Xanadu. Now he was being kicked out of that too.

Suddenly, he swore. The hell with it, sitting here, feeling sorry for himself! He'd have a long day tomorrow, and a rough climb. As he unrolled his sleeping-bag, waiting for the blankets to warm, he wondered; how old *was* Xanadu?

Did it matter? Surely, if men could throw a bridge between the planets, they could build a bridge across the greater gap of time that separated them from these who had once lived on Mars. And if any man could do that, Andy admitted ungrudgingly, that man was John Reade. He pulled off his boots, anchored them carefully with his pack, weighted the whole thing down with rock, and crawled into the sack.

In the comforting warmth, relaxing, a new thought crossed his mind.

Whatever it was that had happened to him at Xanadu, he wasn't quite sure. The bump had confused him. But certainly *something* had happened. He did not seriously consider Reade's warning. He knew, as Reade could not be expected to know, that he had not suffered from a hallucination; had *not* been touched by the fringes of insanity. But he had certainly undergone a very strange experience. Whether it had been subjective or objective, he did not know; but he intended to find out.

How? He tried to remember a little desultory reading he had once done about telepathy. Although he had spoken glibly to Reade about "opening his mind", he really had not the faintest idea of what he had meant by the phrase. He grinned in the dark.

"Well, whoever and whatever you are," he said aloud, "I'm all ready and waiting. If you can figure out a way to communicate with me, come right ahead."

And the alien came.

"I am Kamellin," it said.

*   *   *

I AM KAMELLIN.

That was all Andrew could think. It was all his tortured brain could encompass. His head hurt, and the dragging sense of some actual, tangible force seemed to pull and twist at him. I AM KAMEL-LIN... KAMELLIN... KAMELLIN... it was like a tide that sucked at him, crowding out his own thoughts, dragging him under and drowning him. Andrew panicked; he fought it, thrashing in sudden frenzy, feeling arms and legs hit the sides of the sleeping-bag, the blankets twisted around him like an enemy's grappling hands.

Then the surge relaxed and he lay still, his breath loud in the darkness, and with fumbling fingers untangling the blankets. The sweat of fear was cold on his face, but the panic was gone.

For the force had not been hostile. It had only been—eager. Pathetically eager; eager as a friendly puppy is eager, as a friendly dog may jump up and knock a man down.

"Kamellin," Andrew said the alien word aloud, thinking that the name was not particularly outlandish. He hoped the words would focus his thoughts sufficiently for the alien to understand.

"Kamellin, come ahead, okay, but this time take it easy, take it slow and easy. Understand?" Guardedly, he relaxed, hoping he would be able to take it if some unusual force were thrust at him. He could understand now why men had gone insane. If this—Kamellin—had hit him like that the *first* time—

Even now, when he understood and partly expected what was happening, it was an overwhelming flood, flowing through his mind like water running into a bottle. He lay helpless, sweating. The stars were gone, blanked out, and the howling wind was quiet—or was it that he no longer saw or heard? He hung alone in a universe of emptiness, and then, to his disembodied consciousness, came the beginning of—what? Not speech. Not even a mental picture. It was simply contact, and quite indescribable. And it said, approximately;

GREETINGS. AT LAST. AT LAST IT HAS HAPPENED AND WE ARE BOTH SANE. I AM KAMELLIN.

The wind was howling again, the stars a million flame-bright flares in the sky. Huddled in his blankets, Andrew felt the dark intruder in his brain ebb and flow with faint pressure as their thoughts raced in swift question and answer. He whispered his own question aloud; otherwise Kamellin's thoughts flowed into his and intermingled with them until he found himself speaking Kamellin's thoughts.

"What are you? Was I right, then? Are you martians discarnate intelligences?"

NOT DISCARNATE. WE HAVE ALWAYS HAD BODIES, OR RATHER— WE LIVED IN BODIES. BUT OUR MINDS AND BODIES WERE WHOLLY SEPARATE. NOTHING BUT OUR WILL TIED THEM TOGETHER. WHEN

ONE BODY DIED, WE SIMPLY PASSED INTO ANOTHER NEWBORN BODY.

A spasm of claustrophobic terror grabbed at Andrew, and his flesh crawled. "You wanted—"

Kamellin's reassurance was immediate;

I DO NOT WANT YOUR BODY. YOU HAVE, Kamellin fumbled for a concept to express what he meant, YOU ARE A MATURE INDIVIDUAL WITH A PERSONALITY, A REASONING INTELLIGENCE OF YOUR OWN. I WOULD HAVE TO DESTROY THAT BEFORE YOUR BODY COULD JOIN WITH ME IN SYMBIOSIS. His thoughts flared indignation; THAT WOULD NOT BE HONOURABLE!

"I hope all your people are as honourable as you are, then. What happened to the other expedition?"

He felt black anger, sorrow and desolation, breaking like tidal waves in his brain. MY PEOPLE WERE MADDENED—I COULD NOT HOLD THEM BACK. THEY WERE NOT STABLE, WHAT YOU WOULD CALL, NOT SANE. THE TIME INTERVAL HAD BEEN TOO LONG. THERE WAS MUCH KILLING AND DEATH WHICH I COULD NOT PREVENT.

"If I could only find some way to tell Reade—"

IT WOULD BE OF NO USE. A TIME AGO, I TRIED THAT. I ATTEMPTED TO MAKE CONTACT, EASILY, WITH A YOUNG MIND THAT WAS PARTICULARLY RECEPTIVE TO MY THOUGHT. HE DID NOT GO INSANE, AND WE, TOGETHER, TRIED TO TELL CAPTAIN KINGSLANDER WHAT HAD HAPPENED TO THE OTHERS. BUT HE BELIEVED IT WAS MORE INSANITY, AND WHEN THE YOUNG MAN WAS KILLED BY ONE OF THE OTHERS, I HAD TO DISSIPATE AGAIN. I TRIED TO REACH CAPTAIN KINGSLANDER HIMSELF, BUT THE THOUGHT DROVE HIM INSANE—HE WAS ALREADY NEAR MADNESS WITH HIS OWN FEAR.

Andrew shuddered. "God!" he whispered. "What can we do?"

I DO NOT KNOW. I WILL LEAVE YOU, IF YOU WISH IT. OUR RACE IS FINALLY DYING. IN A FEW MORE YEARS WE WILL BE GONE, AND OUR PLANET WILL BE SAFE FOR YOU.

"Kamellin, no!" Andrew's protest was immediate and genuine. "Maybe, together, we can think of some way to convince them."

The alien seemed hesitant now;

WOULD YOU BE WILLING, THEN, TO—SHARE YOUR BODY FOR A TIME? IT WILL NOT BE EASY, IT IS NEVER EASY FOR TWO PERSON-ALITIES TO CO-INHABIT ONE BODY. I COULD NOT DO IT WITHOUT YOUR COMPLETE CONSENT. Kamellin seemed to be thinking thoughts which were so alien that Andrew could grasp them only vaguely: only the concept of a meticulous honour remained to colour his belief in Kamellin.

"What happened to your original host-race?"

He lay shivering beneath his heated blankets as the story unfolded in his mind. Kamellin's race, he gathered, had been humanoid—as that concept expressed itself, he sensed Kamellin's amusement; RATHER, YOUR RACE IS MARTIANOID! Yes, they had built the city the Earthmen called Xanadu, it was their one technological accomplishment which had been built to withstand time. BUILT IN THE HOPE THAT ONE DAY WE MIGHT RETURN AND RECLAIM IT FROM THE SAND AGAIN, Kamellin's soundless voice whispered, THE LAST REFUGE OF OUR DYING RACE.

"What did you call the city?"

Kamellin tried to express the phonetic equivalent and a curious sound formed on Andrew's lips. He said it aloud, exploringly; "Shein-la Mahari." His tongue lingered on the liquid syllables. "What does it mean?"

THE CITY OF MAHARI—MAHARI, THE LITTLE MOON. Andrew found his eyes resting on the satellite Earthmen called Deimos.

"Sheinla Mahari," he repeated. He would never call it Xanadu again.

Kamellin continued his story.

The host-race, Andrew gathered, had been long-lived and hardy, though by no means immortal. The minds and bodies—"minds", he impressed on Andrew, was not exactly the right Concept—were actually two separate, wholly individual components. When a body died, the "mind" simply transferred, without any appreciable interval, into a newborn host; memory, although slightly impaired and blurred by such a transition, was largely retained. So that the consciousness of any one individual might extend, though dimly, over an almost incredible period of time.

The dual civilisation had been a simple, highly mentalised one, systems of ethics and philosophy superseding one another in place of the rise and fall of governments. The physical life of the hosts was not highly technological. Xanadu had been almost their only such accomplishment, last desperate expedient of a dying race against the growing inhospitality of a planet gripped in recurrent, ever-worsening ice ages. They might have survived the ice alone, but a virus struck and decimated the hosts, eliminating most of the food animals as well. The birth-rate sank almost to nothing; many of the freed minds dissipated for lack of a host-body in which to incarnate.

Kamellin had a hard time explaining the next step. His kind could inhabit the body of anything which had life, animal or plant. But they were subject to the physical limitations of the hosts. The only animals which survived disease and ice were the sand-mice and the moronic banshees; both so poorly organised, with nervous systems so faulty, that even when vitalised by the intelligence of Kamellin's race, they were incapable of any development. It was similar, Kamellin explained, to a genius who is imprisoned in the body of a helpless paralytic; his mind undamaged, but his body wholly unable to respond.

A few of Kamellin's people tried it anyhow, in desperation. But after a few generations of the animal hosts, they had degenerated terribly, and were in a state of complete nonsanity, unable even to leave the life-form to which they had bound themselves. For all Kamellin knew, some of his people still inhabited the banshees, making transition after transition by the faint, dim flicker of an instinct still alive, but hopelessly buried in generations of non-rational life.

The few sane survivors had decided, in the end, to enter the prickle-bushes; spinosa martis. This was possible, although it, too, had drawbacks; the sacrifice of consciousness was the main factor in life as a plant. In the darkness of the Martian night, Andrew shuddered at Kamellin's whisper;

IMMORTALITY—WITHOUT HOPE. AN ENDLESS, DREAMLESS SLEEP. WE LIVE, SOMNOLENT, IN THE DARKNESS, AND THE WIND, AND WAIT—AND FORGET. WE HAD HOPED THAT SOME DAY A NEW RACE MIGHT EVOLVE ON THIS WORLD. BUT EVOLUTION HERE REACHED A DEAD END WITH THE BANSHEES AND SAND-MICE. THEY ARE PERFECTLY ADAPTED TO THEIR ENVIRONMENT AND THEY HAVE NO STRUGGLE TO SURVIVE: HENCE THEY NEED NOT EVOLVE AND CHANGE. WHEN THE EARTHMEN CAME, WE HAD HOPE. NOT THAT WE MIGHT TAKE THEIR BODIES. ONLY THAT WE MIGHT SEEK HELP FROM THEM. BUT WE WERE TOO EAGER, AND MY PEOPLE DROVE OUT—KILLED—

The flow of thoughts ebbed away into silence.

Andrew spoke at last, gently.

"Stay with me for a while, at least. Maybe we can find a way."

IT WON'T BE EASY, Kamellin warned.

"We'll try it, anyhow. How long ago—how long have you, well, been a plant?"

I DO NOT KNOW. MANY, MANY GENERATIONS—THERE IS NO CONSCIOUSNESS OF TIME. MANY SEASONS. THERE IS MUCH BLUR-RING. LET ME LOOK AT THE STARS WITH YOUR EYES.

"Sure," Andrew consented.

The sudden blackness took him by surprise, sent a spasm of shock and terror through his mind; then sight came back and he found himself sitting upright, staring wide-eyed at the stars, and heard Kamellin's agonised thoughts;

IT HAS BEEN LONG—again the desperate, disturbing fumbling for some concept, IT HAS BEEN NINE HUNDRED THOUSAND OF YOUR YEARS!

Then silence; such abysmal grieved silence that Andrew was almost shamed before the naked grief of this man—he could not think of Kamellin except as a man—mourning for a dead world. He lay down, quietly, not wanting to intrude on the sorrow of his curious companion.

Physical exhaustion suddenly overcame him, and he fell asleep.

*   *   *

"Was Mars like this in your day, Kamellin?"

Andrew tossed the question cynically into the silence in his brain. Around him a freezing wind shifted and tossed at the crags, assailing the grip of his gauntleted hands on rock. He didn't expect any answer. The dark intruder had been dormant all day; Andrew, when he woke, had almost dismissed the whole thing as a bizarre fantasy, born of thin air and impending madness.

But now the strange presence, like a whisper in the dark, was with him again.

OUR PLANET WAS NEVER HOSPITABLE. BUT WHY HAVE YOU NEVER DISCOVERED THE ROADWAY THROUGH THE MOUNTAINS?

"Give us time," Andrew said cynically. "We've only been on Mars a minute or two by your standards. What roadway?"

"WE CUT A ROADWAY THROUGH THE MOUNTAINS WHEN WE BUILT SHEIN-LA MAHARI."

"What about erosion? Would it still be there?"

Kamellin had trouble grasping the concept of erosion. Rain and snow were foreign to his immediate experience. Unless the roadway had been blocked by a sandstorm, it should be there, as in Kamellin's day.

Andrew pulled himself to a ledge. He couldn't climb with Kamellin using part, of his mind; the inner voice was distracting. He edged himself backward on a flat slab of rock, unstrapping his pack. The remnant of his morning coffee was hot in his canteen; he drank it while Kamellin's thoughts flowed through his. Finally he asked "Where's this roadway?"

Andrew's head reeled in vertigo, He lay flat on the ledge, dizzily grasping rock, while Kamellin tried to demonstrate his sense of direction. The whirl slowly quieted, but all he could get from the brain-shaking experience was that Kamellin's race had oriented themselves by at least eleven major compass points in what felt like four dimensions to Andrew's experience, oriented on fixed stars—his original host-race could see the stars even by daylight.

"But I can't, and anyway, the stars have moved."

I HAVE THOUGHT OF THAT Kamellin answered. BUT THIS PART OF THE MOUNTAINS IS FAMILIAR TO ME. WE ARE NOT FAR FROM THE PLACE. I WILL LEAD YOU THERE.

"Lead on, MacDuff."

THE CONCEPT IS UNFAMILIAR. ELUCIDATE.

Andrew chuckled. "I mean, which way do we go from here?"

The vertigo began to overcome him once more.

"No, no—not that again!"

THEN I WILL HAVE TO TAKE OVER ALL YOUR SENSES—

Andrew's mental recoil was as instinctive as survival. The terror of that moment last night, when Kamellin forced him into nothingness, was still too vivid. "No! I suppose you could take over forcibly, you did once, but not without half killing me! Because this time I'd fight—I'd fight you like hell!"

Kamellin's rage was a palpable pain in his mind. HAVE YOU NO HONOUR OF YOUR OWN, FOOL FROM A MAD WORLD? HOW COULD I LIE TO YOU WHEN MY MIND IS PART OF YOUR OWN? WANDER AS YOU PLEASE, I DO NOT SUFFER AND I AM NOT IMPATIENT. I THOUGHT THAT YOU WERE WEARY OF THESE ROCKY PATHS, NO MORE!

Andrew felt bitterly ashamed. "Kamellin—I'm sorry."

Silence, a trace of alien anger remaining.

Andrew suddenly laughed aloud. Alien or human, there were correspondences; Kamellin was sulking. "For goodness sake," he said aloud, "if we're going to share one body, lets' not quarrel. I'm sorry if I hurt your feelings; this is all new to me. But you don't have to sit in the corner and turn up your nose, either!"

The situation suddenly struck him as too ridiculous to take seriously; he laughed aloud, and like a slow, pleasant ripple, he felt Kamellin's slow amusement strike through his own.

FORGIVE ME IF I OFFENDED. I AM ACCUSTOMED TO DOING AS I PLEASE IN A BODY I INHABIT. I AM HERE AT YOUR SUFFERANCE, AND OFFER APOLOGIES.

Andrew laughed again, in a curious doubled amusement, some-how eager to make amends. "Okay, Kamellin, take over. You know where I want to go—if you can get us there faster, hop to it."

But for the rest of his life he remembered the next hour with terror. His only memory was of swaying darkness and dizziness, feeling his legs take steps he had not ordered, feeling his hands slide on rock and being unable to clutch and save himself, walking blind and deaf and a prisoner in his own skull; and ready to go mad with the horror of it. Curiously enough, the saving thought had been; Kamellin's able to stand it. He isn't going to hurt us.

When sight and sense and hearing came back, and full orienta-tion with it, he found himself at the mouth of a long, low canyon which stretched away for about twelve miles, perfectly straight. It was narrow, less than fifteen feet wide. On either side, high dizzy cliffs were cut sharply away; he marvelled at the technology that had built this turnpike road.

The entrances were narrow, concealed between rock, and deeply drifted with sand; the hardest part had been descending, and later ascending, the steep, worn-away steps that led down into the floor of the canyon. He had struggled and cursed his way down the two-foot steps, wishing that the old Martians had had shorter legs; but once down, he had walked the whole length in less than two hours—trav-elling a distance, which Reade had covered in three weary days of rock-climbing.

And beside the steps was a ramp down which vehicles could be driven; had it been less covered with sand, Andrew could have slid down!

When he finally came to the end of the canyon road, the nearly-impassible double ridge of mountains lay behind him. From there it was a simple matter to strike due west and intersect the road from Mount Denver to the spaceport. There he camped overnight, awaiting the mailcar. He was awake with the first faint light, and lost no time in gulping a quick breakfast and strapping on his pack; for the mail-cars were rocket-driven (in the thin air of Mars, this was practical) and travelled at terrific velocities along the sandy barren flats; he'd have to be alert to flag it down.

He saw it long before it reached him, a tiny cloud of dust; he hauled off his jacket and, shivering in the freezing air, flagged furiously. The speck grew immensely, roared, braked to a stop; the driver thrust out a head that was only two goggled eyes over a heavy dustkerchief.

"Need a ride?"

Protocol on Mars demanded immediate identification.

"Andrew Slayton—I'm with the Geographic Society—Reade's outfit back in the mountains at Xanadu. Going back to Mount Denver for the rest of the expedition."

The driver gestured. "Climb on and hang on. I've heard about that gang. Reade's Folly, huh?"

"That's what they call it." He settled himself on the seatless floor—like all Martian vehicles, the rocket-car was a bare chassis without doors, seats or sidebars, stripped to lower freight costs—and gripped the rail. The driver looked down at him, curiously;

"I heard about that place Xanadu. Jinxed, they say. You must be the first man since old Torchevsky, to go there and get back safe. Reade's men all right?"

"They were fine when I left," Andrew said.

"Okay. Hang on," the driver warned, and at Andrew's nod, cut in the rockets and the sand-car leaped forward, eating up the desert.

—

Mount Denver was dirty and smelly after the clean coldness of the mountains. Andrew found his way through the maze of army barracks and waited in the officer's Rec quarters while a call-system located Colonel Reese Montray.

He hadn't been surprised to find out that the head of the other half of the expedition was a Colonel in active service; after all, within the limits imposed by regulations, the Army was genuinely anxious for Reade to find something at Xanadu. A genuine discovery might make some impression on the bureaucrats back on Earth; they might be able to revive public interest in Mars, get some more money and supplies instead of seeing everything diverted to Venus and Europa.

Montray was a tall thin man with a heavy Lunar Colony accent, the tiny stars of the Space Service glimmering above the Army chevrons on his sleeve. He gestured Andrew into a private office and listened, with a bored look, up to the point where he left Reade, then began to shoot questions at him.

"Has he proper chemical testing equipment for the business? Protection against gas—chemicals?"

"I don't think so," Andrew said. He'd half forgotten Reade's theory about hallucinogens in spinosa martis; so much had happened since that it didn't seem to make much difference.

"Maybe we'd better get it to him. I can wind things up here in an hour or so, if I have to, I've only got to tell the Commander what's going on. He'll put me on detached duty. You can attend to things here at the Geographic Society Headquarters, can't you, Slayton?"

Andrew said quietly "I'm going back with you, Captain Montray. And you won't need gas equipment. I did make contact with one of the old Martians."

Montray sighed and reached for the telephone. "You can tell Dr. Cranston all about it, over at the hospital."

"I knew you'd think I was crazy," Andrew said in resignation, "but I can show you a pass that will take you through the Double Ridge in three hours, not three days—less, if you have a sand-car."

The Colonel's hand was actually on the telephone, but he didn't pick it up. He leaned back and looked at Andrew curiously, "You discovered this pass?"

"Well, yes and no, sir." He told his story quickly, skipping over the parts about Kamellin, concentrating on the fact of the roadway. Montray heard him out in silence, then picked up the telephone, but he didn't call the hospital. Instead he called an employment bureau in the poorer part of Mount Denver. While he waited for the connection he looked uncertainly at Andrew and muttered "I'd have to go out there in a few weeks anyhow. They said, if Reade got well started, he could use Army equipment—" he broke off and spoke into the clicking phone.

"Montray here for the Geographic. I want twenty roughnecks for desert work. Have them here in two hours." He held down the contact button, dialled again, this time to call Dupont, Mars Limited, and requisition a first-class staff chemist, top priority. The third call, while Andrew waited—admiring, yet resenting the smoothness with which Montray could pull strings, was to the Martian Geographic Society headquarters; then he heaved himself up out of his chair and said "So that's that. I'll buy your story, Slayton, You go down—" he scrawled on a pink form, "and commandeer an Army sand-bus that will hold twenty roughnecks and equipment. If you've told the truth, the Reade expedition is already a success and the Army will take over. And if you haven't—" he made a curt gesture of dismissal, and Andrew knew that if anything went wrong, he'd be better off in the psycho ward than anywhere Montray could get at him.

*   *   *

When Army wheels started to go round, they ran smoothly. Within five hours they were out of Mount Denver with an ease and speed which made Andrew—accustomed to the penny-pinching of Martian Geographic—gape in amazement. He wondered if this much string-pulling could have saved Kingslander. Crammed in the front seat of the sand-bus, between Montray and the DuPont chemist, Andrew reflected gloomily on the military mind and its effect on Reade. What would Reade say when he saw Andrew back again?

The wind was rising. A sandstorm on Mars makes the worst earthly wind look like a breeze to fly kites; the Army driver swore helplessly as he tried to see through the blinding sand, and the roughnecks huddled under a tarpaulin, coarse bandannas over their eyes, swearing in seven languages. The chemist braced his kit on his knees—he'd refused to trust it to the baggage-bins slung under the chassis next to the turbines—and pulled his dustkerchief over his eyes as the hurricane wind buffeted the sand-bus. Montray shouted above the roar "Doesn't that road of yours come out somewhere along here?"

Shielding his eyes, Andrew peered over the low windbreak and crouched again, wiping sand from his face. "Half a mile more."

Montray tapped the driver on the shoulder. "Here."

The bus roared to a stop and the wind, unchallenged by the turbine noise, took over in their ears.

Montray gripped his wrist. "Crawl back under the canvas and we'll look at the map." Heads low, they crawled in among the roughnecks; Montray flashed a pocket light on the "map", which was no more than a rough aerial photo taken by a low flier over the ridge. At one edge were a group of black dots which might or might not have been Xanadu, and the ridge itself was a confusing series of blobs; Andrew rubbed a gritty finger over the photo.

"Look, this is the route we followed; Reade's Pass, we named it. Kingslander went this way; a thousand feet lower, but too much loose rock. The canyon is about here—that dark line could be it."

"Funny the flier who took the picture didn't see it." Montray raised his voice. "All out—let's march!"

"In'a dees' weather?" protested a gloomy voice, touching off a chorus of protest. Montray was inflexible. "Reade might be in bad trouble. Packs, everybody."

Grumbling, the roughnecks tumbled out and adjusted packs and dust-bandannas. Montray waved the map-photo at Andrew; "Want this?"

"I can find my way without it."

A straggling disorderly line, they began, Andrew leading. He felt strong and confident. In his mind Kamellin lay dormant and that pleased him too; he needed every scrap of his mind to fight the screaming torment of the wind. It sifted its way through his bandanna and ate into his skin, though he had greased his face heavily with lanolin before leaving the barracks. It worked, a gritty nuisance, through his jacket and his gloves. But it was his own kind of weather; Mars weather. It suited him, even though he swore as loud as anyone else.

Montray swore too, and spat grit from his throat.

"Where is this canyon of yours?"

A little break in the hillocky terrain led northward, then the trail angled sharply, turned into the lee of a bleak canyon wall. "Around there." Andrew fell back, letting Montray lead, while he gave a hand to the old man from DuPont.

Montray's angry grip jerked at his elbow; Andrew's bandanna slid down and sailed away on the storm, and the chemist stumbled and fell to his knees. Andrew bent and helped the old fellow to his feet before he thrust his head around to Montray and demanded "What the hell is the big idea?"

"That's what I'm asking you!" Montray's furious voice shouted the storm down. Andrew half fell around the turn, hauled by Montray's grip; then gulped, swallowing sand, while the wind bit unheeded at his naked cheeks. For there was now no trail through the ridge. Only a steep slope of rock lay before them, blank and bare, every crevice filled to the brim with deep-drifted sand.

*　　*　　*

Andrew turned to Montray, his jaw dropping. "I don't understand this at all, sir," he gulped, and went toward the edge. There was no sign of ramp or steps.

"I do." Montray bit his words off and spat them at Andrew. "You're coming back to Mount Denver—under arrest!"

"Sir, I came through here yesterday! There was a wide track, a ramp, about eleven feet wide, and at one side there were steps, deep steps—" he moved toward the edge, seeking signs of the vanished trailway. Montray's grip on his arm did not loosen. "Yeah, and a big lake full of pink lemonade down at the bottom. Okay, back to the bus."

The roughnecks crowded behind them, close to the deep-deep-drifted sand near the spires of rock Andrew had sighted as landmarks on either side of the canyon. One of them stepped past Montray, glaring at the mountain of sand.

"All the way out here for a looney!" he said in disgust.

He took another step—then suddenly started sinking—stumbled, flailed and went up to his waist in the loose-piled dust.

"Careful—get back—" Andrew yelled, "You'll go in over your heads!" The words came without volition.

The man in the sand stopped in mid-yell, and his kicking arms stopped throwing up dust. He looked thoughtfully up at the other roughnecks. "Colonel," he said slowly, "I don't think Slayton's so crazy. I'm standing on a step, and there's another one under my knee. Here, dig me out." He began to brush sand away with his two hands. "Big steps—"

Andrew let out a yell of exultation, bending to haul the man free. "That's IT," he shouted. "The sandstorm last night just blew a big drift into the mouth of the canyon, that's all! If we could get through this drift, the rest lies between rock walls and around the next angle, the sand can't blow!"

Montray pulled binoculars from his pocket and focused them carefully. "In farther, I do see a break in the slope that looks like a canyon," he said. "If you look at it quick, it seems to be just a flat patch, but with the glasses, you can see that it goes down between walls… but there's a hundred feet of sand, at least, drifted into the entrance, and it might as well be a hundred miles. We can't wade through that." He frowned, looking around at the sandbus. "How wide did you say this canyon was?"

"About fifteen feet. The ramp's about eleven feet wide."

Montray's brow ridged. "These buses are supposed to cross drifts up to eighty feet. We'll chance it. Though if I take an army sandbus in there, and get it stuck in a drift, we might as well pack for space."

Andrew felt grim as they piled back into the bus. Montray displaced the driver and took the controls himself. He gave the main rocket high power; the bus shot forward, its quickly-extruded glider units sliding lightly, without traction, over the drifted sand. It skidded a little as Montray gunned it for the turn; the chassis hit the drift like a ton of lead. Swearing prayerfully, Montray slammed on the auxiliary rockets, and it roared—whined—sprayed up sand like a miniature sirocco, then, mercifully, the traction lessened, the gliders began to function, and the sandbus skied lightly across the drift and down the surface of the monster ramp, into the canyon.

It seemed hours, but actually it was less than four minutes before the glider units scraped rock and Montray shut off the power and called two men to help him wind up the retractors... the gliders could be shot out at a moment's notice, because on Mars when they were needed, they were needed *fast*, but retracting them again was a long, slow business. He craned his neck over the windbreak, looking up at the towering walls, leaning at a dizzy angle over them. He whistled sharply. "This is no natural formation!"

"I told you it wasn't," Andrew said.

The man from Dupont scowled. "Almost anything can be a natural formation, in rock," he contradicted. "You say you discovered this pass, Slayton?"

Andrew caught Montray's eye and said meekly "Yes, sir."

The sandbus cruised easily along the canyon floor, and up the great ramp at the other end. Montray drove stubbornly, his chin thrust out. Once he said "Well, at least the Double Ridge isn't a barricade any more," and once he muttered "You could have discovered this by accident—delirious—and then rationalised it..."

The Martian night was hanging, ready to fall, when the squat towers of the city reared up, fat and brown, against the horizon. From that distance they could see nothing of Reade's camp except a thin trail of smoke, clear against the purplish twilight. Vague unease stirred Andrew's mind and for the first time in hours, Kamellin's thoughts flickered dimly alive in the corridors of his brain.

I AM FEARFUL. THERE IS TROUBLE.

Montray shouted, and Andrew jerked up his head in dismay, then leaped headlong from the still-moving sandbus. He ran across the sand. Reade's tent lay in a smoking ruin on the red sand. His throat tight with dread, Andrew knelt and gently turned up the heavy form that lay, unmoving, beside the charred ruin.

Fat Kater had lost more than his shirt.

Montray finally stood up and beckoned three of the roughnecks. "Better bury him here," he said heavily, "and see if there's anything left unburned."

One of the men had turned aside and was noisily getting rid of everything he'd eaten for a week. Andrew felt like doing the same, but Montray's hand was heavy on his shoulder.

"Easy," he said. "No, I don't suspect you. He hasn't been dead more than an hour. Reade sent you away before it started, evidently." He gave commands; "No one else seems to have died in the fire. Spread out, two and two, and look for Reade's men." He glanced at the sun, hovering too close to the horizon; half an hour of sunlight, and Phobos would give light for another couple of hours—he said grimly "After that, we get back to the bus and get out of here, fast. We can come back tomorrow, but we're not going to wander around here by Deimos-light." He unholstered his pistol.

DON'T, said the eerie mentor in Andrew's brain, NO WEAPONS.

Andrew said urgently, "Colonel, have the roughnecks turn in their pistols! Kingslander's men killed each other pretty much like this!"

"And suppose someone meets a banshee? And Reade's men all have pistols, and if they're wandering around, raving mad—"

The next hour was nightmarish, dark phantoms moving shoulder to shoulder across the rock-needled ground; muttered words, far away the distant screams of a banshee somewhere. Once the crack of a pistol cut the night; it developed—after the roughnecks had all come running in, and half a dozen random shots had been fired, fortunately wounding no one—that one man had mistaken a rock-spire for a banshee. Montray cursed the man and sent him back to the sandbus with blistered ears. The sun dropped out of sight. Phobos, a vast purple balloon, sketched the towers of the city in faint shadows on the sand. The wind wailed and flung sand at the crags.

An abrupt shout of masculine hysteria cut the darkness; Montray jumped, stumbled and swore. "If this is another false alarm—"

It wasn't. Somebody flashed an electric torch on the sand; Mike Fairbanks, a bullet hole cleanly through his temple, lay on the sand that was only a little redder than his blood.

That left Hansen, Webber—and John Reade.

I CAN FIND THEM: LET ME FIND THEM! BEFORE SOMETHING WORSE HAPPENS—

"Sir, I think I can find the others. I told you about Kamellin. This proves—"

"Proves nothing," grunted Montray. "But go ahead." Andrew felt coldly certain that inside the pocket of his leathers, Montray's finger was crooked around a trigger trained on his heart. Tense and terrified, Andrew let Kamellin lead him. How did he know that this was not an elaborate trap for the Earthmen? For Kamellin led them straight beneath the walls of the city and to an open door—an open door, and three expeditions had blasted without success!

ONE OF MY PEOPLE HAS TAKEN OVER ONE OF YOUR MEN. HE MUST HAVE FOUND THE HIDDEN DOOR. IF ONLY HE IS STILL SANE, WE HAVE A BARE CHANCE...

"Stop there," Montray ordered curtly.

"Stop there," echoed a harsh wild voice, and the dishevelled figure of John Reade, hatless, his jacket charred, appeared in the doorway. "Andrew!" His distorted shout broke into a sobbing gasp of relief, and he pitched headlong into Andrew's arms. "Andy, thank God you're here! They—shot me—"

Andrew eased him gently to the ground. Montray bent over the old man, urging "Tell us what happened, John."

"Shot in the side—Andy you were right—something got Spade first, then Kater fired the tent—Spade rushed him, shot Mike Fairbanks—then—then, Andy, it got me, it sneaked inside me, inside my head when I wasn't looking, inside my head—"

His head lolled on Andrew's shoulder.

Montray let go his wrist with a futile gesture. "He's hurt pretty bad. Delirious."

"His head's as clear as mine. He's fainted, that's all," Andrew protested. "If we bring him around, he can tell us—"

"He'll be in no shape to answer questions," said the scientist from DuPont, very definitely, "not for a long time. Montray, round up the men; we've got to get out of here in a hurry—"

"Look out!" shouted somebody. A pistol shot crashed and the scream of an injured man raised wild echoes. Andrew felt his heart suck and turn over; then he suddenly sank into blindness and felt himself leap to his feet and run toward the voices. Kamellin had taken over!

Spade Hansen, tottering on his feet, stumbled toward them. His shirt hung raggedly in charred fragments. Through some alien set of senses, like seeing double, Andrew sensed the presence of another, one of Kamellin's kind.

IF I CAN GET THROUGH TO HIM—...

Montray cocked, levelled his pistol.

"Hansen!" His voice cracked like a whip, "stand where you are!"

Spade yelled something.

"Po'ki hai marrai nic Mahari—"

YOU FOOL! THEY ARE AFRAID OF US! STAND BACK!

Spade flung himself forward and threw his pistol to the ground at Andrew's feet. *"Kamellin!"* he screamed, but the voice was not his own. Andrew's heart thudded. He stepped forward, letting the dark intruder in his mind take over all his senses again. A prisoner, he heard the alien voice shouting, felt his throat spewing forth alien syllables. There were shouts, a despairing howl, then somewhere two pistols cracked together and Andrew flickered back to full consciousness to see Hansen reel, stumble and fall inert. Andrew sagged, swayed; Montray held him upright, and Andrew whispered incredulously, "You shot him!"

"I didn't," Montray insisted. "Rick Webber burst out of that doorway—fired into the crowd. Then—"

"Is Rick dead too?"

"As a doornail." Montray gently lowered the younger man to the sand beside Reade. "You were raving yourself, for a minute, young Slayton." He shouted angrily at the roughneck who had shot, "You didn't have to kill Webber! A bullet in the leg would have stopped him!"

"He ran right on me with the gun—"

Montray sighed and struck his forehead with his clenched hands. "Somebody make a stretcher for Reade and one for the kid here."

"I'm all right." Andrew shoved Montray's hand aside; bent to look at Reade.

"He's in a bad way," the man from DuPont said. "We'd better get them both back to Mount Denver while there's time." He looked sharply at Andrew. "You had better take it easy, too. You went shouting mad yourself, for a minute." He stood up, turning to Montray.

"I think my theory is correct. Virus strains can live almost indefinitely where the air is dry. If such a plague killed off the people who built the city, it would explain why everyone who's come up here has caught it—homicidal and suicidal."

"That isn't it—"

Montray checked him forcibly, "Slayton, you're a sick man too. You'll have to trust our judgment," he said. He tucked his own coat around Reade and stood up, his face grey in the fading moonlight. "I'm going to the governor," he said, "and have this place put off limits. Forty-two men dead of an unknown Martian virus, that's too much. Until we get the money and the men to launch a full-scale medical project and knock it out, there won't be any more private expeditions—or public ones, either. The hell with Xanadu." He cocked his pistol and fired the four-shot signal to summon any stragglers.

Two of the men improvised a stretcher and began to carry Reade's inert body toward the sandbus. Andrew walked close, steadying the old man's limp form with his hands. He was beginning to doubt himself. Under the setting moon, the sand biting his face, he began to ask himself if Montray had been right. Had he dreamed, then rationalised? Had he dreamed Kamellin? KAMELLIN? he asked.

There was no answer from the darkness in his mind. Andrew smiled grimly, his arm easing Reade's head in the rude litter. If Kamellin had ever been there, he was gone, and there was no way to prove any of it—and it didn't matter any more.

*   *   *

"...therefore, with regret, I am forced to move that project Xanadu be shelved indefinitely," Reade concluded. His face was grim and resigned, still thin from his long illness. "The Army's attitude is inflexible, and lacking men, medics and money, it seems that the only thing to do with Xanadu is to stay away from it."

"It goes without saying," said the man at the head of the table, "that we all appreciate what Major Reade and Mr. Slayton have been through. Gentlemen, no one likes to quit. But in face of this, I have no alternative but to second Major Reade's suggestion, Gentlemen, I move that the Martian chapter of the Geographic Society be closed out, and all equipment and personnel transferred to Aphrodite Base Twelve, South Venus."

The vote was carried without dissent, and Reade and Andrew, escaping the bombardment of questions, drifted into the cold sunlight of the streets. They walked for a long time without speaking. Reade said at last;

"Andy, we did everything we could. Montray put his own commission in jeopardy for us. But this project has cost millions already. We've just hit the bottom of the barrel, that's all."

Andrew hunched his shoulders. "I could be there in three days."

"I'd like to try it, too." Reade sounded grim. "But forget it, Andy. Shein-la Mahara is madness and death. Forget it. Go home—"

"Home? Home where? To Earth?" Andrew broke off, staring. *What* had Reade said?

"Say that again. The name of the city."

"Shein-la Mahari, the city of—" Reade gulped. "What in the *hell*—" he looked at Andy in despair. "I thought I could forget, convince myself it never happened. It left me when Hansen shot me. We've *got* to forget it, Andy—at least until we're on the ship going home."

"Ship, hell! We're not going back to Earth, Reade!"

"Here, here," said Reade, irritably, "*Who's* not going?" Andrew subsided, thinking deeply. Then, with a flash of inspiration, he turned to Reade. "John, who owns the Society's test animals?"

Reade rubbed his forehead. "Nobody, I guess. They sure won't bother shipping a few dogs and chimps out to Venus! I've got authority to release them—I guess I'll turn them over to Medic. Why? You want a dog? A monkey? What for?" He stopped in his tracks, glaring. "What bug have you got in your brain now?"

"Never mind. You're going back to Earth by the next ship."

"Don't be in such a rush," Reade grumbled, "The *Erdenluft* won't blast for a week."

Andrew grinned. "John, those animals are pretty highly organised. I wonder—"

Reade's eyes met his in sudden comprehension. "Good lord, I never thought of that! Come on, let's hurry!"

At the deserted shack where the Society's animals were kept, a solitary keeper glanced indifferently at Reade's credentials and let them in. Reade and Andrew passed the dogs without comment, glanced at and rejected the one surviving goat, and passed on to the caged chimpanzees.

"Well, either I'm crazy or this is it," he said, and listened for that inner answer, the secret intruder in his brain. And after a long time, dimly, it came as if Kamellin could not at once reestablish lapsed contact.

I SHOULD HAVE LEFT YOU. THERE IS NO HOPE NOW, AND I WOULD RATHER DIE WITH MY PEOPLE THAN SURVIVE AS A PRISONER IN YOUR MIND.

"No!" Andrew swung to face the chimpanzee. "Could you enter that living creature without his consent?"

There was a tightness across his diaphragm, as if it wore his own fate, not Kamellin's, that was being decided.

THAT CREATURE COULD NOT GIVE CONSENT.

"I'm sorry, I tried—"

Kamellin's excitement almost burst into speech, NO, NO, HE IS PERFECTLY SUITED, FOR HE IS HIGHLY ORGANISED, BUT LACKING INTELLIGENCE—

"A chimp's intelligent—"

A shade of impatience, as if Kamellin wore explaining to a dull child; A BRAIN, YES, BUT HE LACKS SOMETHING—WILL, SPIRIT, SOUL, VOLITION—

"A chimp can he taught to do almost anything a man can—

EXCEPT TALK, COMMUNICATE, USE REAL REASON. YOU CANNOT ENTIRELY GRASP THIS EITHER, I KNOW. It was the first time Andrew had been allowed to glimpse the notion that Kamellin did not consider Andrew his complete equal. THE BANSHEES ARE THE FIRST STAGE: A PHYSICAL BRAIN, CONSCIOUSNESS, BUT NO INTELLIGENCE. THEY CANNOT BE ORGANISED. THEN YOUR CREATURE, YOUR PRIMATE MAMMAL, INTELLIGENCE BUT NO SOUL. HOWEVER, WHEN VITALISED BY TRUE REASON... Kamellin's thought-stream cut off abruptly, but not before Andrew had caught the concept, WHAT DOES THE EARTH MAN THINK HE IS, ANYHOW?

Kamellin's thoughts were troubled; FORGIVE ME, I HAD NO RIGHT TO GIVE YOU THAT...

"Inferiority complex?" Andrew laughed.

YOU DO NOT FUNCTION ON THIS LEVEL OF YOUR SOUL. YOU'RE AWARE ALMOST EXCLUSIVELY IN YOUR FIVE SENSES AND YOUR REASONING INTELLIGENCE. BUT YOUR IMMORTAL MIND IS SOMEHOW STUNTED: YOU HUMANS HAVE SLID INTO A DIFFERENT TIME-TRACK SOMEHOW, AND YOU LIVE ONLY IN THREE DIMENSIONS, LOSING MEMORY—

"I don't believe in the soul, Kamellin."

THAT IS THE POINT I AM TRYING TO MAKE, ANDREW.

Reade touched his shoulder.

"You give me the creeps, talking to yourself. What now?"

They picked out a large male chimp and sat looking at it while it grimaced at them with idiotic mildness. Andrew felt faint distaste. "Kamellin in that thing?"

Reade chuckled. "Quit being anthropomorphic. *That thing* is a heck of a lot better adapted to life on Mars than you are—look at the size of the chest—and Kamellin will know it, if you don't!" He paused. "After the switch, how can we communicate with Kamellin?"

Andrew relayed the question, puzzled. Finally he said "I'm not sure. We're using straight thoughts and he can't get any notion of the *form* of our language, any more than I can of his. Reade, can a chimp learn to talk?"

"No chimp ever has."

"I mean, if a chimp *did* have the intelligence, the reasoning power, the drive to communicate in symbols or language, would its vocal cords and the shape of his mouth permit it?"

"I wouldn't bet on it," Reade said, "I'm no expert on monkey anatomy, though. I wouldn't bet against it either. Why? Going to teach Kamellin English?"

"Once he leaves me, there won't be any way to communicate except the roughest sort of sign language!"

"Andy, we've got to figure out some way! We can't let that knowledge be lost to us! Here we have a chance at direct contact with a mind that was alive when the city was built—"

"That's not the important part," Andrew said. "Ready, Kamellin?"

YES. AND I THANK YOU ETERNALLY. YOUR WORLD AND MINE LIE APART, BUT WE HAVE BEEN BROTHERS. I SALUTE YOU, MY FRIEND. The voice went still. The room reeled, went into a sick blur—

"Are you all right?" Reade peered anxiously down at Andrew. Past him, they both realised that the big chimpanzee—no, Kamellin!—was looking over Reade's shoulder. Not the idiot stare of the monkey. Not human, either. Even the posture of the animal was different.

Andrew—recognised—Kamellin.

And the—difference—in his mind, was gone.

Reade was staring; "Andy, when you fell, he jumped forward and *caught* you! No monkey would do that!"

Kamellin made an expressive movement of his hands.

Andrew said "A chimp's motor reflexes are marvellous, with a human—no, a *better* than human intelligence, there's practically no limit to what he can do." He said, tentatively, "Kamellin?"

"Will the chimp recognise that?"

"Look, Reade—will you remember something, as a favour to me? He—the chimp—is *not* a freak monkey! He is Kamellin—my close personal friend—and a damned sight more intelligent than either of us!"

Reade dropped his eyes. "I'll try."

"Kamellin?"

And Kamellin spoke. Tentatively, hoarsely, mouthily, as if with unfamiliar vocal equipment, he spoke. "An—drew," he said slowly. "Shein. La. Mahari." They had each reached the extent of their vocabulary in the other's language. Kamellin walked to the other cages, with the chimpanzee's rolling scamper which somehow had, at the same time, a controlled and fluid dignity that was absolutely new. Reade dropped on a bench. "I'll be damned," he said. "But do you realise what you've done, Andrew? A talking monkey. At best, they'd call us a fraud. At worst the scientists would end up dissecting him. We'll never be able to prove anything or tell anyone!"

"I saw that all along," Andrew said bitterly, and dropped to the bench. Kamellin came and squatted beside them, alert, with an easy stillness.

Suddenly Andrew looked up.

"There are about twenty chimps. Not enough. But there's a good balance, male to female, and they can keep up a good birth rate—"

"What in the—"

"Look," Andrew said excitedly, "it's more important to preserve the Martian race—the last few sane ones—than to try convincing the Society—; we probably couldn't, anyhow. We'll take the chimps to Shein-la Mahari. Earthmen never go there, so they won't be molested for a while, anyhow—probably not for a hundred years or so! By that time, they'll have been able to—to reclaim their race a little, gain back their culture, and there'll be a colony of intelligent beings, monkeylike in form but not monkeyish. We can leave records of this. In a hundred years or so—"

Reade looked at him hesitantly, his imagination gripped, against his will, by Andrew's vision. "Could they survive?"

"Kamellin told me that the city was—time-sealed, he called it, and in perfect order." He looked down at the listening stillness of Kamellin and was convinced that the Martian understood; certainly Kamellin's reception of telepathy must be excellent, even if Andrew's was not.

"It was left that way—waiting for a race they could use, if one evolved. Chimps have terrific dexterity, once they're guided by intelligence. They made their food chemically, by solar power, and there are heat units, records—just waiting."

Reade stood up and started counting the chimpanzees. "We'll probably lose our jobs and our shirts—but we'll try it, Andy. Go borrow a sandbus—I've still got good contacts." He scribbled a note on a scrap of paper he found in his pocket, then added grimly "But don't forget; we've still got to be on the *Erdenluft* when it lifts off."

"We'll be on it."

Once again Andrew Slayton stood on the needled desert for a last look at the squat towers of Shein-la Mahari. He knew he would never come back.

Reade, his white shock of hair bent, stood beside him. Around them the crowd of Martians stood motionless, with a staid dignity greater than human, quietly waiting.

"No," Reade said half to himself, "it wouldn't work, Andy. Kamellin might take a chance on you, but you'd both regret it."

Andrew did not move or answer, still looking hungrily up at the glareless ramparts. If I could only write a book about it, he was thinking. The day they had spent had been what every interplanetary archaeologist dreams about in his most fantastic conjectures. The newly-incarnate Martians had been gratefully receptive to Reade's expressive sign-language and the tour of the city was a thing past all their wildest imagination.

Beneath the sand of centuries Shein-la Mahari was more than a city; it was a world. Never would they forget the heart-stopping thrill when a re-inhabited Martian, working with skill and inhuman awareness, had uncovered the ancient machinery of the water supply, connected to the miles-deep underground lakes, and turned great jets of water into hydroponic gardens; seeds long in storage had instantly bubbled into sprouting life. A careful engineer, her monkey-like paws working with incredible skill, had set sealed power units to humming. Rations, carefully time-sealed against emergency, were still edible. Reade and Andrew had shared the strangest meal of their lives with twenty-odd Martians—and it was not the suddenly-controlled chimpanzees whose table manners had seemed odd. Martian conventions were a cultural pattern of unbelievable stability.

Nor would he ever forget the great library of glyphs inscribed on flexible sheets of Vanadium, the power-room of throbbing machinery—

"Forget it," Reade said roughly, "they'll probably send us to Titan—and who knows what we'll find there?"

"Yeah. We've got a spaceship to catch." Andrew climbed into the sandcar, leaning out to grasp Kamellin's paw—sensing that the Martian would understand the gesture, if not the words. "Goodbye, Kamellin. Good luck to all of you." He cut the rockets in and shot away in a thunderstorm of sand. He drove fast and dangerously. He would never see Shein-la Mahari again. He would leave Mars, probably forever. And forever he would be alone...

"They'll make out," said Reade gruffly, and put an arm around his shoulders. To his intense horror, Andrew discovered that he was blinking back scalding tears.

"Sure," he made himself say. "In a few hundred years they'll be way ahead of Earth. Look what seventy-odd pilgrims did in North America, on our own planet! Synthetics—power—maybe even interstellar travel. They'd visited Earth once, before the plagues that killed them, Kamellin told me."

The sandcar roared around the rock-wall and Shein-la Mahari was gone. Behind them Andrew heard a rumble and a dull, groundshaking thunder. The pass behind them crashed in ruin; the Ridge was impassable again. Kamellin and his Martians would have their chance, unmolested by Earthmen, for at least a few years—

"I wonder," Reade mused, "which race will discover the other first...?"

WITHOUT BUGLES

E. C. Tubb

If any writer was determined to show the harsh realities of colonising Mars it was E. C. ("Ted") Tubb (1919–2010). Indeed, all of Tubb's works shout such grittiness that you can taste the perils he relishes describing. Tubb was one of Britain's most prolific writers, but also one of the most talented. Although he could write formulaic work if necessary to pay the bills, he could turn his hand to inventiveness and originality when needed. Tubb is probably best remembered today as the author of the 32-volume series about Earl Dumarest's search to find his home planet, Earth, which began with The Winds of Gath *in 1967, but his work goes way back to 1951 with his first novel* Planetfall, *under the pseudonym King Lang.*

Several of Tubb's stories are set on Mars, but the most rewarding are those that were collected as Alien Dust *in 1955, and follow the first thirty-five years or so of efforts to settle on the planet. The following is the first in that series and demonstrates, right from the start, the dangers that await and the sacrifices that may be necessary.*

THE MAN WRITHED ON THE NARROW COT, AND FOUGHT FOR life. He sat with his head between his knees, his mouth open, a thin trickle of saliva running from one corner down across his unshaven chin.

His hands clenched, twisted, tore at chest and throat. He whimpered, moaned, flung his body in strange convulsions. The skin of his face was blue with strangulation. The sound of his breathing horrible to hear.

They brought oxygen and strapped on the mask. A hypodermic pumped adrenaline into an already overstrained heart. The writhing quietened, the convulsions ceased. Breathing eased and he relaxed.

Strangely he slept.

Dirk Banner turned away feeling slightly sick. He met the cynical gaze of the doctor and jerked his head towards the bed. "Will he recover?"

The doctor, a tall thin man with sparse hair, cold eyes, and an expression of perpetual irritation, shrugged.

"To a degree, yes. Light work only, though. Better find him an inside job."

Dirk snorted. "How could it have happened?"

"He was careless."

"Careless? How do you mean?"

"Worked without a mask. Walked without one. Slept without one. How do I know? But he was careless."

Dirk snarled with baffled anger. "Can you blame him? Do you wear a mask? Do I?"

"Not here. Do you walk around outside without one? If you answer yes to that, I'll prepare a bed. You'll need it."

Dirk flushed. "Sorry, Doc, but it's getting worse. How many now?"

"Twenty hopeless, Fifty over the danger level. All the rest from one to thirty per cent, affected." He dropped a hand on the younger man's shoulder. "Don't let it get you, Dirk. There's nothing that you can do."

"That's what makes it so bad. To see men lying there, helpless, and know there's nothing anyone can do." He turned pleadingly to the doctor. "Is there any hope for them, Doc?"

"None." He gestured wearily. "It's not new this thing. It's been with us for over a hundred years. An industrial disease. Silicosis they called it once, and other names, but it all added up to the same thing. Inhaling dust will block the lungs, cutting down the area available for oxygen absorption. Manual activity is reduced, and if unalleviated, life becomes a constant struggle for oxygen to keep alive." He shuddered. "There are worse deaths, but not many."

Dirk nodded absently, then coming to some decision walked towards the exit. The doctor joined him at the inner door, and while they donned thick coveralls and masks, ventured a question. "Any news?"

"None." His voice sounded hollow through the fabric and filters. "Coming?" He swung open the door and stepped inside the vestibule, waited impatiently for the inner door to be closed, then together they stepped outside.

It was a depressing sight. A huddle of low rounded buildings, dun coloured, adobe constructed, their surfaces smooth and bearing a faint polish. One building bore the appearance of pre-fabrication, glistening with the sheen of scoured aluminium.

From it, as from all the buildings, cables snaked, meeting at a central point, from there disappearing over the horizon. The streets were just lanes between the domes, unpaved, and thickly covered with a fine powdery dust.

Dirk kicked at it disgustedly. It rose at the impact, hanging like smoke in the thin air, settling in a fine film over his coverall.

"Who would have thought that a bit of dust would cause such trouble?"

The doctor started to answer, then checked himself, staring into the sky. It was night. The stars shone clear, scattered thick across the heavens. The twin moons raced for the horizon, and a faint glow warned of a new dawn.

Above their heads a star had moved. It seemed to grow, to lengthen. Then it wasn't a star but a slim pencil of flame.

"The rocket!" he yelled. "The rocket!"

He ran to the administration building, stumbling through the dust, sending it flying in great clouds. Seconds later the wail of a siren cut through the thin air.

Within minutes the entire settlement came alive.

Jud Anders drew deeply on his cigar and sent a fragrant cloud billowing towards the fan. The noses of his audience wrinkled with disgust, and he looked his surprise.

"We've been conditioned to dislike tobacco," explained Dirk patiently, "as well as coffee, milk, alcohol and about everything else you can think of that we can't get here. It helps not to like something which you can't get anyway."

"I see," said Anders. "I'd forgotten." He did not attempt to remove the cigar.

"Why are you here, Anders?" the doctor was abrupt. "You're not here to work, and mass is too important for you to have come just for the ride."

"Why?" Anders grinned. "Well you might call me a one-man commission. Secretary for Extra-Planetary Affairs." He rolled the title on his tongue. "I'm here to report hack to Congress on how things are going."

"He's here to see if you're worth your keep," put in a new voice. "And I'm here to help him do it."

It wasn't what the voice said, it was the tones it said it in. You can condition men to dislike almost anything, but not women, not after living for almost five years without even hearing one. The newcomer received instant and undivided attention.

She stood by the door, swinging a mask in one hand. The bulky coverall hid her body, but that didn't matter. Nothing mattered except that she was feminine. Dirk rose as she came across the crowded room.

"Dirk Banner? My name's Pat Easton. Short for Patricia. Did it throw you off?"

"It did rather," he admitted. "I'd expected a man." He knew now why the rocket crew had been so amused. "Are you the writer?"

"Reporter," she corrected. "Trans-World Communications decided that the public would like to know how its money was being spent. I'm here to find out."

"Pleased to have you with us," lied Dirk politely. "But why you? Why a woman, I mean?"

"I happened to have influence," she admitted calmly. "I wanted to come. After all you are making history. Heroes! Pioneers! The vanguard of all Earth, breaking new frontiers! You know the sort of thing."

"No," said Dirk soberly. "I don't think that I do. And I don't think that you do either."

She flushed, and bit her lip, then deliberately smiled over his shoulder. "Why I know you! Professor Winton isn't it?"

The doctor grinned sheepishly, and took her outstretched hand. "Just call me Doc." he chuckled. "Everyone else does around here. Have you met everyone?" He led her away, acting the host. Dirk stood frowning after them. He was annoyed to find that he felt a tinge of jealousy. He turned to Anders.

"Did you have a nice trip?"

"Nice? If you can call being crushed by acceleration, nauseated by seven weeks of free fall, then to land in the middle of nowhere, having a nice trip—then I had one."

They all laughed. "That's the romance of space flight you keep reading about," chuckled Mason, the diminutive pilot. "The romance our lady friend was talking about."

Hastily Dirk changed the subject. "How's Luna Base getting on? Found that vein of rare ore yet?"

Anders gestured with the cigar. "Found that six months ago. Setting up a proper relay station now. Over three thousand personnel, and growing fast," he beamed. "Those boys are certainly worth their keep. They mine enough uranium to more than pay running costs."

"I've got the news tapes on the ship. I left them until the mail had been distributed," explained Mason. "I thought it would be better to get them settled on mail home first. We're only stopping three days this trip."

"You're staying, of course?" Dirk asked Anders. "The next ship should be due in about three months."

"What makes you think that?" Anders squinted through the cigar smoke. "I'm going back on the same ship, Miss Easton too."

"But I thought that you wanted to investigate the settlement?"

"Well?"

"It'll take more than three days to do that. You've a whole planet to see."

"So what? Listen Banner, all I'm interested in is a straight answer to a straight question."

"And that is?"

"Only this." Anders was obviously enjoying himself. "Congress has poured billions of dollars into this project, When are you going to start paying it back?"

A man next to him spat in utter disgust.

Dirk stood watching the sun set behind the rocket. It was a sight he never tired of, and one he thought that could never be equalled. The slender pencil of gleaming metal resting on wide fins. The desert, flaming with all the reds, oranges and yellows ever imagined. An alien masterpiece.

A faint wind blew from the east, rippling the dust, shaping the dunes into new more fantastic configurations. Little clouds scudded over the plain, rising, falling, eddying, pluming, finally drifting to a halt. Dust. The curse of the planet.

He sighed and turned away, almost knocking down the slight shape behind him. They clung together, striving for balance, and through the plastic of the mask he recognised the reporter. He held her, and suddenly didn't want to let her go.

She wriggled from his arms with an easy motion, and dusted herself down. "Admiring the scenery?"

"I always come to see the rocket," he laughed self-consciously. "A craving for the romantic I suppose you'd call it."

"No. Why should I? I think that it's a perfectly natural thing to do." She stood looking at him. "You don't like me, do you?"

"Of course I do," he stammered, "but…" He steadied under her calm gaze. "I wish that you hadn't come."

"Why?"

"There are nearly two hundred men in the settlement who haven't even heard a woman for almost five years. That's one reason, perhaps the best one."

"And the others?"

He sighed. "Anders is going to be hard enough to handle without Trans-World Communications as well."

"You misunderstand me. We're not against you. Anders takes a pride in being hard-headed. Perhaps a good thing back home where money has to be watched, but not here. Trans-World can help you. That's why I'm here."

"Help? How can they help?"

"Public opinion. If the people can be convinced that you are doing a great thing here, then Anders and all Congress are helpless to do other than help you."

"And can they?"

"Of course," she laughed. "It's the easiest thing in the world. Everyone believes you to be heroes. Brave men battling the unknown," she saw his face and stopped. "I'm sorry. You don't like being regarded as heroes do you?"

"We're not," he said tersely. "We're men doing a job, and all we want is to be left alone to do it our own way."

"I'm entitled to an opinion." She laughed and put out her hands. "Friends?"

"Friends." He grinned and squeezed her hand. "But I still don't like Anders."

"Neither do I, but we must work with him." She took his arm as they walked towards the settlement. "What's that building

over there?" She pointed towards the aluminium dome. "It looks
so new."

"The food plant. The dust keeps it polished. You know that we
live on yeast, I suppose?"

"No. Why do you?"

"Nothing will grow in the desert. At least nothing we know of.
Food can't be imported, we need so much of everything else, so our
first job was to grow our own."

"Do you like it?"

He shrugged. "It's edible." They walked on in silence. Dust
clogged their feet, rising in great clouds around them, settling thickly
on their coveralls. From time to time they wiped the eye windows of
the masks. The sun had almost set, and their shadows danced fitfully
before them, vague in the dying light.

The wind had risen, its passage marked by long rippling plumes across
the desert. A thin whine penetrated the masks, and the air became
heavy with flying particles.

Dirk stopped and looked at the sky.

"What's the matter?"

"I'm not sure," he said absently, "but I think we'd better hurry."
Taking her arm he began loping forward, leaning well into the
wind. Lights gleamed in the settlement. A tractor churned its way
in between the buildings, stopped, and immediately became hidden
in its own fog. Abruptly a siren began to wail.

"What is it?" gasped Pat, straggling to keep up with the now
running Dirk. "Anything wrong?"

"Dust storm," he gasped. "Hurry."

In seconds the storm burst upon them. Pat clung to the one
solid thing in a nightmare of whining wind and choking dust.

Dirk's arm had wrapped round her waist, and dimly she felt him pulling her along. The siren had stopped. A klaxon sounded raucously every few seconds, the sound seeming to come from every direction at once.

She couldn't see. The dust covered the eye windows, and even when she wiped them, it made no difference. Driven by the wind, the dust began to work beneath the coverall. Her skin prickled with irritation, her eyes smarted, the inside of her mouth became coated, her lungs began to burn.

How long it lasted she could never he sure, but suddenly the pressure of the wind dropped. It came again, but this time blowing the dust from her. Through the now clear eye-windows she could see a muffled shape wielding an air hose. Hands fumbled at her mask, something-acrid and nasty filled her mouth, she gagged, spat, gagged again and was suddenly very sick.

The doctor grinned down at her, and turned to Dirk. "She'll be O.K. How about you?"

He leaned against the wall and gasped for breath. Slowly the blue tinge left his skin, but when he straightened it was with an effort. "I'll live," he wheezed. "Take care of her will you, Doc. I'm all in."

"You need adrenaline," grunted the doctor. "Get that coverall off." He stepped away, and turned just in time to catch the fainting man.

Anders pursed thin lips over a fresh cigar, and carefully applied a light. "Hope you don't mind my smoking," he grunted to no one in particular, "but it's barred on the ship." He blew a thin streamer towards the naked bulb.

The doctor coughed and turned to Pat. "Feel better now?"

"Yes, thanks," she smiled gratefully. "I must have been an awful nuisance. Where's Dirk?"

"Checking up on the weather. He won't be long."

Mason sat chewing nervously at his nails. He spat out a shred irritably. "Three days now, and I don't even know if the ship is still standing. Why in hell don't they have windows in these hutches?"

"Wouldn't do much good if there were." Dirk looked pale and worried as he came through the door. "The storms would roughen the glass or plastic, besides, they'd leak." He nodded to the doctor, smiled at Pat. "The ship's still standing though. When we've cleared the dust you'll be able to blast."

"The storm's over then?" Mason jumped to his feet. "I'd better get out there and check the ship." He almost ran through the door.

Anders snorted with relief. "Mason was telling me that if we don't blast today, we'll have to use an alternative course. Add weeks to the trip. Can you get the ship clear?"

"No."

"Now see here, Banner!" Anders slammed his fist on the table. "I've a right to demand that the ship be cleared." He looked shrewdly at Dirk. "I can maybe guess why you don't want us to leave, but you're not helping yourself by keeping us here."

Dirk tensed, then relaxed as the doctor gripped his arm. "I don't want to keep you here Anders, but didn't you come for a reason?"

"I came to investigate. I've written my report." Anders gestured towards the pile of papers before him. "I've been fair Banner, but frankly this settlement isn't worth its keep. Venus Colony needs every ship we can spare. There's virgin territory there Banner, and I'm going to see that this unending drain on public funds is stopped."

In the sudden silence the hiss of the doctor's indrawn breath sounded strangely loud. Pat gave a muffled cry of protest. Dirk said nothing, but from the rest of the men came a murmur. It sounded ugly. Anders blanched.

"I know that you've had your troubles," he protested. "But you must be fair. What have you done in five years?"

"It's all in the reports," Dirk said mildly. "The first year—investigation, exploration, building the settlement, food plant, atomic pile."

"And the other four years?"

"Just keeping alive." Dirk sounded bitter. "It's not been easy, Anders. What did you expect? A uranium mine?"

"Maybe not, but at least you could have done something to offset the cost. New minerals. New plants. Martian artifacts. Anything. For all the good you've done here you might as well have settled in the Sahara."

"No," Pat protested, her face red with anger. "That's not fair. These men have risked everything. Lived from day to day, given up wives, families, comforts, everything." She turned on Dirk and the others. "I know that you don't like being called heroes, but what else are you? Who else, other than men utterly unselfish, would have done what you have done? And because you can't pay for the privilege of living this awful existence, are you to be thrown aside? We'll see what the public thinks about this, Anders. I don't think that you'll sit so smug then."

She sat down her eyes suspiciously bright. Anders sighed. "The young are always romantic, and you, if you'll forgive me, are still very young. The public, my dear, can be made to agree to anything. Just tell them the truth—that they are wasting their money on an ideal—and they will yell to have it stopped. Believe me, I know that, and so do your employers."

"We'll see about that. I want to hear both sides of the story, and so will the peoples of Earth," she turned to Dirk impetuously. "Tell him, Dirk. Make him see how wrong he is. Show him what a wonderful thing, concept, dream of all mankind, this conquest of a new world is!"

Dirk sighed and shifted restlessly in his chair. "I wish I could Pat, but I can't."

"Can't! Why not?"

"Because he's right, Pat. He's right—and you are wrong." He felt as if he had slapped her in the face.

"You see," he explained dully. "Mars is a dead world, I don't mean a dying world, one which is slowly exhausting its natural resources, but a literally dead world. A murdered world. You have heard of radioactive dusts, what they will do, how utterly deadly they are? Mars is the victim of such dusts."

He stopped, his eyes straying around the circle of intent faces. Most of them knew what he had to say, to them it was an old story. To the others it was explanation and excuse. The fan made a steady whirring, sucking the air through the filters. Despite the fan a thin coating of dust lay over everything. He drew a finger across the table.

"Once, how long ago we can only conjecture, there was a war, or maybe it was an accident, and radioactive dust was loose on the planet. You know how such dusts operate. They have a half life of maybe days, or months, even years. Where they are scattered life ceases to exist. All life. Animal. Vegetable. The insectivora. The worms in the soil. Even the bacteria. Everything.

"Where the dust lies becomes a desert. Winds scatter the poisoned soil further afield. The deserts spread, and spread, and spread." He gestured towards the outside of the wall. "The results you have seen."

"But surely the soil can be replanted? Animals imported? Life begin again?" Pat leaned forward vehemently.

"Yes. Given time to find suitable plant life. Time to irrigate. Time to find some means of anchoring the dust. But we haven't got time." Dirk looked at Anders. "Mars isn't a place suitable for a short term investment. It will take years. Billions. Thousands of men. It may take a generation. The prize is a complete new world."

"Doesn't that answer you?" Pat accused. "Isn't that what you want? Why say he's right, when you know different? Anders is wrong. And you know it!"

"No," Dirk said listlessly. "He's not wrong. From the standpoint of immediate results be is right. Why should young blood be wasted on this arid world? Why should we spend a generation on this one planet when there are so many others?" He smiled at her. "You are an idealist. You think of Mars in terms of romance. There is no romance. What have we to offer? A few weeks of free fall, then desolation. Work, more work, and then still more work. And at the end—death."

"No," she protested. "Not death. Life. The life of a planet."

Anders coughed, rustling his papers. "I'm glad that you can see things my way, Banner, but there in another point. Congress has voted a vast sum for this development project. There will have to be an accounting." He lifted a hand at the hum of protest. "I'm not blaming any of you, but we must be realistic. You had the finest equipment available. Over two hundred men, and all the supplies we could send you. What have you done?"

"Lived," the doctor snapped. "At least some of us." He turned to the silent Director, "What's the matter with you, Dirk? Why don't you tell this fat slug where to get off? Do you want to see everything we've done thrown away? If you don't care, think of the rest of us. Snap out of it man."

—

Dirk flushed at the acid tones and glanced half apologetically at the others. "I'm sorry." He stared at Anders, "For the sake of argument I can agree that logically you are correct, but don't go too far. You talk of machines. Equipment. Supplies. I talk of men. At the basis of every civilisation, every development, every monument to Man's greatness, there is one common factor. A simple tiling. A man with a shovel.

"Machines are useless without him. We can do nothing without him. He is the one indispensable. And we haven't got him. We never have had him." He gestured at the paper-littered desk. "You can talk of your two hundred men. What does that really mean? Out of that two hundred, fifty cannot do manual labour. Of the rest twenty are a useless burden. The mere act of keeping alive takes the full-time labour of all but fifty of us. We have fifty men to redevelop an entire planet. We are not supermen, Anders."

"But…"

"But, nothing." Pat turned to Dirk her face shining. "Did they know this back home? Did Congress know?" She smiled triumphantly at Anders. "Wait until the public read of this, why the offices will be swamped with applications from men eager to use a shovel on Mars."

"Will they?" Anders smiled grimly. "I think not. Five years ago, I will agree. Then we could take our pick, and did, but now?" he shook his head. "There are other frontiers. Luna, Venus, the dark side of Mercury. There is life there, the taste of adventure. On Mars?" He shrugged. "Men are very selfish. Give them the promise of wealth, experience, even the pleasure of killing to live, and they will go through hell itself. But what can you offer? An ideal? Work without profit, Life in a dust bowl. The Sahara offers the same. The Matto Grosso more. They are still undeveloped."

"You're a cynic," Pat accused.

"No, my dear," he corrected gently. "A realist. A settlement such as this must be self-supporting to justify its existence, It must not depend on supplies from home. The settlement must expand, take root, produce children. That necessitates women," he smiled at her. "Would you be willing to spend your life here?"

"Why I…" she broke off in confusion.

"To stay here. To bear your children. To live, grow old, die without ever seeing Earth again?" He was gently insistent. "Could you honestly tell women that this was a good place to come. And if you yourself are not willing to settle, how can you persuade others?"

Dirk watched her, heart hammering with emotion. It was foolish he knew, but he desperately wanted her to be willing to stay. She flushed, looked defiant, started to speak then looked up gratefully as a man burst into the room.

Mason swayed, clutched the edge of the table, and tore off his mask. He was deathly pale, and almost gibbered in rage and fright. "For God's sake do something Banner. Your men refuse to let me into the ship!"

They crowded in behind him, a dozen hard-faced men, workers from the blowers and dust clearers. Big men, dust stained, grouping together for mutual support. Dirk recognised them as the latest arrivals; none of them had been on Mars over two years.

He quietened the babble of cross talk and addressed the group. "Who's your spokesman?"

After a mutter of conversation a tall, burly man stepped forward. "I am."

"What's the trouble?"

"No trouble. Before he leaves," he jerked a thumb at Anders, "we want to know where we stand. What's this about abandoning the settlement?"

"Abandoning the settlement?" Dirk looked at them incredulously. "Where did you get that crazy idea?"

"In the mail. My folks tell me that it's common talk that Congress is stopping funds, abandoning the project. We want to know what's going to happen to us!"

Dirk looked at them calmly. "I'm sure that you're mistaken. Mr. Anders is from Congress itself. Maybe he can convince you."

"There's no need to worry," Anders boomed cheerfully. "In the remote event of the settlement being closed you'll all get transportation home. You don't think that we'd leave you here, do you?" He laughed. "Now, how about letting the pilot into the ship? He won't leave without me, and I won't go yet a while."

The men muttered and shifted restlessly. The burly spokesman ignored Anders and looked at Dirk. "O.K. But we're trusting you, Banner, to look out for us. Sec that you do."

They left the room, the half threat hanging on the thin air. Dirk turned slowly and stared at Anders. "Is there anything in what he said?"

"About what?"

"Abandoning the settlement, of course," snarled Dirk. "What did you think I was talking about?"

Anders shrugged. "Must we go through all that again? I thought that you agreed that the settlement was an unsound proposition. I should think that you'd be glad to be relieved. It may take a little time, of course, but everyone will get back home."

Someone laughed. It was the doctor. He had sat unnoticed through the recent excitement. The others, Dirk noted, had left to their various tasks. Despite Anders, life had to go on.

"That's the best joke I've heard since I left home," he chuckled. "Everyone get back home, eh? Why don't you tell him, Dirk? Why don't you show him? I'd like to see him do it," his laughter had a note of hysteria. Anders frowned.

"I don't see anything funny," he complained. "All I'm suggesting is that it may not be so easy to get you all home as quickly as you may like. The demand on ships for Venus…" his voice trailed off.

"In other words," Dirk said bitterly, "the men are right. Congress do intend abandoning the settlement, and us with it."

"No," protested Anders. "Not that. We would never leave the personnel."

"You have no choice," snapped Dirk curtly, He laughed. "Haven't you even guessed yet? Why do you think we are so intent on keeping the settlement alive? I told you that it was a hopeless dream. Pat here thought I was being modest, a shy hero—nothing is further from the truth. We want to leave. All of us. The joke is, we can't. We're stuck with our own private hell, and there's nothing anyone can do about it."

"I don't understand." Pat frowned at Dirk and the doctor. "What are you trying to say?"

"Shall we show them?"

The doctor nodded, climbing to his feet. Together they left the room.

The ward was quiet, cool, and utterly restful. Extra air pressure eased lungs used to gasping at thin air. The twenty cots stretched down two sides, a narrow passage between them. Apparatus stood about, oxygen, wheeled tables loaded with vials and instruments. An attendant nodded as they entered.

"All restful, Doc."

He nodded and stood staring down at the figure in the nearest bed. It was a man, thin, with waxen skin and unkempt hair. Thin hands lay above the covers, the long fingers almost transparent, the knuckles bulging at the joints.

Pillows behind propped him into a sitting position. He stared vacantly before him, his mouth open, and breathed. That was all he did do. Breathe. That was all he could do.

Pat stared down at him with pity. Then moved to the next cot, and the next.

"They are all like this," the doctor kept his voice low as he stood at her side. "Extreme cases, of course, some of the first effects of ignorance."

"What is it?" Like the doctor she kept her voice low.

"Dust. When we first came we thought that the dust was harmless. Annoying, of course, but not too bad. We were wrong."

They joined Anders and Dirk. Anders had a shocked look in his eyes. He led the way to the exit, and wiped a suddenly moist face.

"There are twenty of them, the worst cases. Any effort would kill them, the shock of acceleration would be certain death." Dirk looked at Anders. "Now do you realise why we can't leave?"

"But, Dirk." Pat bit her lip. "Surely those men in there wouldn't want you to sacrifice yourselves. They would understand, It sounds awful I know, but, euthanasia?"

"No. Don't misunderstand me. I've no compunctions about killing, but it wouldn't do any good." He smiled down at her. "You will insist on thinking of us as heroes—heroism doesn't enter into it. They are the very extreme cases. There are others, able to sit, even walk a little, who have to be thought of. They can do no manual work but they can watch meters, keep the books, a dozen little jobs. The shock of acceleration would kill them too."

—

"But what caused it? Why should you all be forced to stay here because a few men are ill?" Pat clutched his arm. "I want to help, but I can't if you won't even try to help yourselves."

"We are trying to help ourselves, the only way we can," he smiled at her look of frustration. "There are about twenty men who could return home and live a normal life. There are about fifty more who could survive the trip, but who would be semi-invalids. Of the rest, those who lived through the trip would be bedridden like the twenty you saw.

"Our only hope of all keeping alive is to keep the fit men here to do the hard work. Not only that, but to get fresh replacements for them when they succumb. So, you see, we are really very selfish."

"But you wear masks. Why does the dust affect you?"

"Show me a single spot within the settlement free from dust, and I'll give you Mars. We can't keep it out. It seeps everywhere. No mask can fully protect us."

Pat nodded, thinking of her experience in the dust storm, the burning at her lungs and the awful irritation of her body. She looked at Dirk in sudden alarm.

"How long have you been here?"

"About four years," he answered absently. "Mason tells me that you're blasting in a few hours."

She shrugged as if the news was unimportant. "How is it that you are free of the dust poisoning?"

"Am I?" he gestured carelessly. "Luck I guess. I've been careful."

"Why lie about it?" The doctor's cynical voice sounded from the door. "She'll be wondering why you don't propose," he grinned at her without humour. "If he won't tell you, I will. Take him to Earth and he will spend the rest of his life in bed. Not a long one at that."

He took Banner's arm and gently led him away from the sob-bing girl.

"She had to know, Dirk. Better now than later."

Behind them the sobs sounded strangely loud. The first ever heard on Mars.

They stood at the edge of the field watching the activity around the rocket. Men, muffled in their coveralls and masks, cleared the last of the stores, loaded on the few crates of dust for the return load. It was pitifully little to send in return for the years of development.

Dirk felt at peace now that Pat knew, somehow something had dissolved between them. It was good not to have to pretend. He smiled down at her.

"Did you enjoy your stay?"

They both laughed. From the foot of the ramp a diminutive figure waved at them. Mason signalling a last farewell. Pat shivered suddenly.

"Cold?"

"No." She was unnaturally curt.

"What do they think of us back home, Pat? The people, I mean?"

"Some think that you're heroes, the rest that you're fools." Still the same dull tone. He took her shoulders and turned her to him.

"What's the matter, Pat? Aren't you on our side any more?"

"Oh, Dirk!" Suddenly she was in his arms, trembling with emotion. "Why does it have to be like this? Why can't you come home?"

"Because of the gravity, darling." The unnatural word came easily to his lips. "With the lesser gravity we need less oxygen, less lung absorption surface." He laughed, trying to cheer her up. "It's not so bad. With you helping us we'll have all the supplies we need, men too." Gently he stroked the quivering figure.

Anders came ploughing through the dust past them, the doctor striding like some ungainly bird beside him. He called out as they passed. "Only five minutes left, Pat. Better get aboard if you don't want to spend the next three months here."

Dirk lifted an arm in acknowledgement. Beside him the girl lifted her head.

"Dirk? Would it hurt to take off the masks for a minute?"

He considered, frowning at the circle of dust cleared from the rocket by the giant blowers. There was no wind; aside from the drifting plumes caused by the feet of Anders and the doctor, the air was clear.

"I guess not. Not for a few seconds, anyway."

"Good. Then take it off." Hands suddenly trembling he did as she asked. Pat blushed as her mask came free. Wordlessly she lifted her lips. To Dirk the kiss was sheer heaven.

Then she was gone, running across the dust to the waiting rocket. He watched her reach the ramp, climb the incline. The port dogged shut, the ramp flung dear. Automatically he replaced his mask.

A warning blast from the ship's siren stirred the air. Flame started from the swelling venturis. Muffled thunder tore at his eardrums, and slowly the rocket lifted towards the stars.

He watched it until it was high overhead. Until the sound of its passage had echoed over the desert and lost itself in silence. Until the finger of flame had dwindled, shrunk to a point, had flickered, and vanished among the thousands of other points glittering in the sky.

He felt a hand on his shoulder. It was the doctor, a bundle under one arm. "She'll be back," he said with calm conviction. "One day she'll come back."

"Why should she?" Dirk asked bitterly. "What have we to offer? Why should anyone but a fool come to Mars? Why would anyone ever come here again?" He turned away, lost in the memory of a kiss.

Mockingly the dust rose around him.

CRUCIFIXUS ETIAM

Walter M. Miller, Jr.

The rarefied atmosphere of Mars is too thin to support life from Earth—it is about one-hundredth the density of Earth's. It is over 95% carbon dioxide and only 2.7% nitrogen and 0.13% oxygen, compared to 78% nitrogen on Earth, 21% oxygen and only 0.038% carbon dioxide. The fact that the Martian atmosphere is composed almost entirely of carbon dioxide had been known since 1947, following detailed analysis via infrared light by the astronomer Gerard Kuiper. Nevertheless, writers persevered in thinking that perhaps humans could survive using breathing apparatus or masks for long enough to be able to build plants for converting the atmosphere. The idea arose that the best candidates for living on Mars would be those who already live in a rarefied atmosphere on Earth, such as Peruvians or Tibetans. The earliest example I have found of that idea was A. E. van Vogt in 'This Joe' (1951), also known as 'The First Martian', but a more detailed use is in the following story.

Walter M. Miller, Jr. (1923–1996) is remembered today almost entirely for his episodic post-apocalyptic novel, A Canticle for Leibowitz (1959), but this more or less marked the end of his writing career, as he was active only during the 1950s and completed some forty stories. Many of these, such as 'Dark Benediction' (1951), 'Let My People Go' (1952) and 'The Darfstellar' (1955) have a deep theme of religious transmogrification, and it is that same soul-searching feeling of sacrifice that makes the following story so powerful.

MANUE NANTI JOINED THE PROJECT TO MAKE SOME DOUGH. Five dollars an hour was good pay, even in 2134 A.D., and there was no way to spend it while on the job. Everything would be furnished: housing, chow, clothing, toiletries, medicine, cigarettes, even a daily ration of one hundred eighty proof beverage alcohol, locally distilled from fermented Martian mosses as fuel for the project's vehicles. He figured that if he avoided crap games, he could finish his five-year contract with fifty thousand dollars in the bank, return to Earth, and retire at the age of twenty-four. Manue wanted to travel, to see the far corners of the world, the strange cultures, the simple people, the small towns, deserts, mountains, jungles—for until he came to Mars, he had never been farther than a hundred miles from Cerro de Pasco, his birthplace in Peru.

A great wistfulness came over him in the cold Martian night when the frost haze broke, revealing the black, gleam-stung sky, and the blue-green Earth-star of his birth. *El mundo de mi carne, de mi alma,* he thought—yet, he had seen so little of it that many of its places would be more alien to him than the homogeneously ugly vistas of Mars. These he longed to see: the volcanoes of the South Pacific, the monstrous mountains of Tibet, the concrete cyclops of New York, the radioactive craters of Russia, the artificial islands in the China Sea, the Black Forest, the Ganges, the Grand Canyon—but most of all, the works of human art, the pyramids, the Gothic cathedrals of Europe, *Notre Dame du Chartres,* Saint Peter's, the tile-work wonders of Anacapri. But the dream was still a long labour from realisation.

Manue was a big youth, heavy-boned and built for labour, clever in a simple mechanical way, and with a wistful good humour that helped him take a lot of guff from whisky-breathed foreman and sharp-eyed engineers who made ten dollars an hour and figured ways for making more, legitimately or otherwise.

He had been on Mars only a month, and it hurt. Each time he swung the heavy pick into the red-brown sod, his face winced with pain. The plastic aerator valves, surgically stitched in his chest, pulled and twisted and seemed to tear with each lurch of his body. The mechanical oxygenator served as a lung, sucking blood through an artificially grafted network of veins and plastic tubing, frothing it with air from a chemical generator, and returning it to his circulatory system. Breathing was unnecessary, except to provide wind for talking, but Manue breathed in desperate gulps of the 4.0 psi Martian air; for he had seen the wasted, atrophied chests of the men who had served four or five years, and he knew that when they returned to Earth—if ever—they would still need the auxiliary oxygenator equipment.

"If you don't stop breathing," the surgeon told him, "you'll be all right. When you go to bed at night, turn the oxy down low—so low you feel like panting. There's a critical point that's just right for sleeping. If you get it too low, you'll wake up screaming, and you'll get claustrophobia. If you get it too high, your reflex mechanisms will go to pot and you won't breathe; your lungs'll dry up after a time. Watch it."

Manue watched it carefully, although the oldsters laughed at him—in their dry wheezing chuckles. Some of them could scarcely speak more than two or three words at a shallow breath.

"Breathe deep, boy," they told him. "Enjoy it while you can. You'll forget how pretty soon. Unless you're an engineer."

The engineers had it soft, he learned. They slept in a pressurised barrack where the air was ten psi and twenty-five per cent oxygen, where they turned their oxies off and slept in peace. Even their oxies were self-regulating, controlling the output according to the carbon dioxide content of the input blood. But the Commission could afford no such luxuries for the labour gangs. The payload of a cargo rocket from Earth was only about two per cent of the ship's total mass, and nothing superfluous could be carried. The ships brought the bare essentials, basic industrial equipment, big reactors, generators, engines, heavy tools.

Small tools, building materials, foods, non-nuclear fuels—these things had to be made on Mars. There was an open pit mine in the belly of the Syrtis Major where a "lake" of nearly pure iron-rust was scooped into a smelter, and processed into various grades of steel for building purposes, tools, and machinery. A quarry in the Flathead Mountains dug up large quantities of cement rock, burned it, and crushed it to make concrete.

It was rumoured that Mars was even preparing to grow her own labour force. An old-timer told him that the Commission had brought five hundred married couples to a new underground city in the Mare Erythraeum, supposedly as personnel for a local commission headquarters, but according to the old-timer, they were to be paid a bonus of three thousand dollars for every child born on the fed planet. But Manue knew that the old "troffies" had a way of inventing such stories, and he reserved a certain amount of scepticism.

As for his own share in the Project, he knew—and needed to know—very little. The encampment was at the north end of the Mare Cimmerium, surrounded by the bleak brown and green landscape of rock and giant lichens, stretching toward sharply defined horizons except for one mountain range in the distance, and hung over by a blue sky so dark that the Earth-star occasionally became dimly visible during the dim daytime. The encampment consisted of a dozen double-walled stone huts, windowless, and roofed with flat slabs of rock covered over by a tarry resin boiled out of the cactus-like spineplants. The camp was ugly, lonely, and dominated by the gaunt skeleton of a drill rig set up in its midst.

Manue joined the excavating crew in the job of digging a yard-wide, six feet deep foundation trench in a hundred yard square around the drill rig, which day and night was biting deeper through the crust of Mars in a dry cut that necessitated frequent stoppages for changing rotary bits. He learned that the geologists had predicted a subterranean pocket of tritium oxide ice at sixteen thousand feet, and that it was for this that they were drilling. The foundation he was helping to dig would be for a control station of some sort.

He worked too hard to be very curious. Mars was a nightmare, a grim womanless, frigid, disinterestedly evil world. His digging partner was a sloe-eyed Tibetan nicknamed "Gee" who spoke the Omnalingua clumsily at best. He followed two paces behind Manue with a shovel, scooping up the broken ground, and humming a monotonous chant in his own tongue. Manue seldom heard his own language, and missed it; one of the engineers, a haughty Chilean, spoke the modern Spanish, but not to such as Manue Nanti. Most of the other labourers used either Basic English or the Omnalingua. He spoke both, but longed to hear the tongue of his people. Even when he tried to talk to Gee, the cultural gulf was so wide that satisfying communication was nearly impossible. Peruvian jokes were unfunny to Tibetan ears, although Gee bent double with gales of laughter when Manue nearly crushed his own foot with a clumsy stroke of the pick.

He found no close companions. His foreman was a narrow-eyed, orange-browed Low German named Vögeli, usually half-drunk, and intent upon keeping his lung-power by bellowing at his crew. A meaty, florid man, he stalked slowly along the lip of the excavation, pausing to stare coldly down at each pair of labourers who, if they dared to look up, caught a guttural tongue-lashing for the moment's pause. When he had words for a digger, he called a halt by kicking a small avalanche of dirt back into the trench about the man's feet.

Manue learned about Vögeli's disposition before the end of his first month. The aerator tubes had become nearly unbearable; the skin, in trying to grow fast to the plastic, was beginning to form a tight little neck where the tubes entered his flesh, and the skin stretched and burned and stung with each movement of his trunk. Suddenly he felt sick. He staggered dizzily against the side of the trench, dropped the pick, and swayed heavily, bracing himself against collapse. Shock and nausea rocked him, while Gee stared at him and giggled foolishly.

"Hoy!" Vögeli bellowed from across the pit. "Get back on that pick! Hoy, there! Get with it—"

Manue moved dizzily to recover the tool, saw patches of black swimming before him, sank weakly back to pant in shallow gasps. The nagging sting of the valves was a portable hell that he carried with him always. He fought an impulse to jerk them out of his flesh; if a valve came loose, he would bleed to death in a few minutes.

Vögeli came stamping along the heap of fresh earth and lumbered up to stand over the sagging Manue in the trench. He glared down at him for a moment, then nudged the back of his neck with a heavy boot. "Get to work!"

Manue looked up and moved his lips silently. His forehead glinted with moisture in the faint sun, although the temperature was far below freezing.

"Grab that pick and get started."

"Can't," Manue gasped. "Hoses—hurt."

Vögeli grumbled a curse and vaulted down into the trench beside him. "Unzip that jacket," he ordered.

Weakly, Manue fumbled to obey, but the foreman knocked his hand aside and jerked the zipper down. Roughly he unbuttoned the Peruvian's shirt, laying open the bare brown chest to the icy cold.

"*No!*—not the hoses, *please!*"

Vögeli took one of the thin tubes in his blunt fingers and leaned close to peer at the puffy, calloused nodule of irritated skin that formed around it where it entered the flesh. He touched the nodule lightly, causing the digger to whimper.

"No, please!"

"Stop snivelling!"

Vögeli laid his thumbs against the nodule and exerted a sudden pressure. There was a slight popping sound as the skin slid back a fraction of an inch along the tube. Manue yelped and closed his eyes.

"Shut up! I know what I'm doing."

He repeated the process with the other tube. Then he seized both tubes in his hands and wiggled them slightly in and out, as if to insure a proper resetting of the skin. The digger cried weakly and slumped in a dead faint.

When he awoke, he was in bed in the barracks, and a medic was painting the sore spots with a bright yellow solution that chilled his skin.

"Woke up, huh?" the medic grunted cheerfully. "How you feel?"

"*Malo!*" he hissed.

"Stay in bed for the day, son. Keep your oxy up high. Make you feel better."

The medic went away, but Vögeli lingered, smiling at him grimly from the doorway. "Don't try goofing off tomorrow too."

Manue hated the closed door with silent eyes, and listened intently until Vögeli's footsteps left the building. Then, following the medic's instructions, he turned his oxy to maximum, even though the faster flow of blood made the chest-valves ache. The sickness fled, to be replaced with a weary afterglow. Drowsiness came over him, and he slept.

Sleep was a dread black-robed phantom on Mars. Mars pressed the same incubus upon all newcomers to her soil: a nightmare of falling, falling, falling into bottomless space. It was the faint gravity, they said, that caused it. The body felt buoyed up, and the subconscious mind recalled down-going elevators, and diving airplanes, and a fall from a high cliff. It suggested these things in dreams, or if the dreamer's oxy were set too low, it conjured up a nightmare of sinking slowly deeper, and deeper in cold black water that filled the victim's throat. Newcomers were segregated in a separate barracks so that their nightly screams would not disturb the old-timers who had finally adjusted to Martian conditions.

But now, for the first time since his arrival, Manue slept soundly, airily, and felt borne up by beams of bright light.

When he awoke again, he lay clammy in the horrifying knowledge that he had not been breathing! It was so comfortable not to breathe. His chest stopped hurting because of the stillness of his rib-case. He felt refreshed and alive. Peaceful sleep.

Suddenly he was breathing again in harsh gasps, and cursing himself for the lapse, and praying amid quiet tears as he visualised the wasted chest of a troffie.

"*Heh heh!*" wheezed an oldster who had come in to readjust the furnace in the rookie barracks. "You'll get to be a Martian pretty soon, boy. I been here seven years. Look at *me.*"

Manue heard the gasping voice and shuddered; there was no need to look.

"You just as well not fight it. It'll get you. Give in, make it easy on yourself. Go crazy if you don't."

"Stop it! Let me alone!"

"Sure. Just one thing. You wanta go home, you think. I went home. Came back. You will, too. They all do, 'cept engineers. Know why?"

"Shut up!" Manue pulled himself erect on the cot and hissed anger at the old-timer, who was neither old nor young, but only withered by Mars. His head suggested that he might be around thirty-five, but his body was weak and old.

The veteran grinned. "Sorry," he wheezed. "I'll keep my mouth shut." He hesitated, then extended his hand. "I'm Sam Donnell, mech-repairs."

Manue still glowered at him. Donnell shrugged and dropped his hand.

"Just trying to be friends," he muttered and walked away.

The digger started to call after him but only closed his mouth again, tightly. Friends? He needed friends, but not a troffie. He couldn't even bear to look at them, for fear he might be looking into the mirror of his own future.

Manue climbed out of his bunk and donned his fleeceskins. Night had fallen, and the temperature was already twenty below. A soft sift of ice-dust obscured the stars. He stared about in the darkness. The mess hall was closed, but a light burned in the canteen and another in the foremen's club, where the men were playing cards and drinking. He went to get his alcohol ration, gulped it mixed with a little water, and trudged back to the barracks alone.

The Tibetan was in bed, staring blankly at the ceiling. Manue sat down and gazed at his flat, empty face.

"Why did you come here, Gee?"

"Come where?"

"To Mars."

Gee grinned, revealing large black-streaked teeth. "Make money. Good money on Mars."

"Everybody make money, huh?"

"Sure."

"Where's the money come from?"

Gee rolled his face toward the Peruvian and frowned. "You crazy? Money come from Earth, where all money come from."

"And what does Earth get back from Mars?"

Gee looked puzzled for a moment, then gathered anger because he found no answer. He grunted a monosyllable in his native tongue, then rolled over and went to sleep.

Manue was not normally given to worrying about such things, but now he found himself asking, "What am I doing here?"—and then, "What is *anybody* doing here?"

The Mars Project had started eighty or ninety years ago, and its end goal was to make Mars habitable for colonists without Earth support, without oxies and insulated suits and the various gadgets a man now had to use to keep himself alive on the fourth planet.

But thus far, Earth had planted without reaping. The sky was a bottomless well into which Earth poured her tools, dollars, manpower, and engineering skill. And there appeared to be no hope for the near future.

Manue felt suddenly trapped. He could not return to Earth before the end of his contract. He was trading five years of virtual enslavement for a sum of money which would buy a limited amount of freedom. But what if he lost his lungs, became a servant of the small aerator for the rest of his days? Worst of all: whose ends was he serving? The contractors were getting rich—on government contracts. Some of the engineers and foremen were getting rich—by various forms of embezzlement of government funds. But what were the people back on Earth getting for their money?

Nothing.

He lay awake for a long time, thinking about it. Then he resolved to ask someone tomorrow, someone smarter than himself.

But he found the question brushed aside. He summoned enough nerve to ask Vögeli, but the foreman told him harshly to keep working and quit wondering. He asked the structural engineer who supervised the building, but the man only laughed, and said: "What do you care? You're making good money."

They were running concrete now, laying the long strips of Martian steel in the bottom of the trench and dumping in great slobbering wheelbarrowfuls of grey-green mix. The drillers were continuing their tedious dry cut deep into the red world's crust. Twice a day they brought up a yard-long cylindrical sample of the rock and gave it to a geologist who weighed it, roasted it, weighed it again, and tested a sample of the condensed steam—if any—for tritium content. Daily, he chalked up the results on a blackboard in front of the engineering hut, and the technical staff crowded around for a look. Manue always glanced at the figures, but failed to understand.

Life became an endless routine of pain, fear, hard work, anger. There were few diversions. Sometimes a crew of entertainers came out from the Mare Erythraeum, but the labour gang could not all crowd in the pressurised staff-barracks where the shows were presented, and when Manue managed to catch a glimpse of one of the girls walking across the clearing, she was bundled in fleeceskins and hooded by a parka.

Itinerant rabbis, clergymen, and priests of the world's major faiths came occasionally to the camp: Buddhist, Moslem, and the Christian sects. Padre Antonio Selni made monthly visits' to hear confessions and offer Mass. Most of the gang attended all services as a diversion from routine, as an escape from nostalgia. Somehow it gave Manue a strange feeling in the pit of his stomach to see the Sacrifice of the Mass, two thousand years old, being offered in the same ritual under the strange dark sky of Mars—with a section of the new foundation serving as an altar upon which the priest set crucifix, candles, relic-stone, missal, chalice, paten, ciborium, cruets, et cetera. In filling the wine-cruet before the service, Manue saw him spill a little of the red-clear fluid upon the brown soil—wine, Earth-wine from sunny Sicilian vineyards, trampled from the grapes by the bare stamping feet of children. Wine, the rich red blood of Earth, soaking slowly into the crust of another planet.

Bowing low at the consecration, the unhappy Peruvian thought of the prayer a rabbi had sung the week before: "Blessed be the Lord our God, King of the Universe, Who makest bread to spring forth out of the Earth."

Earth chalice, Earth blood, Earth God, Earth worshippers—with plastic tubes in their chests and a great sickness in their hearts.

He went away saddened. There was no faith here. Faith needed familiar surroundings, the props of culture. Here there were only swinging picks and rumbling machinery and sloshing concrete and the clatter of tools and the wheezing of troffies. Why? For five dollars an hour and keep?

Manue, raised in a back-country society that was almost a folk-culture, felt deep thirst for a goal. His father had been a stonemason, and he had laboured lovingly to help build the new cathedral, to build houses and mansions and commercial buildings, and his blood was mingled in their mortar. He had built for the love of his community and the love of the people and their customs, and their gods. He knew his own ends, and the ends of those around him. But what sense was there in this endless scratching at the face of Mars? Did they think they could make it into a second Earth, with pine forests and lakes and snow-capped mountains and small country villages? Man was not that strong. No, if he were labouring for any cause at all, it was to build a world so unearthlike that he could not love it.

The foundation was finished. There was very little more to be done until the drillers struck pay. Manue sat around the camp and worked at breathing. It was becoming a conscious effort now, and if he stopped thinking about it for a few minutes, he found himself inspiring shallow, meaningless little sips of air that scarcely moved his diaphragm. He kept the aerator as low as possible, to make himself breathe great gasps that hurt his chest, but it made him dizzy, and he had to increase the oxygenation lest he faint.

Sam Donnell, the troffie mech-repairman, caught him about to slump dizzily from his perch atop a heap of rocks, pushed him erect, and turned his oxy back to normal. It was late afternoon, and the drillers were about to change shifts. Manue sat shaking his head for a moment, then gazed at Donnell gratefully.

"That's dangerous, kid," the troffie wheezed. "Guys can go psycho doing that. Which you rather have: sick lungs or sick mind?"

"Neither."

"I know, but—"

"I don't want to talk about it."

Donnell stared at him with a faint smile. Then he shrugged and sat down on the rock heap to watch the drilling.

"Oughta be hitting the tritium ice in a couple of days," he said pleasantly. "Then we'll see a big blow."

Manue moistened his lips nervously. The troffies always made him feel uneasy. He stared aside.

"Big blow?"

"Lotta pressure down there, they say. Something about the way Mars got formed. Dust cloud hypothesis."

Manue shook his head. "I don't understand."

"I don't either. But I've heard them talk. Couple of billion years ago, Mars was supposed to be a moon of Jupiter. Picked up a lot of ice crystals over a rocky core. Then it broke loose and picked up a rocky crust—from another belt of the dust cloud. The pockets of tritium ice catch a few neutrons from uranium ore—down under. Some of the tritium goes into helium. Frees oxygen. Gases form pressure. Big blow."

"What are they going to do with the ice?"

The troffie shrugged. "The engineers might know."

Manue snorted and spat. "They know how to make money."

"Heh! Sure, everybody's gettin' rich."

The Peruvian stared at him speculatively for a moment.

"Senor Donnell, I—"

"Sam'll do."

"I wonder if anybody knows why... well... why we're really here."

Donnell glanced up to grin, then waggled his head. He fell thoughtful for a moment, and leaned forward to write in the earth. When he finished, he read it aloud.

"A plough plus a horse plus land equals the necessities of life." He glanced up at Manue. "Fifteen Hundred A.D."

The Peruvian frowned his bewilderment. Donnell rubbed out what he had written and wrote again.

"A factory plus steam turbines plus raw materials equals necessities plus luxuries. Nineteen Hundred A.D."

He rubbed it out and repeated the scribbling. "All those things plus nuclear power and computer controls equal a surplus of everything. Twenty-One Hundred A.D."

"So?"

"So, it's either cut production or find an outlet. Mars is an outlet for surplus energies, manpower, money. Mars Project keeps money turning over, keeps everything turning over. Economist told me that. Said if the Project folded, surplus would pile up—big depression on Earth."

The Peruvian shook his head and sighed. It didn't sound right somehow. It sounded like an explanation somebody figured out after the whole thing started. It wasn't the kind of goal he wanted.

Two days later, the drill hit ice, and the "big blow" was only a fizzle. There was talk around the camp that the whole operation had been a waste of time. The hole spewed a frosty breath for several hours, and the drill crews crowded around to stick their faces in it and breathe great gulps of the helium oxygen mixture. But then the blow subsided, and the hole leaked only a wisp of steam.

Technicians came, and lowered sonar "cameras" down to the ice. They spent a week taking internal soundings and plotting the extent of the ice-dome on their charts. They brought up samples of ice and tested them. The engineers worked late into the Martian nights.

Then it was finished. The engineers came out of their huddles and called to the foremen of the labour gangs. They led the foremen around the site, pointing here, pointing there, sketching with chalk on the foundation, explaining in solemn voices. Soon the foremen were bellowing at their crews.

"Let's get the derrick down!"

"Start that mixer going!"

"Get that steel over here!"

"Unroll that dip-wire!"

"Get a move on! Shovel that fill!"

Muscles tightened and strained, machinery clamoured and rang. Voices grumbled and shouted. The operation was starting again. Without knowing why, Manue shovelled fill and stretched dip-wire and poured concrete for a big floor slab to be run across the entire hundred-yard square, broken only by the big pipe-casing that stuck up out of the ground in the centre and leaked a thin trail of steam.

The drill crew moved their rig half a mile across the plain to a point specified by the geologists and began sinking another hole. A groan went up from structural boys: "Not *another* one of these things!"

But the supervisory staff said, "No, don't worry about it."

There was much speculation about the purpose of the whole operation, and the men resented the quiet secrecy connected with the project. There could be no excuse for secrecy, they felt, in time of peace. There was a certain arbitrariness about it, a hint that the Commission thought of its employees as children, or enemies, or servants. But the supervisory staff shrugged off all questions with: "You know there's tritium ice down there. You know it's what we've been looking for. Why? Well—what's the difference? There are lots of uses for it. Maybe we'll use it for one thing, maybe for something else. Who knows?"

Such a reply might have been satisfactory for an iron mine or an oil well or a stone quarry, but tritium suggested hydrogen-fusion. And no transportation facilities were being installed to haul the stuff away—no pipelines nor railroad tracks nor glider ports.

Manue quit thinking about it. Slowly he came to adopt a grim cynicism toward the tediousness, the back-breaking labour of his daily work; he lived from day to day like an animal, dreaming only of a return to Earth when his contract was up. But the dream was painful because it was distant, as contrasted with the immediacies of Mars: the threat of atrophy, coupled with the discomforts of continued breathing, the nightmares, the barrenness of the landscape, the intense cold, the harshness of men's tempers, the hardship of labour and the lack of a cause.

A warm, sunny Earth was still over four years distant, and tomorrow would be another back-breaking, throat-parching, heart-tormenting, chest-hurting day. Where was there even a little pleasure in it? It was so easy, at least, to leave the oxy turned up at night, and get a pleasant restful sleep. Sleep was the only recourse from harshness, and fear robbed sleep of its quiet sensuality—unless a man just surrendered and quit worrying about his lungs.

Manue decided that it would be safe to give himself two completely restful nights a week.

Concrete was run over the great square and trowelled to a rough finish. A glider train from the Mare Erythraeum brought in several huge crates of machinery, cut-stone masonry for building a wall, a shipful of new personnel, and a real rarity: lumber, cut from the first Earth-trees to be grown on Mars.

A building began going up, with the concrete square for foundation and floor. Structures could be flimsier on Mars; because of the light gravity, compression-stresses were smaller. Hence, the work progressed rapidly, and as the flat-roofed structure was completed, the technicians began uncrating new machinery and moving it into the building. Manue noticed that several of the units were computers. There was also a small steam-turbine generator driven by an atomic-fired boiler.

Months passed. The building grew into an integrated mass of power and control systems. Instead of using the well for pumping, the technicians were apparently going to lower something into it. A bomb-shaped cylinder was slung vertically over the hole. The men guided it into the mouth of the pipe casing, then let it down slowly from a massive cable. The cylinder's butt was a multi-contact socket like the female receptacle for a hundred-pin electron tube. Hours passed while the cylinder slipped slowly down beneath the hide of Mars. When it was done, the men hauled out the cable and began lowering stiff sections of pre-wired conduit, fitted with a receptacle at one end and a male plug at the other, so that as the sections fell into place, a continuous bundle of control cables was built up from "bomb" to surface.

Several weeks were spent in connecting circuits, setting up the computers, and making careful tests. The drillers had finished the second well hole, half a mile from the first, and Manue noticed that while the testing was going on, the engineers sometimes stood atop the building and stared anxiously toward the steel skeleton in the distance. Once while the tests were being conducted, the second bole began squirting a jet of steam high in the thin air, and a frantic voice bellowed from the root top.

"Cut it! Shut it off! Sound the danger whistle!"

The jet of steam began to shriek a low-pitched whine across the Martian desert. It blended with the rising and falling OOOO-awwww of the danger siren. But gradually it subsided as the men in the control station shut down the machinery. All hands came up cursing from their hiding places, and the engineers stalked out to the new hole carrying Geiger counters. They came back wearing pleased grins.

The work was nearly finished. The men began crating up the excavating machinery and the drill rig and the tools. The control-building devices were entirely automatic, and the camp would be deserted when the station began operation. The men were disgruntled. They had spent a year of hard labour on what they had thought to be a tritium well, but now that it was done, there were no facilities for pumping the stuff or hauling it away. In fact, they had pumped various solutions *into* the ground through the second hole, and the control station shaft was fitted with pipes that led from lead-lined tanks down into the earth.

Manue had stopped trying to keep his oxy properly adjusted at night. Turned up to a comfortable level, it was like a drug, insuring comfortable sleep—and like addict or alcoholic, he could no longer endure living without it. Sleep was too precious, his only comfort. Every morning he awoke with a still, motionless chest, felt frightening remorse, sat up gasping, choking, sucking at the thin air with whining rattling lungs that had been idle too long. Sometimes he coughed violently, and bled a little. And then for a night or two he would correctly adjust the oxy, only to wake up screaming and suffocating. He felt hope sliding grimly away.

He sought out Sam Donnell, explained the situation, and begged the troffie for helpful advice. But the mech-repairman neither helped nor consoled nor joked about it. He only bit his lip, muttered something noncommittal, and found an excuse to hurry away. It was then that Manue knew his hope was gone. Tissue was withering, tubercules forming, tubes growing closed. He knelt abjectly beside his cot, hung his face in his hands, and cursed softly, for there was no other way to pray an unanswerable prayer.

A glider train came in from the north to haul away the disassembled tools. The men lounged around the barracks or wandered across the Martian desert, gathering strange bits of rock and fossils, searching idly for a glint of metal or crystal in the wan sunshine of early fall. The lichens were growing brown and yellow, and the landscape took on the hues of Earth's autumn if not the forms.

There was a sense of expectancy around the camp. It could be felt in the nervous laughter, and the easy voices, talking suddenly of Earth and old friends and the smell of food in a farm kitchen, and old half-forgotten tastes for which men hungered: ham searing in the skillet, a cup of frothing cider from a fermenting crock, iced melon with honey and a bit of lemon, onion gravy on homemade bread. But someone always remarked, "What's the matter with you guys? We ain't going home. Not by a long shot. We're going to another place just like this."

And the group would break up and wander away, eyes tired, eyes haunted with nostalgia.

"What're we waiting for?" men shouted at the supervisory staff. "Get some transportation in here. Let's get rolling."

Men watched the skies for glider trains or jet transports, but the skies remained empty, and the staff remained close-mouthed. Then a dust column appeared on the horizon to the north, and a day later a convoy of tractor-trucks pulled into camp.

"Start loading aboard, men!" was the crisp command.

Surly voices: "You mean we don't go by air? We gotta ride those kidney-bouncers? It'll take a week to get to Mare Ery! Our contract says—"

"Load aboard! We're not going to Mare Ery yet!"

Grumbling, they loaded their baggage and their weary bodies into the trucks, and the trucks thundered and clattered across the desert, rolling toward the mountains.

The convoy rolled for three days toward the mountains, stopping at night to make camp, and driving on at sunrise. When they reached the first slopes of the foothills, the convoy stopped again. The deserted encampment lay a hundred and fifty miles behind. The going had been slow over the roadless desert.

"Everybody out!" barked the messenger from the lead truck. "Bail out! Assemble at the foot of the hill."

Voices were growling among themselves as the men moved in small groups from the trucks and collected in a milling tide in a shallow basin, overlooked by a low cliff and a hill. Manue saw the staff climb out of a cab and slowly work their way up the cliff. They carried a portable public address system.

"Gonna get a preaching," somebody snarled.

"Sit down, please!" barked the loud-speaker. "You men sit down there! Quiet—quiet, please!"

The gathering fell into a sulky silence. Will Kinley stood looking out over them, his eyes nervous, his hand holding the mike close to his mouth so that they could hear his weak troffie voice.

"If you men have questions," he said, "I'll answer them now. Do you want to know what you've been doing during the past year?"

An affirmative rumble arose from the group.

"You've been helping to give Mars a breathable atmosphere." He glanced briefly at his watch, then looked back at his audience. "In fifty minutes, a controlled chain reaction will start in the tritium ice. The computers will time it and try to control it. Helium and oxygen will come blasting up out of the second hole."

A rumble of disbelief arose from his audience. Someone shouted: "How can you get air to blanket a planet from one hole?"

"You can't," Kinley replied crisply. "A dozen others are going in, just like that one. We plan three hundred, and we've already located the ice pockets. Three hundred wells, working for eight centuries, can get the job done."

"Eight centuries! What good—"

"Wait!" Kinley barked. "In the meantime, we'll build pressurised cities close to the wells. If everything pans out, we'll get a lot of colonists here, and gradually condition them to live in a seven or eight psi atmosphere—which is about the best we can hope to get. Colonists from the Andes and the Himalayas—they wouldn't need much conditioning."

"What about us?"

There was a long plaintive silence. Kinley's eyes scanned the group sadly, and wandered toward the Martian horizon, gold and brown in the late afternoon. "Nothing—about us," he muttered quietly.

"Why did we come out here?"

"Because there's danger of the re-action getting out of hand. We can't tell anyone about it, or we'd start a panic." He looked at the group sadly. "I'm telling you now, because there's nothing you could do. In thirty minutes—"

There were angry murmurs in the crowd. "You mean there may be an explosion?"

"There *will* be a limited explosion. And there's very little danger of anything more. The worst danger is in having ugly rumours start in the cities. Some fool with a slip-stick would hear about it, and calculate what would happen to Mars if five cubic miles of tritium ice detonated in one split second. It would probably start a riot. That's why we've kept it a secret."

The buzz of voices was like a disturbed beehive. Manue Nanti sat in the midst of it, saying nothing, wearing a dazed and weary face, thoughts jumbled, soul drained of feeling.

Why should men lose their lungs that after eight centuries of tomorrows, other men might breathe the air of Mars as the air of Earth?

Other men around him echoed his thoughts in jealous mutter-
ings. They had been helping to make a world in which they would
never live.

An enraged scream arose near where Manue sat. "They're going
to blow us up! They're going to blow up Mars."

"Don't be a fool!" Kinley snapped.

"Fools they call us! We *are* fools! For ever corning here! We got
sucked in! Look at *me*!" A pale dark-haired man came wildly to his
feet and tapped his chest. "Look! I'm losing my lungs! We're all losing
our lungs! Now they take a chance on killing everybody."

"Including ourselves," Kinley called coldly.

"We oughta take him apart. We oughta kill every one who knew
about it—and Kinley's a good place to start!"

The rumble of voices rose higher, calling both agreement and
dissent. Some of Kinley's staff were looking nervously toward the
trucks. They were unarmed.

"You men sit down!" Kinley barked.

Rebellious eyes glared at the supervisor. Several men who had
come to their feet dropped to their haunches again. Kinley glowered
at the pale upriser who called for his scalp.

"Sit down, Handell!"

Handell turned his back on the supervisor and called out to the
others. "Don't be a bunch of cowards! Don't let him bully you!"

"You men sitting around Handell. Pull him down."

There was no response. The men, including Manue, stared up
at the wild-eyed Handell gloomily, but made no move to quiet him.
A pair of burly foremen started through the gathering from its
outskirts.

"Stop!" Kinley ordered. "Turpin, Schultz—get back. Let the men
handle this themselves."

Half a dozen others had joined the rebellious Handell. They were speaking in low tense tones among themselves.

"For the last time, men! Sit down!"

The group turned and started grimly toward the cliff. Without reasoning why, Manue slid to his feet quietly as Handell came near him. "Come on, fellow, let's get him," the leader muttered.

The Peruvian's fist chopped a short stroke to Handell's jaw, and the dull *thuk* echoed across the clearing. The man crumpled, and Manue crouched over him like a hissing panther. "Get back!" he snapped at the others. "Or I'll jerk his hoses out."

One of the others cursed him.

"Want to fight, fellow?" the Peruvian wheezed. "I can jerk several hoses out before you drop me!"

They shuffled nervously for a moment.

"The guy's crazy!" one complained in a high voice.

"Get back or he'll kill Handell!"

They sidled away, moved aimlessly in the crowd, then sat down to escape attention. Manue sat beside the fallen man and gazed at the thinly smiling Kinley.

"Thank you, son. There's a fool in every crowd." He looked at his watch again. "Just a few minutes men. Then you'll feel the Earth-tremor, and the explosion, and the wind. You can be proud of that wind, men. It's new air for Mars, and you made it."

"But we can't breathe it!" hissed a troffie.

Kinley was silent for a long time, as if listening to the distance. "What man ever made his own salvation?" he murmured.

They packed up the public address amplifier and came down the hill to sit in the cab of a truck, waiting.

—

It came as an orange glow in the south, and the glow was quickly shrouded by an expanding white cloud. Then, minutes later the ground pulsed beneath them, quivered and shook. The quake subsided, but remained as a hint of vibration. Then after a long time, they heard the dull-throated roar thundering across the Martian desert. The roar continued steadily, grumbling and growling as it would do for several hundred years.

There was only a hushed murmur of awed voices from the crowd. When the wind came, some of them stood up and moved quietly back to the trucks, for now they could go back to a city for reassignment. There were other tasks to accomplish before their contracts were done.

But Manue Nanti still sat on the ground, his head sunk low, desperately trying to gasp a little of the wind he had made, the wind out of the ground, the wind of the future. But lungs were clogged, and he could not drink of the racing wind. His big calloused hand clutched slowly at the ground, and he choked a brief sound like a sob.

A shadow fell over him. It was Kinley, come to offer his thanks for the quelling of Handell. But he said nothing for a moment as he watched Manue's desperate Gethsemane.

"Some sow, others reap," he said.

"Why?" the Peruvian choked.

The supervisor shrugged. "What's the difference? But if you can't be both, which would you rather be?"

Nanti looked up into the wind. He imagined a city to the south, a city built on tear-soaked ground, filled with people who had no ends beyond their culture, no goal but within their own society. It was a good sensible question: Which would he rather be—sower or reaper?

Pride brought him slowly to his feet, and he eyed Kinley questioningly. The supervisor touched his shoulder.

"Go on to the trucks."

Nanti nodded and shuffled away. He had wanted something to work for, hadn't he? Something more than the reasons Donnell had given. Well, he could smell a reason, even if he couldn't breathe it.

Eight hundred years was a long time, but then—long time, big reason. The air smelled good, even with its clouds of boiling-dust.

He knew now what Mars was—not a ten-thousand-a-year job, not a garbage can for surplus production. But an eight-century passion of human faith in the destiny of the race of Man.

He paused short of the truck. He had wanted to travel, to see the sights of Earth, the handiwork of Nature and of history, the glorious places of his planet.

He stooped, and scooped up a handful of the red-brown soil, letting it sift slowly between his fingers. Here was Mars—his planet now. No more of Earth, not for Manue Nanti. He adjusted his aerator more comfortably and climbed into the waiting truck.

THE TIME-TOMBS

J. G. Ballard

It may seem strange to find a story by J. G. Ballard (1930–2009) in an anthology about Mars. One of the pioneers of the New Wave movement in science fiction, Ballard is more closely associated with stories about the psychological and social collapse of society in such novels as Crash *(1973) and* High Rise *(1975). But to Ballard, this central theme can be explored in many ways. Early in his career it was through such disaster novels as* The Wind from Nowhere *(1961) and* The Drowned World *(1962) as well as through his stories of a decadent society developing new artistic technologies which often reflect their own inner turmoil. Those stories were collected as* Vermilion Sands *(1971). 'The Time-Tombs' (*If, March 1963*), which was written at the same time as most of the* Vermilion Sands *stories, can be seen as something of a companion piece, but with Martian technology which has miraculously survived for millennia. And, who knows just what lies out there.*

Usually in the evenings, while Traxel and Bridges drove off into the sand-sea, Shepley and the Old Man would wander among the gutted time-tombs, listening to them splutter faintly in the dying light as they recreated their fading personas, the deep crystal vaults flaring briefly like giant goblets.

Most of the time-tombs on the southern edge of the sand-sea had been stripped centuries earlier. But Shepley liked to saunter through the straggle of half-submerged pavilions, the warm ancient sand playing over his bare feet like wavelets on some endless beach. Alone among the flickering tombs, with the empty husks of the past ten thousand years, he could temporarily forget his nagging sense of failure.

Tonight, however, he would have to forego the walk. Traxel, who was nominally the leader of the group of tomb-robbers, had pointedly warned him at dinner that he must pay his way or leave. For three weeks Shepley had put off going with Traxel and Bridges, making a series of progressively lamer excuses, and they had begun to get impatient with him. The Old Man they would tolerate, for his vast knowledge of the sand-sea—he had combed the decaying tombs for over forty years and knew every reef and therm-pool like the palm of his hand—and because he was an institution that somehow dignified the lowly calling of tomb-robber, but Shepley had been there for only three months and had nothing to offer except his morose silences and self-hate.

"Tonight, Shepley," Traxel told him firmly in his hard clipped voice, "you must find a tape. We cannot support you indefinitely. Remember, we're all as eager to leave Vergil as you are."

Shepley nodded, watching his reflection in the gold finger-bowl. Traxel sat at the head of the tilting table, his high-collared velvet jacket unbuttoned. Surrounded by the battered gold plate filched from the tombs, red wine spilling across the table from Bridges's tankard, he looked more like a Renaissance princeling than a cashiered Ph.D. from Tycho U. Once Traxel had been Professor of Semantics, and Shepley wondered what scandal had brought him to Vergil. Now, like a grave-rat, he hunted the time-tombs with Bridges, selling the tapes to the Psycho-History Museums at a dollar a foot. Shepley found it impossible to come to terms with the tall, aloof man. By contrast Bridges, who was just a thug, had a streak of blunt good humour that made him tolerable, but with Traxel he could never relax. Perhaps his cold laconic manner represented authority, the high-faced, stern-eyed interrogators who still pursued Shepley in his dreams.

Bridges kicked back his chair and lurched away around the table, pounding Shepley across the shoulders.

"You come with us, kid. Tonight we'll find a mega-tape."

Outside, the low-hulled, camouflaged half-track waited in a saddle between two dunes. The old summer palace was sinking slowly below the desert, and the floor of the banqueting hall shelved into the white sand like the deck of a subsiding liner, going down with lights blazing from its staterooms.

"What about you, Doctor?" Traxel asked the Old Man as Bridges swung aboard the half-track and the exhaust kicked out. "It would be a pleasure to have you along." When the Old Man shook his head Traxel turned to Shepley. "Well, are you coming?"

"Not tonight," Shepley demurred hurriedly. "I'll, er, walk down to the tomb-beds later myself."

"Twenty miles?" Traxel reminded him, watching reflectively. "Very well." He zipped up his jacket and strode away towards the half-track. As they moved off he shouted: "Shepley, I meant what I said!"

Shepley watched them disappear among the dunes. Flatly, he repeated: "He means what he says."

The Old Man shrugged, sweeping some sand off the table. "Traxel... he's a difficult man. What are you going to do?" The note of reproach in his voice was milk, realising that Shepley's motives were the same as those which had marooned himself on the lost beaches of the sand-sea four decades earlier.

Shepley snapped irritably. "I can't go with him. After five minutes he drains me like a skull. What's the matter with Traxel, why is he here?"

The Old Man stood up, staring out vaguely into the desert. "I can't remember. Everyone has his own reasons. After a while the stories overlap."

They walked out under the proscenium, following the grooves left by the half-track. A mile away, winding between the last of the lava-lakes which marked the southern shore of the sand-sea, they could just see the vehicle vanishing into the darkness. The old tomb-beds, where Shepley and the Old Man usually walked, lay between them, the pavilions arranged in three lines along a low basaltic ridge. Occasionally a brief flare of light flickered up into the white, bonelike darkness, but most of the tombs were silent.

Shepley stopped, hands falling limply to his sides. "The new beds are by the Lake of Newton, nearly twenty miles away. I can't follow them."

"I shouldn't try," the Old Man rejoined. "There was a big sand-storm last night. The time-wardens will be out in force marking any new tombs uncovered." He chuckled softly to himself. "Traxel and Bridges won't find a foot of tape—they'll be lucky if they're not arrested." He took off his white cotton hat and squinted shrewdly through the dead light, assessing the altered contours of the dunes, then guided Shepley towards the old mono-rail whose southern terminus ended by the tomb-beds. Once it had been used to transport the pavilions from the station on the northern shore of the sand-sea, and a small gyro-car still leaned against the freight platform. "We'll go over to Pascal. Something may have come up, you never know."

Shepley shook his head. "Traxel took me there when I first arrived. They've all been stripped a hundred times."

"Well, we'll have a look." The Old Man plodded on towards the mono-rail, his dirty white suit flapping in the low breeze. Behind them the summer palace—built three centuries earlier by a business tycoon from Ceres—faded into the darkness, the rippling glass tiles in the upper spires merging into the starlight.

Propping the car against the platform, Shepley wound up the gyroscope, then helped the Old Man onto the front seat. He pried off a piece of rusting platform rail and began to punt the car away. Every fifty yards or so they stopped to clear the sand that submerged the track, but slowly they wound off among the dunes and lakes, here and there the onion-shaped cupola of a solitary time-tomb rearing up into the sky beside them, fragments of the crystal casements twinkling in the sand like minuscule stars.

Half an hour later, as they rode down the final long incline towards the Lake of Pascal, Shepley went forward to sit beside the Old Man, who emerged from his private reverie to ask quizzically: "And you, Shepley, why are you here?"

Shepley leaned back, letting the cool air drain the sweat off his face. "Once I tried to kill someone," he explained tersely.

"After they cured me I found I wanted to kill myself instead." He reached down to the hand-brake as they gathered speed. "For ten thousand dollars I can go back on probation. Here I thought there would be a freemasonry of sorts. But then you've been kind enough, Doctor.

"Don't worry, we'll get you a winning tape." He leaned forward, shielding his eyes from the stellar glare, gazing down at the little cantonment of gutted time-tombs on the shore of the lake. In all there were about a dozen pavilions, their roofs holed, the group Traxel had shown to Shepley after his arrival when he demonstrated how the vaults were robbed.

"Shepley! Look, lad!"

"Where? I've seen them before, Doctor. They're stripped." The Old Man pushed him away. "No, you fool, about three hundred yards to the west, in the shadow of the long ridge where the big dunes have moved. Can you see them now?" He drummed a white fist on Shepley's knee. "You've made it, lad. You won't need to be frightened of Traxel or anyone else now."

Shepley jerked the car to a halt. As he ran ahead of the Old Man towards the escarpment he could see several of the time-tombs glowing along the sky-line, emerging briefly from the dark earth like the tents of some spectral caravan.

II

For ten millennia the Sea of Vergil had served as a burial ground, and the 1,500 square miles of restless sand were estimated to contain over twenty thousand tombs. All but a minute fraction had been stripped by the successive generations of tomb-robbers, and an intact spool of the 17th Dynasty could now be sold to the Psycho-History Museum at Tycho for over 3,000 dollars. For each preceding dynasty, though none older than the 12th had ever been found, there was a bonus.

There was no corpses in the time-tombs, no dusty skeletons. The cyber-architectonic ghosts which haunted them were embalmed in the metallic codes of memory tapes, three-dimensional molecular transcriptions of their living originals, stored among the dunes as a stupendous act of faith, in the hope that one day the physical re-creation of the coded personalities would be possible. After five thousand years the attempt had been reluctantly abandoned but out of respect for the tomb-builders their pavilions were left to take their own hazard with time in the Sea of Vergil. Later the tomb-robbers had arrived, as the historians of the new epochs realised the enormous archives that lay waiting for them in this antique limbo. Despite the time-wardens, the pillaging of the tombs and the illicit traffic in dead souls continued.

"Doctor! Come on! Look at them!"

Shepley plunged wildly up to his knees in the silver-white sand, diving from one pavilion to the next like a frantic puppy.

Smiling to himself, the Old Man climbed slowly up the melting slope, submerged to his waist as the fine crystals poured away around him, feeling for spurs of firmer rock. The cupola of the nearest tomb tilted into the sky, only the top six inches of the casements visible below the overhang. He sat for a moment on the roof, watching Shepley dive about in the darkness, then peered through the casement, brushing away the sand with his hands.

The tomb was intact. Inside he could see the votive light burning over the altar, the hexagonal nave with its inlaid gold floor and drapery, the narrow chancel at the rear which held the memory store. Low tables surrounded the chancel, carrying beaten goblets and gold bowls, token offerings intended to distract any pillager who stumbled upon the tomb.

Shepley came leaping over to him. "Let's get into them, Doctor! What are we waiting for?"

The Old Man looked out over the plain below, at the cluster of stripped tombs by the edge of the lake, at the dark ribbon of the gyro-rail winding away among the hills. The thought of the fortune that lay at his fingertips left him unmoved. For so long now he had lived among the tombs that he had begun to assume something of their ambience of immortality and timelessness, and Shepley's impatience seemed to come out of another dimension. He hated stripping the tombs. Each one robbed represented, not just the final extinction of a surviving personality, but a diminution of his own sense of eternity. Whenever a new tomb-bed emerged from the sand he felt something within himself momentarily rekindled, not hope, for he was beyond that, but a serene acceptance of the brief span of time left to him.

"Right," he nodded. They began to cleave away the sand piled around the door, Shepley driving it down the slope where it spilled in a white foam over the darker basaltic chips. When the narrow portico was free the Old Man squatted by the time-seal. His fingers cleaned away the crystals embedded between the tabs, then played lightly over them.

Like dry sticks breaking, an ancient voice crackled:

> Orion, Betelgeuse, Altair,
> What twice-born star shall be my heir,
> Doomed again to be the scion—

"Come on, Doctor, this is a quicker way." Shepley put one leg up against the door and lunged against it futilely. The Old Man pushed him away. With his mouth close to the seal, he rejoined:

Of Altair, Betelgeuse, Orion.

As the doors accepted this and swung back he murmured: "Don't despise the old rituals. Now, let's see." They paused in the cool, unbreathed air, the votive light throwing a pale ruby glow over the gold drapes parting across the chancel.

The air became curiously hazy and mottled. Within a few seconds it began to vibrate with increasing rapidity, and a succession of vivid colours rippled across the surface of what appeared to be a cone of light projected from the rear of the chancel. Soon this resolved itself into a three-dimensional image of an elderly man in a blue robe.

Although the image was transparent, the brilliant electric blue of the robe revealing the inadequacies of the projection system, the intensity of the illusion was such that Shepley almost expected the man to speak to them. He was well into his seventies, with a composed, watchful face and thin grey hair, his hands resting quietly in front of him. The edge of the desk was just visible, the proximal arc of the cone enclosing part of a silver inkstand and a small metal trophy. These details, and the spectral bookshelves and paintings which formed the backdrop of the illusion, were of infinite value to the Psycho-History institutes, providing evidence of the earlier civilisations far more reliable than the funerary urns and goblets in the anteroom.

Shepley began to move forward, the definition of the persona fading slightly. A visual relay of the memory store, it would continue to play after the code had been removed, though the induction coils would soon exhaust themselves. Then the tomb would be finally extinct.

Two feet away, the wise unblinking eyes of the long dead magnate stared at him steadily, his seamed forehead like a piece of pink transparent wax. Tentatively, Shepley reached out and plunged his hand into the cone, the myriad vibration patterns racing across his wrist. For a moment he held the dead man's face in his hand, the edge of the desk and the silver inkstand dappling across his sleeve.

Then he stepped forward and walked straight through him into the darkness at the rear of the chancel.

Quickly, following Traxel's instructions, he unbolted the console containing the memory store, lifting out the three heavy drums which held the tape spools. Immediately the persona began to dim, the edge of the desk and the bookshelves vanishing as the cone contracted. Narrow bands of dead air appeared across it, one, at the level of the man's neck, decapitating him. Lower down the scanner had begun to misfire. The folded hands trembled nervously, and now and then one of his shoulders gave a slight twitch. Shepley stepped through him without looking back.

The Old Man was waiting outside. Shepley dropped the drums onto the sand. "They're heavy," he muttered. Brightening, he added: "There must be over five hundred feet here, Doctor. With the bonus, and all the others as well—" He took the Old Man's arm. "Come on, let's get into the next one."

The Old Man disengaged himself, watching the sputtering persona in the pavilion, the blue light from the dead man's suit pulsing across the sand like a soundless lightning storm.

"Wait a minute, lad, don't run away with yourself." As Shepley began to slide off through the sand, sending further falls down the slope, he added in a firmer voice: "And stop moving all that sand around! These tombs have been hidden here for ten thousand years. Don't undo all the good work, or the wardens will be finding them the first time they go past."

"Or Traxel," Shepley said, sobering quickly. He glanced around the lake below, searching the shadows among the tombs in case anyone was watching them, waiting to seize the treasure.

III

The Old Man left him at the door of the next pavilion, reluctant to watch the tomb being stripped of the last vestige of its already meagre claim to immortality.

"This will be our last one tonight," he told Shepley. "You'll never hide all these tapes from Bridges and Traxel."

The furnishings of the tomb differed from the previous one's. Somber black marble panels covered the walls, inscribed with strange goldleaf hieroglyphs, and the inlays in the floor represented stylised astrological symbols, at once eerie and obscure. Shepley leaned against the altar, watching the cone of light reach out towards him from the chancel as the curtains parted. The predominant colours were gold and carmine, mingled with a vivid powdery copper that gradually resolved itself into the huge, harplike headdress of a reclining woman. She lay in the centre of what seemed to be a sphere of softly luminous gas, inclined against a massive black catafalque, from the sides of which flared two enormous heraldic wings. The woman's copper hair was swept straight back off her forehead, some five or six feet long, and merged with the plumage of the wings, giving her an impression of tremendous contained speed, like a goddess arrested in a moment of flight in a cornice of some great temple-city of the dead.

Her eyes stared forward expressionlessly at Shepley. Her arms and shoulders were bare, and the white skin, like compacted snow, had a brilliant surface sheen, the reflected light glaring against the black base of the catafalque and the long sheathlike gown that swept around her hips to the floor. Her face, like an exquisite porcelain mask, was tilted upward slightly, the hooded, half-closed eyes suggesting that the woman was asleep or dreaming. No background had been provided for the image, but the bowl of luminescence invested the whole persona with immense power and mystery.

Shepley heard the Old Man shuffle up behind him.

"Who is she, Doctor? A princess?"

The Old Man shook his head slowly. "You can only guess. I don't know. There are strange treasures in these tombs. Get on with it, we'd best be going."

Shepley hesitated. He started to walk towards the woman on the catafalque, and then felt the enormous upward surge of her flight, the pressure of all the past centuries carried before her brought to a sudden focus in front of him, holding him back like a physical barrier.

"Doctor!" He reached the door just behind the Old Man. "We'll leave this one, there's no hurry!"

The Old Man examined his face shrewdly in the moonlight, the brilliant colours of the persona flickering across Shepley's youthful cheeks. "I know how you feel, lad, but remember, the woman doesn't exist, any more than a painting. You'll have to come back for her soon."

Shepley nodded quickly. "I know, but some other night. There's something uncanny about this tomb." He closed the doors behind them, and immediately the huge cone of light shrank back into the chancel, sucking the woman and the catafalque into the darkness. The wind swept across the dunes, throwing a fine spray of sand onto the half-buried cupolas, sighing among the wrecked tombs.

The Old Man made his way down to the mono-rail, and waited for Shepley as he worked for the next hour, slowly covering each of the tombs.

On the Old Man's recommendation he gave Traxel only one of the canisters, containing about 500 feet of tape. As prophesied, the time-wardens had been out in force in the Sea of Newton, and two members of another gang had been caught red-handed. Bridges was in foul temper, but Traxel, as ever self-contained, seemed unworried at the wasted evening.

Straddling the desk in the tilting ballroom, he examined the drum with interest, complimenting Shepley on his initiative. "Excellent, Shepley. I'm glad you joined us now. Do you mind telling me where you found this?"

Shepley shrugged vaguely, began to mumble something about a secret basement in one of the gutted tombs nearby, but the Old Man cut in: "Don't broadcast it everywhere! Traxel, you shouldn't ask questions like that—he's got his own living to earn."

Traxel smiled, sphinxlike. "Right again, Doctor." He tapped the smooth untarnished case. "In mint condition, and a 15th Dynasty too."

"Tenth!" Shepley claimed indignantly, frightened that Traxel might try to pocket the bonus. The Old Man cursed, and Traxel's eyes gleamed.

"Tenth, is it? I didn't realise there were any 10th Dynasty tombs still intact. You surprise me, Shepley. Obviously you have concealed talents."

Luckily he seemed to assume that the Old Man had been hoarding the tape for years.

Face down in a shallow hollow at the edge of the ridge, Shepley watched the white-hulled sand-car of the time-wardens shunt through the darkness by the old cantonment. Directly below him jutted the spires of the newly discovered tomb-bed, invisible against the dark background of the ridge. The two wardens in the sand-car were more interested in the old tombs; they had spotted the gyrocar lying on its side by the monorail, and guessed that the gangs had been working the ruins over again. One of them stood on the running board, flicking a torch into the gutted pavilions. Crossing the mono-rail, the car moved off slowly across the lake to the northwest, a low pall of dust settling behind it.

For a few moments Shepley lay quietly in the slack darkness, watching the gullies and ravines that led into the lake, then slid down among the pavilions. Brushing away the sand to reveal a square wooden plank, he slipped below it into the portico.

As the golden image of the enchantress loomed out of the black-walled chancel to greet him, the great reptilian wings unfurling around her, he stood behind one of the columns in the nave, fascinated by her strange deathless beauty. At times her vivid luminous face seemed almost repellent, but he had nonetheless seized on the faint possibility of her resurrection. Each night he came, stealing into the tomb where she had lain for ten thousand years, unable to bring himself to interrupt her. The long copper hair streamed behind her like an entrained time-wind, her angled body in flight between two infinitely distant universes, where archetypal beings of superhuman stature glimmered fitfully in their own spontaneously generated light.

Two days later Bridges discovered the remainder of the drums.

"Traxel! Traxel!" he bellowed, racing across the inner courtyard from the entrance to one of the disused bunkers. He bounded into the ballroom and slammed the metal cans onto the computer which Traxel was programming. "Take a look at these—more Tenths! The whole place is crawling with them!"

Traxel weighed the cans idly in his hands, glancing across at Shepley and the Old Man, on lookout duty by the window. "Interesting. Where did you find them?"

Shepley jumped down from the window trestle. "They're mine. The Doctor will confirm it. They run in sequence after the first I gave you a week ago. I was storing them." Bridges cut back with an oath. "Whaddya mean, storing them? Is that your personal bunker out there? Since when?" He shoved Shepley away with a broad hand and swung round on Traxel. "Listen, Traxel, those tapes were a fair find, I don't see any tags on them. Every time I bring something in I'm going to have this kid claim it?"

Traxel stood up, adjusting his height so that he overreached Bridges. "Of course, you're right—technically. But we have to work together, don't we? Shepley made a mistake, we'll forgive him this time." He handed the drums to Shepley, Bridges seething with barely controlled indignation. "If I were you, Shepley, I'd get those cashed. Don't worry about flooding the market." As Shepley turned away, sidestepping Bridges, he called him back. "And there are advantages in working together, you know."

He watched Shepley disappear to his room, then turned to survey the huge peeling map of the sand-sea that covered the facing wall.

"You'll have to strip the tombs now," the Old Man told Shepley later. "It's obvious you've stumbled on something, and it won't take Traxel five minutes to discover where."

"Perhaps a little longer," Shepley replied evenly. They stepped out of the shadow of the palace and moved away among the dunes; Bridges and Traxel were watching them from the dining-room table, their figures motionless in the light. "The roofs are almost completely covered now. The next sandstorm should bury them for good."

"Have you entered any of the other tombs?"

Shepley shook his head vigorously. "Believe me, Doctor, I know now why the time-wardens are here. As long as there's a chance of their being resurrected we're committing murder every time we rob a tomb. Even if it's only one chance in a million it may be all they themselves bargained on. After all, one doesn't commit suicide because the chances of life existing anywhere are virtually nil."

Already he had come to believe that the enchantress might suddenly resurrect herself, step down from the catafalque before his eyes. While a slender possibility existed of her returning to life he felt that he too had a valid foothold in existence, that there was a small element of certainty in what had previously seemed a random and utterly meaningless universe.

IV

As the first dawn light probed through the casements, Shepley turned reluctantly from the nave. He looked back briefly at the glowing persona, suppressing the slight pang of disappointment that the expected metamorphosis had not yet occurred, but relieved to have spent as much time awaiting it as possible.

He made his way down to the old cantonment, steering carefully through the shadows. As he reached the monorail—he now made the journey on foot, to prevent Traxel guessing that the cache lay along the route of the rail—he heard the track hum faintly in the cool air. He jumped back behind a low mound, tracing its winding pathway through the dunes.

Suddenly an engine throbbed out behind him, and Traxel's camouflaged half-track appeared over the edge of the ridge. Its front
four wheels raced and spun, and the huge vehicle tipped forward
and plunged down the incline among the buried tombs, its surging
tracks dislodging tons of the fine sand Shepley had so laboriously
pushed by hand up the slope. Immediately several of the pavilions
appeared to view, the white dust cascading off their cupolas.

Half-buried in the avalanche they had set off, Traxel and Bridges
leapt from the driving cab, pointing to the pavilions and shouting at
each other. Shepley darted forward, put his foot up on the mono-rail
just as it began to vibrate loudly.

In the distance the gyro-car slowly approached, the Old Man
punting it along, hatless and dishevelled.

He reached the tomb as Bridges was kicking the door in with a
heavy boot, Traxel behind him with a bag full of wrenches.

"Hello, Shepley!" Traxel greeted him gaily. "So this is your treasure trove."

Shepley staggered splay-legged through the sliding sand, brushed
past Traxel as glass spattered from the window. He flung himself on
Bridges and pulled the big man backwards.

"Bridges, this one's mine! Try any of the others, you can have
them all!"

Bridges jerked himself to his feet, staring down angrily at Shepley.
Traxel peered suspiciously at the other tombs, their porticos still
flooded with sand. "What's so interesting about this one, Shepley?"
he asked sardonically. Bridges roared and slammed a boot into the
casement, knocking out one of the panels. Shepley dived onto his
shoulders, and Bridges snarled and flung him against the wall. Before
Shepley could duck he swung a heavy left cross to Shepley's mouth,
knocking him back onto the sand with a bloody face.

Traxel roared with amusement as Shepley lay there stunned, then knelt down, sympathetically examining Shepley's face in the light thrown by the expanding persona within the tomb. Bridges whooped with surprise, gaping like a startled ape at the sumptuous golden mirage of the enchantress.

"How did you find me?" Shepley muttered thickly. "I double-tracked a dozen times."

Traxel smiled. "We didn't follow you, chum. We followed the rail." He pointed down at the silver thread of the metal strip, plainly visible in the dawn light almost ten miles away. "The gyro-car cleaned the rail, it led us straight here. Ah, hello, Doctor," he greeted the Old Man as he climbed the slope and slumped down wearily beside Shepley. "I take it we have you to thank for this discovery. Don't worry, Doctor, I shan't forget you."

"Many thanks," the Old Man said flatly. He helped Shepley to sit up, frowning at his split lips. "Aren't you taking everything too seriously, Traxel? You're becoming crazed with greed. Let the boy have this tomb. There are plenty more."

The patterns of light across the sand dimmed and broke as Bridges plunged through the persona towards the rear of the chancel. Weakly Shepley tried to stand up, but the Old Man held him back. Traxel shrugged. "Too late, Doctor." He looked over his shoulder at the persona, ruefully shaking his head in acknowledgement of its magnificence. "These 10th Dynasty graves are stupendous. But there's something curious about this one."

He was still staring at it reflectively a minute later when Bridges emerged.

"Boy, that was a crazy one, Traxel! For a second I thought it was a dud." He handed the three canisters to Traxel, who weighed two of them in one hand against the other. Bridges added: "Kinda light, aren't they?"

Traxel began to pry them open with a wrench. "Are you certain there are no more in there?"

"Hundred per cent. Have a look yourself."

Two of the cans were empty, the tape spools missing. The third was only half full, a mere three-inch width of tape in its centre. Bridges bellowed in pain: "The kid robbed us. I can't believe it!" Traxel waved him away and went over to the Old Man, who was staring in at the now flickering persona. The two men exchanged glances, then nodded slowly in confirmation. With a short laugh Traxel kicked at the can containing the half reel of tape, jerking the spool out onto the sand, where it began to unravel in the quietly moving air. Bridges protested but Traxel shook his head.

"It *is* a dud. Go and have a close look at the image." When Bridges peered at it blankly he explained: "The woman there was dead when the matrices were recorded. She's beautiful all right—as poor Shepley here discovered—but it's all too literally skin deep. That's why there's only half a can of data. No nervous system, no musculature or internal organs—just a beautiful golden husk. This is a mortuary tomb. If you resurrected her you'd have an ice-cold corpse on your hands."

"But why?" Bridges rasped. "What's the point?"

Traxel gestured expansively. "It's immortality of a kind. Perhaps she died suddenly, and this was the next best thing. When the Doctor first came here there were a lot of mortuary tombs of young children being found. If I remember he had something of a reputation for always leaving them intact. A typical piece of highbrow sentimentality-giving immortality only to the dead. Agree, Doctor?"

Before the Old Man could reply a voice shouted from below, there was a nearby roaring hiss of an ascending signal rocket and a vivid red star-shell burst over the lake below, spitting incandescent fragments over them. Traxel and Bridges leapt forwards, saw two men in a sand-car pointing up at them, three more vehicles converging across the lake half a mile away.

"The time-wardens!" Traxel shouted. Bridges picked up the tool bag and the two men raced across the slope towards the half-track, the Old Man hobbling after them. He turned back to wait for Shepley, who was still sitting on the ground where he had fallen, watching the image inside the pavilion.

"Shepley! Come on, lad, pull yourself together! You'll get ten years!"

When Shepley made no reply he reached up to the side of the half-track as Traxel reversed it expertly out of the moraine of sand, let Bridges swing him aboard. "Shepley!" he called again. Traxel hesitated, then roared away as a second star-shell exploded.

Shepley tried to reach the tape, but the stampeding feet had severed it at several points, and the loose ends, which he had numbly thought of trying to reinsert into the projector, now fluttered around him in the sand. Below, he could hear the sounds of flight and pursuit, the warning crack of a rifle, engines baying and plunging, as Traxel eluded the time-wardens, but he kept his eyes fixed on the image within the tomb. Already it had begun to fragment, fading against the mounting sunlight. Getting slowly to his feet, he entered the tomb and closed the battered doors.

Still magnificent upon her bier, the enchantress lay back between the great wings. Motionless for so long, she had at last been galvanised into life, and a jerking syncopated rhythm rippled through her body. The wings shook uneasily, and a series of tremors disturbed the base of the catafalque, so that the woman's feet danced an exquisitely flickering minuet, the toes darting from side to side with untiring speed. Higher up, her wide smooth hips jostled each other in a jaunty mock tango.

He watched until only the face remained, a few disconnected traces of the wings and catafalque jerking faintly in the darkness, then made his way out of the tomb.

Outside, in the cool morning light, the time-wardens were waiting for him, hands on the hips of their white uniforms. One was holding the empty canisters, turning the fluttering strands of tape over with his foot as they drifted away.

The other took Shepley's arm and steered him down to the car.

"Traxel's gang," he said to the driver. "This must be a new recruit." He glanced dourly at the blood around Shepley's mouth. "Looks as if they've been fighting over the spoils."

The driver pointed to the three drums. "Stripped?"

The man carrying them nodded. "All three. And they were 10th Dynasty." He shackled Shepley's wrists to the dashboard. "Too bad, son, you'll be doing ten yourself soon. It'll seem like ten thousand."

"Unless it was a dud," the driver rejoined, eyeing Shepley with some sympathy. "You know, one of those freak mortuary tombs."

Shepley straightened his bruised mouth. "It wasn't," he said firmly.

The driver glanced warningly at the other wardens. "What about the tape blowing away up there?"

Shepley looked up at the tomb spluttering faintly below the ridge, its light almost gone. "That's just the persona," he said. "The empty skin."

As the engine surged forward he listened to the three empty drums hit the floor behind the seat.

STORY SOURCES

All of the stories in this anthology are in the public domain unless otherwise noted. The following gives the first publication details for each story and the sources used.

'The Time Tombs' by J. G. Ballard, first published in *If*, March 1963.

'Ylla' by Ray Bradbury, first published in *Maclean's Magazine*, January 1950 under the title 'I'll Not Look for Wine'.

'Measureless to Man' by Marion Zimmer Bradley, first published in *Amazing Stories*, December 1962.

'Letters from Mars' by W. S. Lach-Szyrma first published in two separate parts of 'Letters from the Planets' in *Cassell's Family Magazine*, April and October 1887.

'The Forgotten Man of Space' by P. Schuyler Miller, first published in *Wonder Stories*, April 1933.

'Crucifixus Etiam' by Walter M. Miller, Jr, first published in *Astounding SF*, February 1953.

'Without Bugles' by E. C. Tubb, first published in *New Worlds* #13, January 1952.

'The Great Sacrifice' by George C. Wallis, first published in *The London Magazine*, July 1903.

'A Martian Odyssey' by Stanley G. Weinbaum, first published in *Wonder Stories*, July 1934.

'The Crystal Egg' by H. G. Wells first published in *The New Review*, May 1897.

The cover illustration is by Chesley Bonestell (1888–1986), considered by many to be the dean of science-fiction artists. His work has adorned not only such books as *The Conquest of Space* by Willy Ley (1949) and *Beyond Jupiter: The Worlds of Tomorrow* (1972) with Arthur C. Clarke, but was also central to the films *Destination Moon* (1950), *War of the Worlds* (1953) and *Conquest of Space* (1955). His artistic career extended for eighty years from 1905 till his death. He was awarded a Special Achievement Hugo in 1974 and has both an asteroid and a crater on Mars named after him.